Pickled

by

Deany Ray

Chapter One

FIRST DAY AT WORK! I wedged my old Corolla into the first space that I found, although the fit was tight. Someone's pickup truck was encroaching on my space. *Can't you see the line, dude? Learn to drive,* I thought.

Parking, I could see, was gonna be an issue but we'd known that all along. The busiest laundromat in town was just to the left, and *Bill's Grab and Go* was a few buildings to our right. Come to think of it, our little corner might have been the hottest spot in Springston, Massachusetts. What was not to love? Just about everyone in town craved a good orange slushy (which came free with a foot-long hot dog), and there was just no getting around the need to wash your undies.

Marge said that our prime location would save us a lot of time. "Throw your blouses in the wash, grab a taquito for a fast lunch, then head off to your desk to finish your reports." It sounded like a good plan except some of those taquitos looked a little old and I could throw my laundry into the wash at my parents' house. Because – yes, it was sad but true – I,

Charlotte Cooper (who was trying my best *not* to be a loser) lived with my mom and dad at the age of twenty-nine.

But it was starting to look like (Fingers crossed!) that might change real soon. Celeste and Marge, my best amigos, were hopeful that CMC Services would be pulling in the big bucks within the first six months. To the outside world, we worked as technology consultants, but that was just a ruse. I didn't know a hard drive from a four-wheel drive. I didn't know a download from a downpour. What exactly was a megabyte? I didn't have a clue.

But that was not a problem because – are you ready for the secret? – we were undercover investigators. And hopefully our first case would come rolling in at any minute. Any day now....

Although today was the official start of our new endeavor, my girls had been putting feelers out for business while I moved my things from Boston. We'd hoped to start our first day with a case, so we'd feel like real detectives, but we'd had no luck.

"Good morning, super spies!" With my arms wrapped around a small box, I used my hips to swing the door wide open. I put my purse down in a chair, set the box down on the floor, looked around and smiled. The place was pretty small, but we didn't need a big space. We'd be out and about most days, not behind a desk – hopefully.

"Hey, Charlie. How's it going?" Marge was on her knees, putting together a three-tiered shelf. All I could see of my friend was her ample rear as she bent down to tighten a screw. She straightened up and giggled. "The gang's all here. I guess we're officially in business." Her voice always rose to a squeak when she got excited – and she got excited quite a lot.

The office seemed to be taking shape. The week before, we'd loaded my oldest brother's pickup with all manner of supplies, both practical and fun. Marge had picked out three large posters in black frames for the walls. Colored blobs blended together and swirled into shapes that, at least to me, could be most anything – or perhaps they were only meant to be a sea of abstract green and yellow. We knew less about art than we did about technology, our *supposed* specialty.

Of course, Marge saw all kinds of things she loved when she stared up at the posters. Now she walked over to study one. "I see elephants!" she cried. "Oh, and I see apples too. And can't you see the little pears on the right dancing above that squishy shape that looks like a flying saucer?"

Celeste scowled at the pictures. "They must carry some funky kind of fruit at your grocery store."

I didn't see a thing, but the colors were nice; they brightened up the room.

"Now, all we need is that sign they promised." Celeste put both hands on her hips and stared out the window as if it might somehow magically appear. "They promised me a sign. You can never trust a single thing that comes out of the mouth of any man." Some guys from the Springston Police were supposed to have put it up before our opening day. It was an odd assignment for police, but Celeste's ex-husband, Bert, was the brand-new chief, and she had some goods on him. I was hoping that one day, after too many rum and cokes, she might tell me what was up with the new top cop in town. But I didn't think I'd ever find out. The girl could hold her liquor.

Celeste pointed to a desk in the back-left corner of the room. "Charlie, there's your desk." She grinned. "And you might just find a little something siting there on top."

"Celeste made cookies!" Marge squeaked. "Because it's our first day."

I looked eagerly at the cellophane package tied in a pink bow. Cookies were my favorite way to celebrate – or to do most anything: to sooth myself, to help me ponder big decisions, or to answer the age-old question, *what should I do now?* And the answer was always easy: I should scarf down more cookies.

"Thank you. You're the best." I gave Celeste a hug. I could smell the hairspray that held in place the bright red tower of hair that meant you could always spot Celeste in any crowded room. I knew she had a drawer full of scarves that she would put to good use when we went undercover. With her jeweled belts, copious charms and bling, and stiletto heels (in every hue), there was nobody who stood out more than my vibrant friend Celeste. There was nobody seemingly less-suited for a life undercover. But I noticed she'd toned things down today with a light blue blouse and khaki pants and a pair of simple flats.

She noticed me checking out her outfit. "Oh, I know! I thought the same thing." She sighed. "This just isn't me! It just about killed me to come out of the house looking like the dullest plain jane in the world. No red lipstick, no rings, no bracelets, not a sparkle to be found. And would you look at this?" She held out her hands for my inspection. The long nails were pale instead of their usual bright green or red or pink. "I'm sure people were talking about me," she said. *"Didn't that girl's mama ever tell her to put a little color on her face before she goes out in public?"*

"Well, the real Celeste can still come out and play at night," I said. "The real Celeste lives on!"

"Girl, you got that right." She began loading some paper and folders into the top drawer of her desk, which sat across the room from mine.

Although her shelf was still a little wobbly, Marge began to fill it with supplies: binoculars, pepper spray, a child's pink tape recorder, then she opened a bag, and out came the sharpest knives that I'd ever seen. Marge had the demeanor of a favorite aunt, the kind who'd sneak you extra cookies when your mother had said no. But there must have been a ninja inside my giggly friend and if *Angry Marge* ever got set loose on some bad guy, I'd advise him to stand back. Despite the impressive display of weapons that she'd set out on the shelves, I knew she had something else in store for anyone who meant her harm: the little pistol in her flowered purse. She liked to call it her *persuader.* And persuade it did.

I'd seen Marge in action just the month before, when we'd run into a little spot of trouble that involved some *real* bad dudes. At the time, I was a secretary for the police in Boston, and my boss had talked me into a little bit of spy work in Springston, my hometown, that almost got me killed. Then, just when things got *really* bad, Marge morphed into a superhero who made my attacker beg for mercy. And I'd thought she was just a giggly waitress from my father's diner.

We're good at this, we thought. So, we went into business.

The case last month had been really something. Before that, I'd never imagined my clumsy, awkward self as the undercover type. My adventures all began when the police in Boston linked a drug case to a cell phone they traced to my hometown. So, my captain sent me back to Springston to see if I could pick up on some useful hometown gossip. As it turned out, I *solved* the case, thanks to a little luck, but mostly thanks to my new friends, Celeste and Marge, who – at the time – were waitressing for my dad. It turned out they had lots of skills that didn't have a thing to do with grabbing extra ketchup or refilling cups of coffee.

They were ready for something new. And I was tired of writing reports on crime without getting in on all the action. That's how CMC Services was born into the world. It stood for Charlie, Marge, and

Celeste (or Celeste, Marge, and Charlie, depending on who you asked).

The Springston police chief had promised he'd put us on some cases, and hopefully other agencies would decide to do the same once we had a solved case on the books. It helped, of course, that the new chief in town was anxious to keep Celeste from telling what she knew. Luckily, we had more going for us than that. My new besties and I had exactly what it took to get to the bottom of any case they could throw at the three of us. We were three smart women. Not to mention, we didn't look like cops, so nobody would suspect us.

We looked like any group of girlfriends out and about the town: one of us soft and round, clasping her hands in delight at every little thing; the other tall and serious, with a cigarette clamped between her lips; and the other (that one would be me) trying not to trip over her clumsy feet and to keep her glasses from slipping off her nose.

Marge was the sweet and innocent type that people loved to tell their troubles to. And if one of those persons happened to be the bad guy we were after? Then – Bingo! – the case would be solved and in the books. She sometimes seemed flustered and, well, a little bit naive. But you never knew when a stroke of brilliance would come bubbling out.

As for Celeste, she was the perfect partner in solving the mysteries of an unjust world. Packed into the deep furrows of her brow was the wisdom that came from many years of taking names and kicking ass. Anything we might run into in the world of crime would not surprise Celeste. "I have seen some *stuff*," she liked to say. But she wouldn't tell us what – or not much, at least.

I'd asked my dad about her, but he knew less than me.

"We all loved her at the diner," he said, "but she didn't talk about her life. Asked lots of question about other people's lives and gave them great advice. She's lived in town her whole life, but nobody seems to know a lot about Celeste."

She was an enigma in *Coiffures Par Excellence, Red, Number 8*. I'd seen it on her bathroom counter.

Perhaps one day Marge and I – ace detectives that we were – could solve the mystery of our co-worker. All I knew was that she hid a big heart behind her ever-present scowl. That was good enough for now.

And then there was me. 5'6", light-brown hair – shoulder length – gold-green eyes hidden behind glasses with a black frame. Very average and very non-spectacular. I wasn't sure exactly what I had to offer. Experience answering the phone for the police in Boston and writing up reports? The number of burglaries in the month of March, the increase in violent crimes from 2014 to 2015. Would those skills really help us? I wasn't sure. I just knew I needed a big change. The change needed to include excitement and challenge and – most of all – a paycheck. And so here I was.

I tasted one of Celeste's cookies. Peanut butter. Yum. I liked working here already.

Marge handed me a flier. "What do you think of this one, hon? I thought I'd ride around and hand it out to the police and sheriffs in Billington, Dolton and some other little towns. I thought a radius of twenty miles might be a good place for us to start." She winked at me, then glanced over at Celeste. "Got any exes in *those* departments? Any incentives for *those* guys to send some business our way?" Celeste had lots of former boyfriends, plus more than one ex-husband.

Celeste rolled her eyes. "Very funny. No."

Marge put some fliers in her large purse. "Charlie, come and ride with me. Let's see what kind of crime is brewing out in the world today. Let's see who might need the three of us to go check something out."

I looked down at the paper that she'd handed me. *CMC Services – For When You Want to Hire the Best. We Blend in with Any Crowd While Keeping Our Ears Open to Get the Info that You Need.*

"Thish looks exshellaa," I said, my mouth all full of cookies. The snickerdoodles were delicious. And I couldn't wait to try the pecan sandies.

Celeste studied Marge's stash of weapons and supplies. "You know, Marge, if someone peeped into our window on their way to put a load of clean clothes into one of those dryers over there, we might not exactly look like technological consultants. Not with all of this stuff sitting right here by the door for anyone to see."

Marge thought about it. "Hmm."

Celeste frowned. "Now, I'm no computer guru but I don't think pepper spray or binoculars would do a darn thing to get a laptop up and working. People might get an inkling that we're up to something else," she said.

Marge nodded. She seemed happy to have a decision to ponder on this first day on the job. "I think perhaps the bottom drawer of my desk would be a better place."

"Exshellaa," I repeated. I really should save some cookies for my coffee break.

Celeste began unloading more supplies. "Marge, I think you had a good idea about distributing those fliers. Maybe head to Brownsville too. I know their department is short staffed now, two officers out with mono. And Charlie, you go with her, see if we might be able to drum up a little business."

"Surely there's some crime that needs solving somewhere," Marge said. "It can get mean out there on the streets of Springston."

"I hope you're right," I said. Oh! That sounded bad. Not that I wanted to wish some horrific crime on our pretty little corner near the coast of Massachusetts. But I hoped *something* was going on *somewhere* that required the services of three very nosy, highly resourceful women. I needed money fast before my parents drove me crazy. My mother thought the answer to anything was a séance, a cleansing of my aura, or a yoga class with some of her ancient students who always seemed in danger of getting stuck in some beginner pose. She taught classes at our house – often right outside my window, and with the music turned up loud.

I never knew when she might run after me to warn me about my horoscope or – even worse – to ask about my sex life. Not that I had a sex life. But still...some subjects should be way off limits with your mother. Just...absolutely ewww!

My whole family was bonkers. My father was the world's oldest fan of awful jokes. I could hardly ever make it out the door without having to guess the answer to the latest one that some customer had told him. The knock-knocks were the worst.

And my youngest brother, Brad...well, my brother hadn't moved off the couch except for bathroom breaks and meals since...hmm, I don't know when. Oh, wait, I know when. Since last week, when he landed a job at the post office sorting out the mail. He should be given a medal for holding on to a job for that long.

So, trust me – I had to get some funds and quick. Maybe I'd been foolish to quit my job in Boston. But I had gotten so darn tired of doing the same old boring things every single day. I was trying hard to be a grownup, to have a career and not a job. Plus, my cool factor had just been amped up in a major way, from administrative assistant to undercover detective.

Marge and Celeste had both offered me their guest rooms. But we'd be working together all day and, as much as I loved my friends, we might need a break from one another when we weren't solving crimes.

Although I would have felt like Springston's own Kardashian living with Celeste. She had quite a place: a sprawling white brick two-story with a big back porch and an in-ground swimming pool. Kind of fancy, you might say, for someone who'd ended up serving customers at the diner after a string of businesses failures. I wondered if her ex had paid her through the nose when they got divorced. Or was it family money? The Ortiz clan was kind of shady, per the whispers on the streets. Nobody really knew what Celeste's brothers and uncles and grandma did to make their money.

Celeste wasn't telling. She was good at keeping secrets. Her standard answer to nosy questions was a simple wink. But one thing I knew for sure: there wasn't one darn thing shady about Celeste.

And however she got the money, it helped to pay our rent on the first floor of the three-story building in the heart of town.

"Thanks for getting the rent," I said as I unpacked a few things onto my desk: a plant that was almost dead (I could not afford a new one) and a picture of a cat I used to own before she ran away. I needed to find more friends, go out and do the kinds of things that people do in pictures that they put into frames. I had to get a life. My new life in Springston might just be the beginning of it. *Baby-steps*, I told myself.

"I'll pay you back as soon as possible," I said as I stuck some gum and candy bars and pens into my drawers. Celeste and Marge were splitting the rental payments until we got some work to pad my bank account.

"Oh, don't feel bad about it, hon," Marge squeaked. "We couldn't do this without you. It gives us a certain *savoir faire* – to be associated with someone *from the police in Boston*." She whispered the last five words with a kind of reverent awe. Marge was easily impressed.

"And besides," Celeste chimed in, "we'll all be making money soon. Because I have some news! The chief promised me last night that we'd get a case today from the PD here in Springston. And hopefully, Marge's fliers will bring in some cases too."

Today? She must know something good. Or maybe the chief just wanted to put a stop to the endless phone calls he must have been getting from his ex. And why not throw some work our way? We were gonna be good at this; I was absolutely sure.

I looked around our little office. Celeste had brought in a lavender and blue oriental rug from one of her spare rooms. She'd also managed to get some computer stuff to make us seem legit: old laptops and cords and all of that.

"Hey, Charlie," Marge cooed. "Have you seen Alex lately? I think Alex has a crush on someone in this room! And her initials are CC."

She loved nothing more than a good romantic story, but she could cool it any day now with all this talk of Alex Spencer. We'd worked with him on the drug thing. He was undercover for the Springston cops. Well, we haven't exactly worked *with* him, it was more that we bumped into each other while trying to solve the case.

I spun in my new desk chair to see how it would move. "I want nothing to do with Alex," I said. "Alex is a jerk." A gorgeous jerk. Hmm. I wondered why I hadn't seen the guy around.

Marge took a spin in her chair too, then rolled it close to mine. "Oh, I think you really like him. I've seen the way you look at him. And the way he looks at you."

No way did I flirt with Alex. I absolutely didn't.

"And you'd make the cutest couple," Marge said. "We should think of an excuse to call him over here. We must need help with *something*."

Great. Now I had Marge – and my mother too – trying to fix my love life. Was I that pathetic?

"No way. I don't like Alex. Don't you remember how he acted? Mr. Know-It-All!" The guy couldn't stand it when he found out that I was on the case. He'd acted like his royal self was the only one entitled to have official information. Which hadn't stopped me and my waitress friends from solving the whole thing. Ha! While he and his colleagues were clueless to the max that it was their *own chief* who was running the drug ring.

Which meant that the police chief in Springston went to jail and that Bert, Celeste's ex, was hired to take his place. Which led to my new job. Funny how things work.

Of course – in addition to pissing me off – Alex had kind of saved me, too. On more than one occasion. He'd even pulled me from an empty grave. It was easy to get in trouble when you were on the run from some criminal in a graveyard who was armed and mad. It didn't help that I tended to be unlucky...and very, very clumsy. What also didn't help, was Alex's dreamy bright blue eyes. He's six

17

feet of hard muscle, has short, dark-brown hair and looks like a model from the cover of a magazine. Although he annoys me as hell, I'm getting all melty every time I see him.

I was thinking about those eyes when I was startled by the phone.

All three of us stared at it in silence, then Celeste jumped to pick it up. "CMC Services. Good morning. You're speaking to Celeste." A serious look came across her face as she listened to the caller. "What? When?"

I whispered to Marge. "Are those fumes that come out of her ears?"

"Yeah. Must be something really serious."

"Have you ever seen Celeste really mad?" I asked.

Marge pondered for a few seconds. "I really don't know. She always looks so composed. Oh, but once, someone cut her off and took the parking space she was eyeing. So, she accidentally hit his back fender." Marge used her fingers as quotation marks as she said the word *accidentally*.

I swallowed hard. "But hadn't she damaged her own car too?"

"Nah. It helped that he drove a Ferrari and she drove a beat-up truck," Marge grinned.

18

I made a mental note to myself to always let Celeste have whichever parking space she wants.

Celeste continued talking on the phone. "You've got to be kidding me!"

"Oh, this looks bad," Marge said and backed away.

I followed suit.

"Well, *of course* we can!" Celeste said. "We'll solve the crap out of that baby!" She slammed down the phone.

"What's wrong?" I asked her.

"We got a case."

"A case! We've got a case!" Marge jumped up and down in anticipation. This was feeling real.

Celeste stood up and headed toward the door. "Grab your purses, ladies. The team is going out."

"Going out to where?" I asked.

"We're going to the zoo."

"The *zoo*?" Marge and I asked the question at the same time.

"Emergency!" said Celeste in a clipped, official voice. "A red panda has escaped."

Chapter Two

A CASE! I WAS EXCITED. But Celeste was pissed. I could tell she wasn't happy when she popped a stick of gum into her mouth. That was never a good sign.

"Those danged police!" she said as we all squished into Marge's car. "This is their way of saying we're not good enough. They don't think we have the chops to take on a bigger case."

A bigger case? But this was Springston! What was she expecting? Our town was quiet, mostly upper middle class. Not the kind of place where serial killings and million-dollar heists were the order of the day. At least, not that we've been aware of. Still, I was feeling a little let down too. Surely something else was up that could benefit from the work of three smart sleuths. Perhaps a missing person? Some kind of drug cartel scheme?

Celeste reached up to tighten the scarf that held down her mass of hair. The shocking bright red color was hidden now in silky folds of beige. She looked less like Celeste than ever.

"They don't trust us yet," she said. "Of course, my ex was very happy to call in with the news that

I'd be chasing some dang panda. He said it was the perfect job for the new wonder girls in town. He was having too much fun! And, I have to tell you, the jerk has a lot of nerve. He said he'd be sure to call us anytime a cat got stuck up in a tree – unless the tree was too tall, and he thought we might get hurt."

"He didn't!" Marge cried out in horror. "I'm gonna kill that Bert."

Whoops. The ex might be willing to help keep CMC in business, but he wasn't playing nice.

"Oh, but I gotta tell you, I love this case," Marge squeaked as she took a curve too fast. "The pandas are my favorite. With their itty bitty paws and their itty bitty noses and their itty bitty cheeks…"

Celeste angrily smacked her gum. "We get it, Marge. Just drive."

I was glad Celeste had spoken up. Every time Marge thought of another precious, itty bitty part, she sped up a little more. Her driving was pretty scary even when she wasn't cooing over furry animals. Yet anytime we traveled, she was the designated driver. Why was that? I wondered. Because my car was full off old sweaters and empty grocery bags and used candy wrappers?

"But we'll show them," Celeste said. "We'll find that panda so fast that they won't know what hit them. They'll be begging for the wonder girls to take on their next case. We'll be the best damn animal rescue service Springston has ever seen. Your cat stuck in a tree? You know who to call." The sarcasm was not lost on me. She chewed her gum so hard I was afraid she'd break her jaw. "I ought to charge him double the next time that they need us," she said. "We ought to charge an asshole rate."

As we got closer to the zoo, I thought about all the other times I had gone to visit. Something struck me then. "When you think about it," I said to my friends, "this case is kind of huge. This is important stuff. You know how Springston feels about those two red pandas."

Our town did adore its zoo, and especially the pandas. There were two of them: twins named Lou and Len. A city treasure had escaped! This was an ordinary town with an extraordinary zoo, built with money from a lifelong resident who'd taught my geology class sophomore year at Springston High. Tim Banyan's old torn sweaters had never given any hints that he had a lot of money. But he'd left the town a legacy when he died in 2008 with no heirs, a secret fortune and a passion for animals of all kinds.

There were no bigger stars in this town than the beloved Len and Lou. There was a naming contest and parade in 2012 when the zoo acquired the baby twins. I had a red panda t-shirt and a red panda coffee mug. Most people made a beeline for the pandas on any visit to the zoo. You'd probably catch them sleeping. But sometimes, if you were lucky, they'd peer curiously at you, as if they might be wondering what you were doing there.

Each year on their birthday, the whole town celebrated at the Panda Festival that went on all over town. Almost every merchant ran a special for patrons who wore red: free fries with a burger, free popcorn at the movies, five percent off for a style and perm...

"I love the pandas too," I said. "And if we find him, we'll be heroes. We'll be heroes our first week!"

Celeste turned to look at me in the backseat. "Not *if* we find the panda, but *when*." she said. "We will absolutely find him. And we can't be heroes, Charlie. Because we're undercover."

"Oh, yeah. I forgot."

"We'll be secret heroes," Marge said. "I've always loved a secret." She nodded to herself. "We do it for the safety of the citizens, not for the fame and fortune." She slammed on her brakes to keep from rear ending a Honda Civic whose driver wasn't traveling at Marge's breakneck speed. So much for the safety of Springston citizens.

It wasn't that she wanted to get to the zoo as soon as possible to get her hands on that panda. She always stepped hard on the gas as if every situation was an emergency. The next thing that I knew, she'd be begging for a siren for her official spy-mobile. Although that would surely be a tipoff that we weren't just fixing laptops.

I thought about the missing panda as we got closer to the zoo. It wouldn't be an easy case, but I loved a challenge. With a human, after all, you could kind of guess some of the places your target might be hiding. But what would a panda do with an unexpected day to roam about the town? Who could really know? Except, perhaps, a trio of very bright detectives if they put their minds to work.

And then, that's when it hit me: this *was* an emergency, a red panda was running loose in Springston! A panda didn't know to cross only on a crosswalk. He could knock down the ladder or the cans of bright white paint at Greenway Park where crews were building a gazebo. A panda might attack the little sample cups at the Apple Butter Festival going on downtown. So many things could go wrong. I hoped we'd find him quick.

But how? They didn't teach these things in school, or in the self-help section (where I sometimes spent my time, reading up on how to organize my stuff, set goals, be my best and most fit self... None of it seemed to take).

The zookeepers might have a hint on where a panda might go. They could tell us his likes and dislikes. Leafy areas? Quiet places? Or was he, perhaps, a curious panda who might run straight toward the action? Which this week might just mean the Apple Butter Festival. Or perhaps the new Crestview Crescent Mall that opened just last year.

Celeste continued to angrily snap her gum, her thoughts still stuck on the chief. "Bert and I are gonna have a little talk when this panda's safely in its cage. Do you know what the creep had the absolute nerve to come out and say to me? That he'd send more cases our way if he thought they weren't too much for us to handle. I can tell you one thing right now: he'd better toe the line or else his guys will have a great time hearing all the ways their boss used to..."

I leaned closer, but all I heard were angered mutterings. Dang. Close, so very close.

Soon we pulled up to the zoo. Well to be exact, Marge zoomed right past the zoo, then sped into the parking lot of a grocery store to turn her car around. That didn't make me feel great about our chances of success. How can you find a panda if you can't find the zoo?

The parking lot was a little less than half full. It was, after all, a Monday; the older kids were all in school. This was the time for toddlers and mothers pushing strollers, along with retired couples. Nobody in Springston ever grew too old for the zoo.

We pulled past the lighted sign held up by a metal tiger wearing green sunglasses and by a metal zebra in a safari hat. *We're So Happy that You've Come to the Springston Zoo!* Celeste tightened up her scarf. Unlike the tiger and the zebra, Celeste did not look happy.

Marge got out and began loading items into her purse: the knife, the hot pink tape recorder, the binoculars. "Go Team Panda!" she said as she pumped her fist into the air. Then she locked the car door.

"Quiet!" Celeste hissed. "They might not have made it public yet that the panda's missing." She took a deep and calming breath. "Okay, here's the plan. You girls walk around, act like you're just visitors, and keep your eyes wide open. I'll go check

26

in with the director, then I'll come and find you. Keep your cell phones on."

Undercover zoo girl. This might be a kick. It beat writing dull reports. How many speeding tickets had there been in August? How many burglaries in June? Ho hum. Life was way too short. A cool breeze brushed my face and brought the smell of popcorn. In the background, I could hear some kind of tinny music. I'd always loved the zoo. I was starting to feel good about my brand-new life.

As we walked quickly to the entrance, Celeste continued to fill us in, talking in a low voice. "They're doing everything they can to find his little guy. Animal Control is on it too. We're the reinforcements. I'll just show them my I.D. at the ticket counter, say we're guests of the director. Bert set that one up, at least, so we won't have to pay."

Marge hurried to keep up. "Do the employees know? That a panda has escaped?"

"Maybe. I'm not sure." Celeste stopped just before the ticket counter to pull her license from her purse. "But let's assume they don't know. And whether or not they have that information, we can't let them know who we are."

"Ohhh," Marge whispered knowingly. "Because we're undercover."

Celeste looked at me and rolled her eyes. "You get an A-plus, Marge. Yes, we're undercover. That kind of is the point."

We left Celeste at the front gate, and Marge took my arm with an air of great excitement. "What should we go see first? I love the elephants! And let's go find the snakes. Hey, I think they sell cotton candy."

The smell of sunscreen filled the air as we made our way through the clumps of visitors and peeked into some cages. *Hello, funny otter. Please don't get me wet.* We watched as a girl stood on tiptoes on a wooden box to feed one of three giraffes who bent toward her with its massive neck.

I turned toward a jingling sound and saw the Tiny Tots Train making its slow way past us. The crowd of children and mothers onboard smiled and waved at us, unaware of the ensuing crisis in this place of *Animals, Friends and Fun!* – the slogan that had been in place since the zoo first opened.

I heard a tiny redhead in the first train car call out to her mother. "Can we see the pandas next? I want to see the pandas."

A toddler behind her smiled. "Me go see the pandas!"

I noticed he had a t-shirt with the pandas' picture. I had a similar one at home. Most everybody did. In black letters across the top it said *Panda-monium at the Zoo*. A wave of sadness hit me. At least one panda was still left for the kids to see. I also felt filled up with a sense of great importance. It felt good to matter on this sunny, breezy day.

A small boy began to wail beside me when his ice cream scoop landed on the pavement. I stared at the oozing mess. Was that chocolate swirl? It might be nice to have a little something sweet to get the brain cells moving.

Marge looked very thoughtful. Sometimes I could almost swear that she could read my mind. "You know," she said, "if we bought some snacks, we might look more like tourists. Because you know that it's important that we blend in with the crowd." She looked carefully around her and whispered the last words.

We headed to the ice cream truck that was parked nearby; we studied the pictures on the side.

"First decision of the case!" Marge said.

"Shhh!" I said. She needed to work a little bit more on her undercover skills.

She picked a strawberry shortcake bar. I picked a rainbow pop.

Then we headed toward the panda cage. I didn't need one of the small green maps that I saw everywhere, abandoned on benches and sticking out of the trash. I loved to visit the pandas almost every chance I got. They were absolutely precious. Not that I'd been home that much in the last few years. I loved my family; they were great. But I'd found that it was easier to love them from a distance.

The names were still on the cage with one of the happy-looking signs in the shape of brightly colored paws that were attached to all the cages. *Meet Zoo Friends: Len and Lou.* A small blue and white sign to the side gave fun facts about the pair. I didn't need to read it; I knew all about Springston's favorite cuddly duo. I knew that their huge tails (that made them look like red raccoons) helped them balance when they were climbing (or sleeping) in a tree. I knew what their favorite food was: bamboo.

Now, Len was sleeping soundly on a branch. These two loved to snooze. They seemed to even have less energy than my brother Brad. These were lazy pandas. Sleeping and eating all day, it seemed like a nice life. Was Lou napping, too, wherever he had gone?

An employee passed by with a bucket, most likely making the rounds to see that all the animals were fed. Several others were doing the same, all wearing the trademark bright red shirt with the zoo logo on the back. With a pockmarked face and close-cropped hair, the dude looked like he could be a recent high school grad. If kids here didn't opt for college, the zoo was often a first choice as a cool place to get a job.

"Excuse me. Where is Lou?" I asked him, taking care to use my very best, oh-so-nonchalant, undercover voice.

He looked kind of nervous, or perhaps just in a hurry. "Lou is, unfortunately, not available for viewing." The answered seemed rehearsed. Had they given them all a script? Then he gave us a quick nod and rushed over to the next cage. There, he busied himself throwing fish to the seals, who thanked him and begged for more with eager, happy barks.

"Oh, look! It's the monkeys," Marge cried, glancing around the corner. "Let's go see the monkeys."

"In a minute, Marge. Let's stay here a little longer. Do you think pandas snore?" I slowly walked around the cage. If we were going to find a clue, this might well be the place. After all, here we were, at the crime scene, so to speak. Len didn't move a muscle. I wondered if he ever lost his balance in his sleep and fell right off the branch.

I looked closely at the cage and the area around it. Did anything seem different? (Well, there was one missing panda.) Nothing looked out of place. I'd been here a million times.

As usual, there was a crowd milling around the cage. A child beside me hugged her mother, sobbing. "I wanted to see Lou! I wanted to show him the picture that I drew of him," she cried. She held a crayoned drawing in her hand.

The mother gently ran her fingers through the girl's long hair. "I'm sure that Lou's just resting. We'll come back next week. You can show the picture to his brother when he wakes up from his nap."

Yes, we had to find that panda. I lowered my voice, linking elbows with my friend. "Okay. We'll see the monkeys like you wanted. But let's walk very slowly, and if we see a big group, let's just kind of hang real close, see what we can hear. We are at work, you know. Hey, look. The Snack Shack looks kind of busy. We might hear something there."

We followed some mothers with strollers to the open-air dining area filled with picnic tables. We both ordered sodas. We picked a table where we could listen in on the conversation of three employees on a break. If anyone had good info, it would be the people who were at work that morning when the panda disappeared. At least, I guessed that's when it happened. Celeste would have to fill us in.

We didn't learn a thing, at least not about the case. We learned that one employee's mother had stayed out past two a.m. with her handsome (married) boss.

"Spying can be fun!" Marge squeaked. Then she frowned. "I just wish I'd heard a name to go with that last story."

We learned that pork was on special that week at the grocer's, and that soy sauce, sesame oil and Worcestershire made a perfect marinade. Marge grabbed her notebook and jotted down the recipe. "Oh, goodness. Yum," she said.

We learned that dancing slowly with a baby could lull him back to sleep. "That's one that I haven't tried," said another mother as she tried to soothe a wailing infant.

Marge kicked me in the ankles. "Remember that one, Charlie, if you get serious with Alex."

I rolled my eyes. "No way is that happening." I had a hard time getting a real, grown-up life. Making babies was not high on my to-do list right now. And with Alex? No way. It's funny how things turn out. When I was little, I imagined I'd have a big family and a house with a big front yard by the time I was thirty. It seemed so far away. And here I was, at age twenty-nine, living with my parents and looking for escaped pandas.

Since no one seemed to be talking about the missing panda, I stood up from the table and prepared to leave. I grabbed the world's worst matchmaker by one arm and said it was time to go. "Let's go see your monkeys before you marry me off to some guy that I don't even like."

A small crowd had gathered near the exhibit that housed the lively long-armed capuchin monkeys. With their mischievous antics and almost human faces, they always drew lots of fans. A handler stood in a roped-off area where kids could shake hands with a monkey and get their pictures made. Groups could enter one family at a time.

"Oooh, let's do it, Charlie," Marge said. She pulled me into line.

"You notice we're the only ones who don't have a kid."

She pouted. "You're allowed to still have fun once you pass a certain age. Because that's only fair."

"Don't forget," I whispered. "We're supposed to be keeping our ears wide open. We're on duty here."

The handler, a young blonde in her twenties, handed a water bottle to a small boy beside her. "Do you like to drink cold water on a hot day like today?" she asked.

The little boy nodded, looking eager. He glanced over at the monkey in the handler's arms. The girl gave the audience a bright smile. "Well, Max likes water too." Apparently, that was the name of the black and white monkey whose arms were draped around her neck. "Why don't you hand the bottle to Max?" she said to the boy, then she gently put the monkey down.

Marge clasped her hands in glee, guessing what was next.

The boy gently put the bottle into Max's hand. Then the audience clapped as the monkey unscrewed the bottle top and took a long, slow sip of water.

Families posed with the monkey. Kids held it or shook its hand, with the handler standing close by, keeping a watchful eye on the monkey's mood.

And it was no wonder that she stayed on high alert. I loved to watch the monkeys, but they could get a little crazy. When a monkey got extra cranky, handlers had been known to end the show a little early to whisk the star attraction off to take a little break. Can you say temperamental? Hollywood stars have nothing on these little guys.

When it was our turn for the meet and greet, Marge scooped the monkey up into her arms and almost touched her nose to his. "How is the wittle monkey wonkey? Aren't you a cutie wootie?" she sang into his ear in her high pitched squeaky voice. She rocked him back and forth in a little dance.

The monkey looked a little startled, and, really, who could blame him? That meant that he was worked up when she placed him in my arms. Whoops. I felt trouble brewing. And what was she doing anyway? I never asked to hold a monkey! What was I? Ten years old?

Maybe Max sensed I wasn't thrilled to play a role in his little show. Or perhaps he was still freaked out by my over-excited friend, who continued to coo into his ear, sounding like a dying bird.

Whatever the reason, he grabbed my hair and yanked it hard. The crowd gasped as I begin to scream. Then, before I knew it, he was sitting on my head. But he didn't let go of my hair. That monkey had a grip.

"Get him off me! Get him off me!" I screamed, startling the wild creature, whose attack had grown more frenzied. Why couldn't we have gotten lucky and had this guy run away?

The handler swept the creature into her arms, along with some strands of my hair, giving him a soothing hug as she shot me the evil eye.

"I'm sorry," she said to the crowd. "I need to take Max for a rest."

The crowd grumbled in disappointment, and two kids began to wail. "I wanted to hold Max! That lady scared the monkey," one girl cried out to her mother.

"It's okay. Let's get an ice cream," said the tired-looking woman, sending me a glare. "Max is feeling a little sad, but he'll feel better soon."

"Hmm," Marge said, smoothing down my hair. "That monkey seemed to like everyone but you."

Great. My talent for repelling guys worked for monkeys too. I pushed my glasses up my nose and at least tried to get out of there with a little dignity. And then I noticed that some of the kids were watching me and laughing.

"Your hair," Marge whispered who had noticed my confusion. "Hon, I hate to have to tell you, but your hair is a mess."

I felt the top of my head. My hair, which I'd so carefully straightened that morning, was shooting out in all directions. This keeps getting better. *What a lovely day at the zoo*, I groaned in my head.

Suddenly, Celeste appeared amid the children, half of whom were laughing while the others sobbed.

"What's going on?" she asked, confused. Then she looked at me and frowned. "Did you brush your hair today?"

"I did, but...oh, never mind," I said.

Marge pouted like a child reporting to her mother. "I got to hold the monkey! For just a little while, but then it was Charlie's turn...and Charlie hurt the monkey's feelings."

"Let's just get out of here," I said and stomped away.

I didn't bother to explain, and Celeste somehow got the idea that it was better not to ask.

"You two need to get your act together," she said as we walked away. "You weren't exactly what I'd call blending into the crowd."

***

Back in Marge's car, Celeste lit a cigarette and reported what she'd learned. "Apparently, some employee got really slack last night. He went in to feed the pandas and left the door wide open. Who forgets to shut the door when you work at the blooming zoo?"

Well, that's a bad day at work, I thought. "How long was it open?"

Marge started up the car and drove us out of the parking lot, which by now had filled up a little more since some schools had let out for the day. It was not a weekend crowd, but the zoo always did a steady business.

"Nobody knows for sure how long it was before the panda saw his chance and ran." Celeste blew a ring of smoke. "It was a few hours until closing time when another worker found the cage door open."

"It couldn't have been open too long," Marge said. "Or don't you think that Len would have made a run for freedom too?"

"Maybe not," I said. "Those pandas love to sleep. Poor guy. I bet he's missing his twin right now. Don't you know that freaks the poor guy out? They're always here together." I gazed out the window at the clouds. "So. They have no clue where he might have run to?"

"No. They say that they've looked everywhere, but this is a big town. They called in extra staff and searched the premises all night and all the nearby streets. But they did it very quietly in the hours before they closed. They didn't want the guests to know that anything was wrong."

"Too bad it happened on a Sunday," I said. "It probably made it harder that there was a weekend crowd." You'd think someone would have noticed him: a small red panda with a big striped tail hanging around the ticket office, near the snake exhibit, under a table at the Snack Shack or scarfing up some chips. That would have certainly made for a day to remember at the zoo.

"So. I got some information." Celeste held her cigarette out the window to let some of the smoke escape. "A tiny little crash course on red pandas and their habits."

"Oooh," Marge said, starting to speed up. "This is so much fun."

Celeste frowned. "No, Marge, it's far from fun. It's an animal on the loose. He could be hurt or causing havoc. Who knows what could happen."

"You're right. But still..." Marge said, slowing down a little. "What did you find out?"

"Okay, Wonder Girls, here a description of our subject." Celeste reached into her blue expensive leather bag. She fished out a notebook, which she opened to read. "It seems that our missing person has distinct white marks on his face. And they gave me pictures. I'm not one for animals, but I have to say: he is quite a cutie." She looked back at the notebook. "He's twenty-two inches long, and his tail's almost as long as the rest of his whole body. Pandas mostly eat bamboo, but also fruits and insects when the weather's warm like this."

"Insects. That's disgusting." Marge scrunched her whole face into a frown. "Why in the world would they do that?"

"Marge! Because they're pandas!" I said.

"They are more active when it gets dark." Celeste continued to read out loud from her notes.

"It's like they're party people!" Marge squeaked. "Lou knows that life's more fun when the sun goes down." She turned around to wink at us. "And do you know what? He's right."

Celeste let loose her honking laugh. "The best kind of misbehavior is what happens after dark. Lou's my kind of guy."

"What else do we know about him?" I asked. "Anything at all that might be a clue about where we should look first?"

"Well, keep your eyes focused up above you. Our boy's favorite place to hang is high up in the treetops."

"Noted," said Marge.

"Cool," I said.

"And here's something interesting," Celeste said, flipping to a new page. "Animals in captivity sometimes take on habits that are different from the norm for the species that's in question."

"So, he's a one-of-a-kind little panda boy," Marge said. "That's good. Who wants to go searching anyway for some old boring panda?"

Celeste smiled. "This panda likes to eat pickles. Lots and lots of pickles."

"I can relate," Marge said. "I myself have been known to enjoy a pickle, especially on a burger."

"We don't need to know your dietary habits. Because you're not missing, Marge." Celeste lifted the cigarette to her mouth again.

I leaned back in my seat. "Weird. How did they find out about the pickles?"

"Somehow, Lou got hold of a pickle that some visitor dropped inside the cage. And they said he just went crazy. That's when the zookeepers got together and decided: if something that simple can make a little panda's day, why not give him more? They have two vets on staff. They said it wouldn't hurt him."

"Does Len like pickles too?" I asked.

Celeste shook her head. "Len's a hot dog fan."

"I have an idea," Marge said as we pulled onto the street that led to our new office. "Let's all go home to take a break. Cookies, naps, whatever. I've got Criminal Minds on TiVo, and there's a good one that's up next. Then let's meet at Green Acres Park at nine since our new friend Lou seems to get more active after dark."

"That sounds good," I said. "It will be easier to spot him if he's on the go and not sound asleep." But too bad it would be pitch black. "Everyone bring flashlights," I said.

Celeste gave us a thumbs up. "Rest up, girls, and save your energy so we can find this little guy!"

Marge slammed on the brakes and brought the car to a screeching halt. "Hang on, Lou. We're coming! And we're bringing pickles."

Chapter Three

I HAD THREE HOURS AT HOME BEFORE I had to head back out to meet the girls. Perhaps I could use my burgeoning detective skills to avoid my crazy family. Thank goodness it was a huge house with a basement and a big back porch. Lots of places to hide out! But noises seemed to carry. My father liked to turn the volume way up when he watched his football games. My mother sang while she fixed dinner, and I'm afraid she missed more notes than she ever hit. My brother might be snoring on the couch – or staring at some computer game with irritating sound effects. Sometimes all the noises seemed to be competing to see which was the loudest.

I was not off to a good start. As soon as I walked in, I spotted my brother Brad collapsed onto the sofa. He had a dazed look in his eyes as if he'd just worked a double shift fighting fires or performing rescues on some stormy mountain top.

"Can you bring me a beer?" he called. "While you're in the kitchen?"

"I'm not in the kitchen. I'm heading up the steps." Make that tiptoeing up the steps. I'd been hoping he wouldn't notice that I'd walked in the door.

"Then can you *go* to the kitchen? Pleeeease?" He sounded like he might be dying.

"Why would I go to the kitchen?"

"Because that's where we keep the beer."

"I don't care to have a beer right now but thank you for the offer."

He should just come out and say it: *I'm absolutely helpless, and I'd much prefer for someone else to wait on me hand and foot. Please don't make me stand up. That's just way too hard!*

"Charlie, please!" he wailed as I got further up the steps. "My job is absolutely brutal."

I paused. This might be entertaining. "What about your job is brutal, Brad? Did you get a paper cut? Pick up a stack of letters that was way too heavy? Did someone forget to add a stamp? Do you need a back rub with that beer?"

He sat up and stared down at the floor. "It's just so absolutely boring. And they make me hand off the stacks of mail so fast that there's no time to even pee. Or to visit with that redhead who's so hot at the Mexican restaurant down the street." He grinned. "I think she likes me, Charlie."

What was she, crazy? On second thought, I doubted that she even knew my brother's name. Of course, I didn't tell him that. Let him have his fantasies amid the piles of other people's bills and all the slick ads for insurance and window repairs that must cross his desk.

I sighed. All of a sudden, I felt really tired. The events of the day seemed to hit me all at once. I'd set up a new office, taken a harrowing ride with Marge, had a huge fight with a monkey, and been jeered at by a crowd. I sunk down on the steps. "Hey Brad, will you get me a beer?"

"Sure." He shrugged, stood up, went into the kitchen and came back with two cold ones. Wow, so he *can* move.

"Thanks. That was really nice." I joined him on the couch.

"How was your first day?" he asked, then leaned back with his beer.

What would someone say to that – if they'd really spent their day coaxing malfunctioning computers to act the way they should? What would such a person even do once they got to work and opened a laptop that needed...whatever laptops need when they cease to work? Even my own computer sometimes left me stumped, when I tried to do the simplest things.

"It was non-stop busy," I said. "Such a crazy day. We...interfaced a lot and...then we did...rebooting..." I paused to think. "And then we...did some things with some worrisome, very problematic...very sensitive...pixels." At least, I thought that was a word. "And we fixed some technical kind of...doodads." That was all I had. I couldn't remember any other words that sounded vaguely technical.

"Awesome, man." He nodded.

"Are Mom and Dad at home?"

"Dad's still at work, I guess," he said, tipping back his beer. My father often worked late at his restaurant, where the meatloaf and mile-high burgers were the stuff of epicurean dreams, and where people loved to gather to talk about town gossip. My dad had owned Jack's Diner since I was a little girl.

Brad stretched out a long leg. "Mom is in the garden. She made us some cookies."

That got my attention. My mother had dozens of cookie recipes, and every single one was fabulous. She made cookies for every holiday and found all kinds of excuses to get out her yellow mixing bowl. She might make cookies because it was our night to watch Dancing with the Stars. She sometimes even baked two dozen brownie bites because it was a Tuesday. In other words, you never knew around our house when you might be surprised by pecan wafers or by my personal favorite – sugar cookies with colored sprinkles.

Brad interrupted my sweet reverie. "And I left a few for you."

A few?

"Gee, Brad. That was very thoughtful of you. Thanks a lot."

"Hey, no problem, Sis." I guess he was too tired to understand a concept like sarcasm. I wondered if chaos would soon descend upon our lovely town when people all over Springston began opening their mailboxes to find other people's mail. How would they pay their bills? Get their weekly coupons from the grocery? Could a town function without mail? Perhaps we would find out.

I headed into the kitchen to check out the colorful plastic containers where my mom kept all her goodies. She had left a note, which I was almost afraid to read. A missive from Barbara Cooper might be sweet or it might be just plain bizarre.

To Charlie! I listened to some classic rock while I baked these cookies. I wanted the good energy from

*the music to flow into every bite. Hope your first day
was awesome, Mom.*

Well, that was nice. It looked like Brad had
scarfed down a ton of them already. So, obviously,
the energy transfer hadn't worked. Which was really
just too bad. If anybody needed energy, it would
surely be my brother. But, man, did those cookies
look good. My mom could turn out some winning
sweets even as her mind spun its zany thoughts.

Yum. There were lemon bars and chocolate-
pumpkin cookies. My day was getting better.

I took a few from each container and fixed
myself a plate, then I sat down with my laptop at the
kitchen table. I logged on to some apartment sites.
One gorgeous complex looked especially intriguing.
The units all featured tiny porches with views of
grassy expanses and, beyond that, Lake Glun where
I'd gone boating as a teen. I had already made plans
to tour the complex the next day. Not that I could
even halfway afford the rent, but a girl could dream.

Then my mind began to spin nightmarish
fantasies, as it did when I got tired. What if we never
got another case? What if I never got a paycheck? I
stuffed a cookie in my mouth. What if I ended up like
Brad, who'd lived at home forever? It didn't seem to
bother him, living with our parents at the age of

49

thirty-two. He was content to stay there as long as they would have him, as long as my mother would cook his meals and do his laundry, as long as my father would bring home leftover ribs and steaks and gravy when he came home from Jack's.

Hey buddy, I wanted to say to him. *Living at home with Mom and Dad is not exactly a ticket for impressing that redhead you seem to like so much.* Oh, but never mind. Brad would never plan a date; that would be too much work. It would mean he had to get up off the couch.

I imagined what it would be like: stuck at home forever as my hair turned gray, my eyesight dimmed, and my knees went bad. Would I join forces with my mother, chanting and humming to try to "center myself" and "reach a peaceful state" as the gun fights on Brad's TV shows got louder and louder still while he grew deaf in his old age? And the whole time we'd be leaping in fright every time that we discovered the plastic mega spiders my dad set out to scare us? Plastic bugs and whoopee cushions and fake nasty-tasting gum. My father loved it all. That vision of my future called for one – no, two – no, three – yummy lemon squares.

I immediately turned back to the advertised apartments. I checked listings in Springston and the surrounding areas, filtering by price. Because of my lack of savings, I was forced to narrow my search to the cheapest ones. The row of pictures for those listings was not a pretty sight. I enlarged the picture of the first one. Absolutely no way! The front steps were missing lots of bricks, and most of the doors had peeling paint. It looked like the kind of place that your parents would tell you to avoid going to at night. Which would put you in a quandary if that's where you kept your bed.

The next one was just as bad. *Three Oaks Landing*, it was called. But not an oak in sight. Just weeds and lots of trash. Couldn't they at least have cleaned it up to make a proper picture?

Like it or not, I seemed to be stuck for the time being at my parents' house. Had it been a moronic move to quit my job in Boston just when I'd been offered a nice-sized raise?

I had to think of something else, so I did some research on red pandas. What better way to cheer yourself than with fuzzy wuzzy little darlings? I read that they were shy. And that they sometimes wrapped their bushy tails around themselves for warmth. But – surprise! – no information at all on where a precious little fur ball might wander on a day of newfound freedom out and about the town.

I wandered back into the den to see what Brad was watching. No way! He was watching a cartoon! And not only was he watching, he was laughing uncontrollably at the antics of two mice running from a cat. Brad seemed to especially like the way that the cat's legs would spin just like a wheel when he ran really fast.

"Oh man, oh man. Did you see that?" he asked me, laughing so hard that he could barely breathe. "Genius. Wouldn't you love to see the cat do that again?"

Get me out of here right now!

"Say, Brad. Why aren't you at work right now?" I asked.

"Oh, I thought I came down with a cold this morning, so I called in sick," he said, without taking his eyes off the TV screen and chugging the last of his beer.

"Right."

I vowed to find that panda so fast that the police would pay us double and assign us five more cases. I had to get out of that house.

***

I left the house at 6:15 p.m. That would give us a little daylight to look around the park before the

52

sun went down. Then we could search the area under the darkened sky that supposedly appealed to our furry runaway. Just as I got to the end of the drive, I remembered something. I ran back into the kitchen and grabbed a bowl and two pickle jars from my mother's cabinet. I hoped she wasn't planning to make deviled eggs or potato salad.

The girls were waiting for me when I pulled up to the southern edge of the park. Celeste put her finger to her lips.

"Better not make too much noise," Marge said, taking care to talk in a quiet voice. "We don't want to frighten Lou." I didn't try to argue, but that sounded kind of lame. If anyone was used to human voices, it had to be a panda living in a zoo.

I filled up my mother's bowl with pickles and left it at the bottom of a tree, then we ducked behind some bushes. How's that for an answer to the age-old question "What did you do at work today?"

Marge had come prepared with binoculars, a notebook and tape recorder and a spool of yellow crime tape. She must have bought every object that she'd seen cops use to solve a crime on her TV shows. Where did you go to get crime tape, anyway? From the police in Springston? And why the tape recorder? Was she gonna interview the panda if we somehow found him? We could put the binoculars to use, at least. I wished I'd thought of that as well. I could have brought some too. Dad used to keep binoculars in the closet in the front hall. He used them to watch the birds.

I stayed quietly behind my bush and I did a lot of thinking. When your job for the evening is to hide behind a bush, you have lots of time to think, which isn't a good thing when you're despondent about your life and when you're prone to worry. That's when I had a startling thought. It hit me that *maybe* we weren't at all the smart detectives we thought we were.

"Celeste!" I hissed.

She poked her head out from behind a nearby bush and gave me a questioning look.

"What do we do if this panda really does show up? How are we going to catch it and get it to the zoo?"

Celeste frowned.

Marge peeked out from another bush. "Do you think it would let me pick it up?"

I had my worst thought of the night right then and there: I imagined Marge with the panda, cooing to the poor thing and freaking it out, just like she'd scared the monkey. If there were zoologists around to record the sight as he beat it out of there, they might see Lou making record time as the fastest panda ever. Then we'd never catch him.

I sighed.

Celeste frowned again. "Damn. I need a cigarette. We should have thought this through."

I tried to come up with something, but my idea was pretty lame. "Maybe we can use the bowl of pickles to lure the panda to the car, then drive him to the zoo." Well, that was certainly a sentence I thought I'd never say.

Of course, what did it matter? What were the chances that the panda would appear that very night in that very park in the very tree that we were peering up at?

Oh, well. I decided to just enjoy the night. It was a lovely evening in August, but there weren't a lot of people out. I made a mental note that this could be a nice place to escape when I needed a little peace and quiet, away from my mother's chanting to the universe and my brother's loud cartoons.

A couple passed us, walking their basset hound who sniffed at the pickles. The husband looked at the bowl, confused. "Someone," he said, "left their pickles in the park. Isn't that the strangest thing?"

The dog barked happily and nuzzled both their faces. Dogs love everybody; they don't care if you're broke or if you're a big loser who doesn't have a clue about how to do your job. I decided that I should find an apartment that would let me have a dog. On second thought, I couldn't even keep plastic plants looking fresh and alive, so maybe getting a dog was not such a great idea.

We saw one determined jogger, frowning from the exertion of running up the hills along the path, where the lights were just starting to come on. Probably I should jog. If I had to stay too long in the same house with my mother and her endless supplies of cookies, I'd need more exercise. Cookies. Why had I not brought cookies? Why should Lou be the only one who got a little snack? If he even showed.

After what seemed to be forever, we heard a rustling in the tree above us. I looked up, trying to make something out. There was more rustling. Something was there. Something was moving down the tree! It looked like a massive reddish-colored cat. I looked closely. I'd seen that face a million times through the bars of a cage. I'd seen it on my favorite coffee mug and my second favorite t-shirt. We'd found him. It was Lou!

Celeste's head popped out, then Marge's. Lou moved toward the pickles. It worked! Our pickle-plan worked!

"I say we pick him up," Marge said. She tiptoed a little closer.

"No way, Marge." I whispered.

"Marge, take a step back from the panda," Celeste said. It was halfway between an order and a plea.

We all moved toward him slowly. I thought about calling someone. The chief of police? Animal control?

Lou sniffed hungrily at the pickles as if he didn't notice us or didn't care that we were there. After all, this panda was used to people. He looked kind of pleased. He started to nibble at the pickles and seemed to enjoy them. Hmm, that was a funny looking pickle. Wait...what the...?

"What is that he's nibbling on?" I asked.

"It's the pickles, hon. You brought them, remember?" Marge said.

"No, he has something else there."

We moved a little closer to take a look. Lou had a pickle in his mouth that definitely did not look like a pickle. Was it...could it be? I stared wide-eyed.

It was. It was a finger.

Chapter Four

CELESTE PEERED DOWN AT THE PANDA. "Don't tell me that's a..." She put both hands on her hips. "Okay, girls, stand back," she barked. "That's surely not a pickle."

"Just gross! Lou has someone's finger!" I said. I couldn't bear to look. Suddenly, it didn't seem like the smartest thing to be out there in the dark. Would Lou really hurt us? Or was someone lurking close by who was capable of butchering another human being?

"No way. That's just silly." Marge grabbed her binoculars to get a better look. Then she did a little shuffle step as if she'd seen a mouse. "Ewww!"

Lou startled at the shrieking, then he calmly put down the finger to nibble on a pickle.

"Put those down right now," I said to Marge. "The binoculars just make it worse." Why take something ghastly and make it ten times bigger?

"Right." Marge closed her eyes and took a breath. Then she leapt into ninja mode, grabbing her "persuader" from her purse.

I gasped. She was aiming at the finger, not the panda. But the panda was pretty close to the place the bullet might well land.

"Hold your horses, cowgirl." Celeste put up a hand. "A finger by itself won't jump up and grab you. Not unless it's attached to a hand that's attached to an arm that's attached to a shoulder, that's…"

"Okay!" I yelled, freaked out. "Celeste, we understand! Stop reciting body parts. And Marge, you need to calm down." Ha. Like I was the one to talk. "Celeste is right. No way can a finger get you. Unless you're in a horror movie. But still, just absolutely ewww!" I shuddered at the thought of the bloody, hairy thing that should be on someone's hand, not laying in the dirt.

Marge put the gun away. "Sorry." She stared down at the finger and scrunched her nose up in disgust. "I was just startled; that's all. No persuader needed."

I made myself take a tiny peek. I was, after all, an investigator on the case. I had to act official! But what I wanted to do for real? Was to sink down into the soft grass and burst into tears. The finger had bits of dried blood on it, and it just looked so very sad and helpless without its hand and arm. A finger without a person, that's not how things should work.

Then I thought of something.

"Um, girls?" I made it a point to keep a close eye on the panda. "Do you think that maybe we should concentrate on Lou first and *then* figure out the finger thing?"

I didn't want to let him get away and lose the very first subject we'd ever apprehended in our new official role. The panda might take off any second; the finger would…it would just lay there on the ground. Unlike the little panda, it wasn't about to flee.

The job suddenly felt real. We needed to take action. This was disgusting – and exciting in a very weird way. We had (almost) caught a panda! And a bonus finger! Now…what to do with them?

Lou munched on some pickles, stopping to look up and stare at us. Then he picked up the finger with his teeth. I put my hand over my mouth and tried not to be sick. Perhaps my stomach was too weak to do this kind of work. But Celeste was made of tougher stuff. She calmly extracted the finger, very gentle, from Lou's mouth.

"Well, at least if we lose the panda, he won't get away with this," she said, holding the finger in the air.

Seemingly happy to share his finger, Lou went back to eating pickles as if he were at some weird buffet in a lovely park where leaves and pickles and fingers were all served up at once. Just a normal night out in the woods when one escapes the zoo.

"So, what do I do with this while we catch the panda?" Holding the finger at a distance, Celeste looked around for a place to tuck it away, out of the reach of Lou. But we had a problem. When your culprit loves to climb trees, not much is out of reach.

Celeste glanced at Marge's floral purse.

"Oh, no you don't," Marge said. "That's a name-brand purse right there with an adjustable strap and a vintage pattern too." It looked like the kind of purse that had lots of pockets. A pocket for your phone, a nice hook for your keys. But probably no stray pouch in case you found a bloody finger. Okay, this was disgusting.

"Charlie, you should grab the panda," Celeste said, taking charge.

"Me? Why me? I've already had...an unfortunate encounter with an animal today."

"But he looks so sweet," Marge cooed. "Don't you want to pick him up?"

He did look soft and cuddly. But I imagined that the owner of the finger wouldn't call him sweet. If it was Lou who'd done it, I might have to throw away my beloved panda shirt when this case was through. Lou might no longer be my favorite animal from the zoo once I got to know him better.

"You pick him up!" I said to Marge.

"Not Marge; she can't do it," Celeste said in a firm voice. "With the way she coos at animals and babies, he'll take off for sure."

I guessed she had a point.

Marge pouted. "I could sing him a little song." She began to make a noise that was more of a high-pitched whine, really, than a melody.

"No!" Celeste and I yelled at the same time.

I studied the panda, who was now eating the last pickle from the bowl. "I think Celeste should grab him." A tiny part of me wanted to be the one to do it; I wanted to be brave. But I mostly just wanted to go home and have this day be over. I wanted to eat a cookie and then to crawl into my bed.

"I'll be glad to pick him up if one of you would take charge of this." Celeste held out the finger.

Oh.

Celeste moved closer. "Does anyone have a pocket?"

"Ewww," Marge and I said in unison as we collided with each other, backing away from Celeste and that awful, awful thing that she had in her hand. How could she even touch it? Suddenly, writing reports at the old precinct in Boston seemed like a cushy job.

That's how it fell to me to pick up the furry creature who was studying the three of us with wide-eyed curiosity. I had to be the one to grab him. Because between a finger and a panda, I'd take a panda any day.

I approached Lou very slowly with my arms spread out. I picked him up but didn't know exactly how to hold him. Just as I expected, he put up a fight, brushing his backside against my face once I got my arms around him. And I got a bonus science lesson. Who knew that a bowl of pickles would made a panda fart? This was the worst job ever.

Gagging with disgust, I let go of my hold on Lou and then watched helplessly as he scrambled up a tree. We had lost our runaway! It was all my fault that we could not return, triumphant, to the zoo with one farting panda, delivered safe and sound.

Plus, the smell was awful. I could barely breath. How could that much stink come from one small animal? I bent down to gag.

I turned to see if my friends were angry. Instead, they were laughing so hard they couldn't catch their breath. They'd moved back ten feet to escape the dreadful smell. Between Marge's shrieks and the honking sound coming from Celeste, there were enough weird noises in the air to send the panda into a full-fledged panic. I heard his quick footsteps as he scrambled even higher up the tree and further from our reach.

"Well," Celeste said when she had caught her breath. "I tried to read up on every possible situation we might face with this panda. But that wasn't covered in the books: how to hang on to a subject when he farts right in your face."

They burst into more gales of laughter.

Humph. Celeste didn't read up on everything (nor did I, apparently). Or she'd have studied how to catch him!

"I'm afraid he's disappeared again," Marge said. She began to coo again. "Come back, little panda!"

I was trying hard not to gag again. "He disappeared all right. But he left his smell behind."

That, of course, set off my laughing friends again. Who knew this was a party?

We decided to divide and conquer, with each of us taking several pickles from the second jar that I'd left in the car and searching a small section of the park for both the smelly panda and a victim with a bloody hand.

"I'll take the east side," Celeste said. "And Marge can take the west. Charlie, you search in the middle. If you find our friend Lou, grab him very gently."

"And then what?" I asked.

"Hold your breath for one thing." Marge scrunched up her nose. "And make sure that his bottom is aimed the other way."

"But what do I do for real?" I asked, exhausted and annoyed. "We have to have a plan."

Nobody said a word. Nobody really knew.

"Try to get him to the car, I guess, the best way that you can," Celeste said at last. "Marge, go make sure that it's unlocked."

I hoped that one of us could catch the panda and wrap this thing up quick. And I really hoped that someone wasn't me.

Before Marge headed to the car, Celeste talked her into taking the finger and stashing it in her purse. "I can't very well catch a panda with one hand and hold on to a bloody finger with the other," Celeste said. "I'm an investigator here; I'm not an acrobat."

But Lou, it seemed, was long gone. We had frightened him, and he had left me wishing for a very long and soapy shower. After twenty minutes, we met back at the car. There was still work to do. Now there was a second mystery: whose finger did we have?

"It belongs to a male, I think," Celeste said. "It's not a dainty finger."

"It might be a pinky," Marge ventured. "It looks small to me."

I tried to turn my thoughts from *ewww*! into investigative mode. How best to find the owner? My fellow detectives joined me in silent contemplation. We all came up short.

It was Marge who broke the silence. "Does anyone know if the park has a lost and found?" That set us all to laughing. I really couldn't help it. It wasn't funny, but it somehow was.

When I caught my breath, I tried once again to scramble for an answer, a clue about where we might go from there. "Why would Lou do a disgusting thing like bite off somebody's finger?"

This was disappointing. The red pandas were heroes here in Springston. Kids dressed up like the pandas every Halloween; they drew the pandas' pictures to hang up on the fridge. The boy next door had even named his kitten Lou.

"Oh, I still believe in Lou!" Marge cried. "I don't think that panda has a mean bone in his body."

"What he did to me was pretty mean," I said. I still could smell the stink. It had settled in my clothes.

"That wasn't aggression," Celeste said. "That was tummy trouble."

"Lou didn't bite off that finger. He's way too sweet and cute," Marge said. "I think he found the finger. After the unfortunate event." Then her eyes grew wide. "Maybe he found it in the park. Maybe someone who does disgusting things is in this park with us."

"That does it," I said. "We need to get out of here. We have to take the finger to the police and report this."

Celeste put up a hand. "Now, hold your horses right there. If we can solve this thing ourselves, we can show them what we're worth. They assign us to find a panda like we're some kind of joke. And instead we nab some bad guy who's maiming people in the park. Somebody's hurt – real bad. Someone needs our help."

"This could be an awesome case," Marge said. "The Finger Fiasco and the Panda."

Celeste sighed. "The case doesn't need a title, Marge. It's not a TV show."

"But it might be on TV someday. This might be a case that makes the TV shows." Marge got all dreamy eyed.

"But before you practice your quotes for the TV," Celeste said, "we need to find the owner of the finger."

"We could call hospitals," I offered. "That could narrow it down. How many recent patients could there be who came in without their finger? But then, on second thought, lots of medical places have sprung up all around here since I moved away. It might take forever to call every single one. And I think you kind of have to hurry with a missing body part. It's not like you can wait forever before it's reattached. At least, I think that's right."

"That's what I think too," Marge said. "I think I saw it on TV."

Celeste frowned. "And it might seem suspicious too: three women asking around about a missing finger. They'll wonder why we didn't just take it to the cops. It would seem odd, I guess, us trying to track down the victim on our own. Since we're not on official business." She winked. "At least, not as far as anyone can tell."

"Day one!" Marge chirped. "And we haven't blown our cover." She looked thoughtful. "I hope that I get to use my crime-scene tape and my tape recorder soon. I got the tape recorder for half price." She had always taken great pride in her shopping skills.

Celeste looked at me and shrugged.

"Whatever, Marge," I said. "I'm sure you'll use them soon. I don't think we have a choice here. We should take this to the police. The hospitals will talk to them. And they can search the park in case the victim's still out here somewhere hurt."

Celeste thought about it. "I suppose you're right. We need to get the finger to them quick." She grinned. "I hope my ex is there. I'd love to give the finger to our brand-new chief. Pun intended."

I'm sure she already had.

I shrugged. "He could get a fingerprint, I guess."

"And I just know that asshole will take the credit for our finger find!" Celeste said. She was a little fired up now. "This is no way to stay in business."

"Just because he has the finger doesn't mean we can't be the ones to solve the mystery," I said. "Because we found it first, that gives us the right to look for the bad guy too – and also for the victim. *If* there is a bad guy at all. We still don't know what's up with the finger. There's a victim for sure."

"Well, that settles that. We'll look for both the pinky people!" Marge said.

***

I was beyond exhausted when we got to the station. It was already dark outside. But somebody somewhere was...well, they were incomplete. A finger is important! A person needs their parts.

The few cops scattered across the room looked at each other and grinned when they noticed us. That made it clear: they knew exactly who we were.

"We need a detective, please." Celeste sounded more official than she looked at the moment. Her shirt was covered with stains after our adventure. Her blue scarf was coming loose, but still made a valiant effort to hide her fire-engine-colored hair.

A heavyset older man took a bite out of an apple as he looked us over. "I don't suppose that you three ladies have a panda in that bag?" He nodded toward Marge's purse. He could barely suppress his laughter over his stupid joke. "Have you come to bring the little guy in for questioning? Better let him out now. It might be hard for him to breathe."

A younger cop put down the file he'd be reading and propped his feet up on his desk. "How's it going, ladies, with that missing-person case? Did the panda leave a note? Did he have enemies that might have some kind of motive to do him any harm?" The others laughed, rewarding his lame efforts to be funny.

I saw Celeste begin to fume. Any redder and her face might just match her hair.

The apple guy shrugged and aimed his core across the room, making an impressive landing in a trashcan almost four feet away. "Well, you ladies have a tough one. I don't guess the panda has a cell phone to help you trace his whereabouts?"

"It's an important case," Marge said, banging her purse down hard on the reception desk. "Lou deserves to be rescued just as much as anybody else."

The younger cop walked over to the desk and leaned across it, facing Marge. "Lady, you got that one right. You know what the song says about our good friends at the zoo. Right, guys?" He glanced back at the others.

Well, dang. I knew what was coming.

They all joined in, singing the theme song for the zoo. The ads played all day on the radio. The cops sang very loudly and very much off key.

Come to the zoo to play.

Oh, happy, happy day!

Friends both old and new

Are waiting just for you.

"Hold the music, maestro." Celeste's voice was firm. "We need a detective, not a choir."

But by then, they were getting into it, swaying with their arms around each other, building up to their big finish.

Who will meet you there?

A snake? A bird? A bear?

They're waiting just for you

At the zoo, the zoo, the zoo.

One cop mooed, another oinked; another let loose with a bray. They finished with jazz hands and turned around three times, kicking their feet up in the air.

Oh, they were having fun.

I hated being laughed at. "That doesn't sound like any zoo I've ever been to," I said indignantly. "That sounds like a farm."

Celeste glared as the men high-fived one another. "Perhaps they missed that little worksheet like my nephew had in school. You know, *Match the baby animal to its cozy home*. I think that it's in first grade that you learn to tell the difference between the zoo and the farm."

Marge was skipping in place with glee. "Sing the song again!"

"Don't you dare!" Celeste yelled. She rubbed her forehead as if she felt a migraine coming on.

I looked to the left and noticed Alex, leaning against the door that led to the administrative offices. There was no way around it; the man was looking *fine*. His dark brown hair was a little longer than before – and it still looked so very soft. His eyes were even dreamier than I had remembered – and seemed to be dancing with amusement over my current plight.

Wasn't that always the way when it came to me and him? I always was the one in some dopey situation, and he got to stand there looking all official and amused. It had happened time and time again with the case we'd worked on earlier. But then, who had caught the bad guys? Not you, Mr. Hottie, with your hint of a moustache and your muscles straining against your shirt and your...Geez. Pay attention, Charlie!

"Now," Celeste said, "the reason we came in here is..."

"We didn't find a panda...yet. But we found a little something else." Like a proud child bringing home a prize, Marge slowly opened her bag and pulled out the finger.

The cops gasped.

"Not so funny now, is it?" I said.

The cops were struck dumb with silence as Alex walked closer to take a look. He didn't look amused anymore; he had his cop face on. "What's up with that thing?"

Humph. "A hello would be nice," I said. I hadn't seen the guy in weeks. I wondered how my hair looked. Snap out of it, Charlie. This is not the time to think about your hair.

He was way too engrossed to notice anyway. He was frowning at the finger. "Where did you..." he started. "Okay, I'll tell you what. Let's talk in my office."

We left the impromptu choir behind and walked into his office. We took seats in the cheap-looking orange chairs that were placed around his desk.

"You're working late," I said.

He leaned back in his big desk chair. "I was just about to wrap things up for the night." He glanced at the finger, which Marge was stroking like a pet that needed comforting. "But now we seem to have a little situation. Okay, what's the story?"

Celeste began the explanation. "Well, I guess that you're aware Bert has hired the three of us…"

He grinned. "Yeah. He's hired you to go chasing after Springston's favorite panda."

"We've already had a sighting at the park downtown," Celeste told him proudly. "The panda was there tonight."

"But he got away from Charlie!" Marge interrupted. "'Cause he farted in her face."

There went any chance I had of appearing even a little bit mysterious or sexy.

Alex stared then laughed out loud. "I've had subjects punch me, shooting at me but none of the jerks I've chased down have tried to get away by setting off a stink bomb in my face."

We filled Alex in on how we found the finger and I thought I saw the corners of his mouth twitch upwards.

"It's a pinky, right?" Marge asked enthusiastically.

Alex took a closer look. "Yeah, looks like it."

"Do you think the panda might have…uh…done this?" I asked.

Alex studied the finger one more time. "Don't think so. Do you see the cut right here?"

We all stared at the finger in disgust.

"It's a clean cut," Alex said. "Even if the panda nibbled on it, you can still see that someone – a person – cut this finger off."

A wave of nausea hit my stomach.

Celeste shifted in her chair. "I believe that time is of the essence with a severed body part. I suggest you phone the hospitals and see if we can reunite this finger as soon as possible with its rightful owner."

"I'll get my colleagues on it. Hang on. I'll be back." He took the finger from Marge and placed it in a small see-through bag he got from a drawer. Then he left the room to tell the men to begin making phone calls in search of a patient in need of a finger.

When he returned, he took us to another office, where a middle-aged woman gave us a tired smile.

Alex made the introductions. "Agnes, I'd like you to meet the independent investigators the chief recently brought in. I'm afraid I'm going to need you to stay a little longer. I'll need you to run some prints."

"No problem," she said.

"I'll be right back," Alex said and left the room.

Agnes turned to us. "Is the suspect already here?"

"Uh…It's actually a victim," I said.

She sighed. "So, they're in bad shape, huh? Brought in without I.D.?" And without an arm, a head…

"Kind of. He was brought in…in a purse," I said.

Startled, Agnes put her hand up to her heart. "What do you mean? In a purse?" She stood. "Where is the victim now?"

"I gave it to Alex. Alex has it now. In a bag," Marge squeaked.

Agnes looked like she might faint.

Alex rushed right back with the finger. "Here. It's not a person, really," he explained to Agnes. "Or…I guess it's part of one. Hopefully you can tell us who might have lost this finger."

"We think the victim's male. Cause of the size and all." Celeste studied the finger once again.

Agnes looked like she was happy just to breathe. "It might take a while to get a name if it's in the database. A day or two at best."

She shook her head when she noticed the surprise on Marge's face. "Oh, I know that's not the timeline that you might expect. We're not like those cops on TV – solving major crimes in the space of sixty minutes. Here in the real world, things move a little slower than they do on CSI." She smiled. "But those cops are fun to watch. I love me some CSI."

Marge bounced up in excitement. "Oh! Did you see the one...?"

Celeste took her gently by the elbow. "No. We all have work to do." Then she turned to Alex. "Did your guys call any hospitals yet?"

"Yeah. Nothing suspicious so far," Alex said.

The local hospitals, it seemed, had nothing to report yet. All new patients in the area had come into the waiting room with all their parts attached.

I wondered what that could mean. It didn't seem like good news. If the victim hadn't shown up to ask for help for his mangled hand, he might be in really bad shape.

Alex sighed. "Well, I have to finish up some reports, and I suggest you ladies go home. We'll work with the medical experts to keep the finger in the best shape that we can."

Did he just want us out of there so he could dig up clues all by himself and get all the credit for wrapping up the case? Alex loved his glory; he loved to be "the man." But there was nothing we could do right now. It had been a long day. I wanted a cookie and my pillow.

Alex cleared his throat. "Oh, and by the way, I wish you ladies would consider laying low for now. We've had some...developments. There's a reason to think that some serious things might be going down. I'm glad you found the finger. Great detective work. But for now at least, I wouldn't hang around the parks or in the woods at night. That would not be wise." He looked straight at me. "I really mean it this time. I'm talking danger here."

"But we have to job to do." Celeste was getting angry once again. "And to find a panda, you need to search a lot of trees. The parks, the woods, the countryside – that's where we need to be."

"And pandas get more active when the sun goes down," I said, hoping to sound smart. "That means that we're nocturnal too. At least until the case is solved."

He sighed, exasperated. "I'm telling you it's not safe."

I was getting pissed off. "Hey pal, we're detectives. We can't just run and hide anytime we think we might get hurt. Do you also have a curfew?" I looked up at the clock. "Oh, Alex, better hurry home. Look how dark it is. Are all police officers off duty after daylight hours until further notice because the dark has gotten way too scary?"

"Okay, Charlie, chill. I'm just trying to protect you. And things for me are about to get real busy. I can't go running off to save you if you get in trouble. You seem to have a knack for...uh...unfortunate incidents."

Well. The guy had a lot of nerve. I never once had asked this jerk to come and save me. Not one single time! He just seemed to be on hand to see me at my worst.

"Thank you for the warning," Celeste told him smoothly. "I know that there are some here who'd rather we get lost. But we will do our job." She looked him in the eye. "And we will kick ass."

Alex held both hands in the air. "Hey, lady, I'm not taking sides between you and your ex. I'm keeping it real, that's all."

Marge opened her purse and fished out her little notebook. "You spoke of developments and danger. What exactly did you mean?"

He just shook his head. "You know that's confidential."

Celeste stared him down. "Unless you happen to be discussing it with people who are colleagues on the case."

"I wasn't talking about the panda. The things I'm talking about don't fall into the Department of Lost Pandas."

I pulled her away toward the door before things could go downhill even more. Then I turned to Alex. "Will you at least just let us know if you get an info on our finger?"

"*We* found the finger, after all!" Marge squeaked.

He looked up to the ceiling as if to say, "what did I do to deserve this?". Instead he said, "I will be in touch."

But he did not look glad about it.

Outside, a mild evening breeze was picking up. I took in a long breath and let it out.

"I think we each have earned a coffee," Celeste said.

That sounded good to me. We all knew just where to go.

Chapter Five

THINGS WERE BUSY AT JACK'S, almost every table filled, despite the lateness of the hour. I found comfort in that fact. If I never found a job where I could make real money, at least my dad would always have the funds to keep his only daughter fed. People would always have a taste for the world's best meatloaf, cheeseburgers and hash browns too. People knew that every Tuesday there was a soup and sandwich special, and that every Friday there was peanut butter pie.

First, we headed to the restroom where Celeste washed her hands three times. So did I, even though I hadn't touched the finger. It was bad enough to have stood within a few feet of someone's body part. And then there was that panda...

Then we settled into a corner booth and scanned the menu for ideas. That was just a habit, really. As former waitresses at Jack's, we all knew the food by heart.

"Nothing with pickles, please," I said. "Nobody else can fart on me today."

The snorts from Celeste and squeaks from Marge startled a young waitress, who rushed up to our table. We ordered three large mochas. Hey, we had more than earned huge quantities of both caffeine and chocolate.

The waitress reached into the pocket of her apron to take out her pad and pencil. Her nametag identified her as Amy. She looked as exhausted as I had sometimes felt when I would help my dad by waiting tables and refilling drinks on extra busy days.

"So," Amy said nervously. "That will be four...no, three...lattes? Coffees? Medium? Or extra-large? No, wait..." She looked like she might burst into tears right then and there. "I am so absolutely sorry. This is just my second day. And all day it's been so busy, I can't even remember the simpler orders..."

"Oh, don't worry about it one bit. That's fine," Celeste said in a soothing voice. "The first thing that you need to do is to stop and breathe."

"All together now," Marge chirped. "Breathe in deep." We all inhaled. "Now, slowly let it out," Marge said.

Four people exhaled all at once. Already I felt better.

"Just write each order down, slowly," Celeste continued to instruct. "And if you forget, just ask! Customers here are happy; customers at Jack's are the forgiving kind. After all, you're the hero. You're about to bring them a plate of something extra fine."

Amy smiled. "I never thought of it like that. Three cappuccinos – no, three mochas – will soon be on their way."

Celeste nodded in approval. "See? You're getting it already." She still sounded like Celeste, although her tower of hair was mostly hidden and her nails no longer blue.

We watched Amy walk away.

"That was nice, Celeste," I said. "Now, I wish you could give us a pep talk on how to catch a panda. And how to solve the pinky-finger mystery before that butthead Alex does."

Celeste gave my hand a pat. "We're learning, girls. We're learning. It's didn't take us long to find that panda, after all."

I frowned. "A lot of good it did us."

"Oh, I think we're doing great," Marge said. She leaned forward and spoke in her official investigative voice. "We spotted the fugitive panda. We picked up on some suspicious happenings out there in the woods. Most importantly, we retrieved key evidence in the case." She made a face. "*Disgusting* evidence. Although who knows what it means..." Suddenly, she turned bright red and fell completely silent. She stared off toward a point somewhere behind me, then burst into a fit of giggles.

I looked at Celeste, confused. "I don't get the joke."

Celeste grinned. "Oh, I don't think it's a joke. I think it's that fry cook!" She pointed her head to indicate the spot where Marge was looking.

I turned to see Ralph, my father's newest hire, peeping from the window between the kitchen and the dining room. He looked to be somewhere in his forties, with a round and weathered face and an extra happy grin.

"A hard worker, that one is," my dad had said the week before. "I hope this one stays a while." Fry cooks were notoriously hard to keep around; it was not an easy job.

He pointed at Marge and winked. Once again, she blushed, then she winked back at him. There was a shyness there, combined with a surprising sense of confidence in her ability to hold this man's attention. It was delightful, really, to watch this temptress side of Marge. Then she primly brushed at her long skirt and smoothed down her dark blond hair.

I started at her, open-mouthed. "Bouncing butter cookies! What the heck is going on?"

"I think the two of them are about to be an item," Celeste said in a low tone.

That sent Marge into another fit of giggles, this time mixed with squeaks. It was like Minnie Mouse getting high.

Celeste leaned back in her seat. "They met on the last day that we worked here. Our last day was Ralph's first." She sighed. "The course of true love never did run smooth. Shakespeare got that one right."

Well, that was a surprise. "Shakespeare? Really? I thought you'd be more into modern romance. Or maybe paperback true crimes." I hadn't been able to finish *Macbeth* back in my high school English class, although I'd somehow earned a B on my final paper.

"If you want romance *and* murder, Shakespeare's your guy," Celeste said. "Have you read Shakespeare? Someone's always killing someone. Or falling helplessly in love, just like you and Marge." She shook her head. "What is it, anyway, with you girls and the fry cooks?"

Alex had gone undercover as a fry cook at my father's diner the last time I'd gotten mixed up with an investigation. I guessed Ralph was his replacement. Hmm. This might be good – or great even. The next time that Marge dared to tease me about that obnoxious Alex, I could hit her right back with some observations about her own romantic prospects.

Celeste finished with her story. "These two lovebirds here haven't even exchanged one word with each other, except when your father introduced them. I keep telling Marge he's shy, and that sometimes a modern woman of the world must make the first move. Once that happens, *bam*! It's fireworks all the way!"

Marge turned red again. But she was saved from further teasing by the arrival of three mochas and three large bowls of cinnamon ice cream.

Amy studied the table with its arrangement of cups and bowls. "I think I got it right."

We didn't bother to correct her. Who could argue with ice cream?

"Okay," Marge said as Amy hurried off to take another order. "Let's get down to business. How should we investigate this bloody-pinky thing? Because I want to solve this case as well as find the missing panda. Double victory. Someone needs to catch the hacker dude before he strikes again. That's one badass dude right there. And who loses their little finger and doesn't go to the hospital? At least we'll know the victim if we run into him." She gazed around at the crowded restaurant. "Should we have a look around? See if someone's missing something?"

Celeste rolled her eyes. "I'm not sure that's be the best way to investigate. In that kind of situation, a person would go after some medical attention and not the meatloaf special."

"But first things first," I said. "You girls have to remember that, officially, our job is to find the panda and return him to the zoo. That's the thing we've been assigned by the guy who'll sign our check. And I need a paycheck bad."

"Okay, let's have brainstorm session." Marge fumbled in her purse and got out her notebook, which she put down on the table.

"Eww! I said, staring at the little cardboard book.

Marge looked startled. "What?"

"Don't put that on the table." I glanced over at her purse. "Did the notebook touch the...you know?" This could be a problem. I might not ever be able to eat another meal in the presence of The Purse.

"No!" Marge said. "It's fine. The..." I could tell she was trying very hard to sound official. One mark of a good investigator, after all, is not to get freaked out by the yuckiness that sometimes was a big part of the job. She took a long, deep breath, and then she began again. "The recently retrieved personal item of an unknown person in distress was wrapped up in a napkin I had left over from the last time I ordered a churro special with hot sauce from the convenience store."

Yikes. That did not go a long way in making me feel better. I looked down sadly at my ice cream. I'd lost my appetite.

Marge pulled a pen out of her purse and set it near my coffee. Ewww!

"Now," she said. "Let's make a list of all the places we could go to look for a cutie patootie little panda." She paused. "Or a person with one less finger than they had the day before."

Suddenly, a sick feeling filled my stomach. What if there wasn't a live person who matched up with the finger? What if, instead, there was a body? But I didn't share that thought with my friends. The day had been so full of so many awful things. I'd save that scary thought for another time.

Nobody could think of anything for Marge to write down on her list, so we just enjoyed our mochas. I could drink a little coffee, but I still couldn't eat. When we were more rested, we could make a plan.

I saw Marge getting a sad look in her eyes. She began to worry about how Lou might be doing alone out in the woods. "Oh, that poor little panda! Do you think he's cold and hungry?" She looked like she might cry. "Do you think that fuzzy wuzzy little panda is scared and all alone?" Then she eyed my ice cream. "Are you going to eat that?"

I pushed the ice cream towards her. Sweets always seemed to help *me* stop a flood of tears.

***

The next morning came too quickly. I'd told Celeste and Marge that I'd be in at noon. First, I was headed out to look at some apartments. I was hoping against hope that some miracle deal on a decent complex was out there waiting – a deal that would fit my tiny budget and save me from my family.

When I got down to the kitchen, my mother was pouring herself a cup of coffee, humming some song, while my brother seemed to scarf his food down like there was no tomorrow. My dad was making pancakes. Ooooh, I loved it when that happened! His pancakes were big and fluffy and full of chocolate chips. It was almost like digging into the softest, giant cookie and covering the whole thing up with butter and maple syrup. Apparently, I got my appetite back.

Of course, my father's pancakes always came with a bad joke.

"There's my little princess," he yelled as I poured some coffee. As if I were an eight-year-old, and hard of hearing too. "Hey, Charlie, here's a question."

"It's way too early, Dad. No jokes before my coffee."

"Why did the Red Sox cook up pancakes?"

Might as well get it over with. "I don't know, Dad. Why?"

"Because they already had the batter."

My mother and I groaned while my brother yelped with laughter.

"Brad!" my mother said, picking up some oranges. "You know to keep your mouth shut while it's full of food."

I tried to erase that picture from my head. I would not let my brother spoil my appetite. It had been way too long since I'd had my dad's pancakes.

Distressed, my mother looked up from squeezing a pitcher of fresh orange juice, which I also loved. "No wonder the energy in this house feels absolutely off. Between the terrible jokes, the lack of manners..."

With a big smile, my father handed me a plate of steamy goodness. "Hope you have an appetite. Other people pay good money for these things when they come out to the diner. And very rarely is the meal prepared and served by Jack himself." My dad was quite the cook. Occasionally he would pop into the diner kitchen, giving tips on the perfect way to dice an onion or season a pork chop. He might even whip a dish up if the spirit moved him.

He stood back, proud, and watched as I took the biggest bite I could and closed my eyes in pleasure.

"Charlie," my father said. "If you could stop by the diner later, we could use your help. The computer's acting screwy. It won't stop freezing up."

"Oh, Dad. Have you met me? I can turn my laptop off and on. Beyond that, I'm pretty clueless."

The kitchen fell strangely silent.

"But Sis," Brad said, "how can you stay in business as a technology consultant? If you're a computer moron?"

Leaping lemon drops! Had I just blown my cover?

I tried to fix it quickly. "Ha ha, Brad, you idiot, don't you recognize a joke?"

My mother brought the orange juice. "Children, be polite. Careful of the energy. The energy in this house is way off today."

"That was a stupid joke," he groused. "Dad's jokes are so much better."

Okay, that was a close one.

Brad's fork was a silver blur as he shoveled bites of pancake into his mouth.

"What's the emergency?" I asked him. "Do you think your food will disappear if you don't eat fast enough?"

He looked genuinely stressed, a look I wasn't used to on my newly employed brother. What worries, after all, would an expert couch potato have? That the battery would die on the remote control?

"I can't be late again," he said. "If I do, they'll fire my ass."

Since when was he concerned about being fired? This was a new aspect of Brad. Maybe he finally decided to be a grown-up.

"Language," my mother said as she pulled a bottle of sage out of a kitchen drawer and began spraying around my brother.

I felt some of it on my face as she continued to energetically spray sage around the room.

"Mother," I said, ducking down. "Don't spray me in the eyes."

My father took a seat. "Brad, I'm glad to see you're serious about doing a good job."

"Yeah. The Employee of the Month gets two hundred dollars and tickets to the Celtics."

So much for unselfish motives. But at least he was up and off the couch.

I stood and gave my dad a kiss. "This girl has got to run. But those pancakes were the best, Dad. I'll see you guys tonight."

My mother looked concerned. "Be careful out there, sweetheart. Do you promise that you will? You should all three remember that it's a Libra moon. I myself plan to stay inside all day. I've cancelled all my classes."

I poured some coffee into one of those to-go cups and headed for my car.

Second day into the I-wanna-live-on-my-own-and-have-an-awesome-career plan. Things could only get better. I'd hoped. But with the missing panda and the cut-off pinky, my hope started to vanish.

Traffic was light, as mostly everybody was already at work or at school. Thirty minutes later, I pulled into the driveway of Escape Option Number One. It didn't look half bad: a brick ranch house located about ten minutes from my office. The resident had advertised on the real estate website that he had a room to rent.

The landlord opened the door before I could even knock. A tall man, somewhat elderly with a big smile on his face; he seemed a friendly sort. Except that – shoot me now – why was he standing on the front porch in his tighty whities?

Don't look, don't look, don't look.

The house, the street, the big trees: they'd all looked so inviting. But I was afraid that this first stop on my rental tour would have to go into the "hell, no" category.

But I might as well go in and look, just to be polite. That seemed to be the easiest way to make a graceful exit.

I introduced myself and stepped in, trying hard not to look directly at the astonishingly – almost sparkling – white color of his underwear. The den was very neat, the kitchen was clean and spacious with a nice stove that I would have never used if I decided to move in. There was a big fridge. Now, that would have been a plus. I'd be bringing home lots of takeout, I supposed. It was a nice house, the walls painted in soothing colors. Half Naked Man seemed to be a neatnik. No empty cups or messy stacks of papers.

The TV was dark and silent. No stupid commercial blared into my ears, no brother sprawled across the couch, no mother asked nosy questions about whether I might consider a sperm donor if no man came along.

Perhaps this might not be so bad. Perhaps I could gift this man with several pairs of nice dress slacks. Or perhaps Half Naked Man was just a crazy uncle who'd snuck out of his bedroom while his caregiver took a break. Tomorrow he might very well be on a plane back home. Perhaps the real landlord would show up any minute in a button-down shirt and jeans. "Never mind Uncle Jake," he'd say. "I thought that he was sleeping."

But I had no such luck.

"I've lived here eighteen years," Tighty Whitey said proudly. He showed me the space that would have been my bedroom: smallish, pink and neat.

He also pointed out his room, which connected right to mine. "Side by side," he said. "Isn't that swell and cozy?"

Well, no. It most certainly was not. I'd have to pass through his room to get in and out of mine. What had the builder been smoking when he designed this house? The whole thing was just too weird.

I thanked him for the tour. "I'll be in touch," I said, as I walked, ran, then leapt into my car.

Hmm. This was going well.

All the other options made me want to weep as well. One apartment was a single room with the shower way too close to where I would be eating dinner. Another complex would give me more space, but the bathroom was shared with others on the hall, including an older woman who loved to talk. In the ten minutes that it took me to escape her in the hallway, I learned all about her five cats and her worthless son. I learned who was sleeping with someone else's husband in another apartment unit that was two floors up, and who was dying a slow and painful death on One Life to Live. Which I could watch with her in the afternoons, she offered with a bright smile. She could make some tea!

"No thank you," I told her. "I really have to go."

I knew that often it was a poor girl's fate to have to settle for a roommate. So I tried to be optimistic when I rang the bell at a lovely townhouse whose occupant, a secretary at a bank, was looking for another girl to share the rent and the payment for the utilities. But the whole place reeked of pot, and given my potential roomie's very mellow conversation, I figured she must have started smoking with her morning java.

The last stop was a pretty space where I could live blessedly alone. There were neat rows of flowers, a well-kept lawn, and fresh coats of paint on every door. But the apartment manager told me there was a catch. The vacant apartment was on the second floor above a field that was set up for games of archery.

She took me up and showed me the vacant one-bedroom space. She gave me a defeated frown when she saw me looking out the window at the archery equipment. "The sport seems very popular," she said. "Who knew so many people liked to play with bows and arrows."

I wondered. Were they loud, these people who played archery? It might not be too bad if they didn't start too early. Perhaps I could even try to play the game myself. It might be fun to learn. And imagine how convenient. I did need exercise. My new job seemed quite physical, and I was out of shape.

"You'd have to keep the windows shut." The manager came to stand beside me and gaze out at the field.

Oh.

"The arrows come that close?"

"Really, really close."

I looked around. The place would be fine, I guess, if I could live with the arrows. Could an arrow pierce a window? Would I be safe huddled in the corner? I guessed this was another *no*.

I thought about my tiny place in Boston, which I used to complain about non-stop. The kitchen had been barely big enough to give a person room to turn around. But it was quiet when I wanted quiet. The couch was an ugly brown, but it was soft and comfy. From the bedroom window on a clear day, you could catch a breeze that smelled of Upper Mystic Lake. And you'd never ever catch an arrow or a whiff of pot.

I pointed the car toward the office. I needed to somehow turn this job into a decent paycheck.

Chapter Six

I ARRIVED TO FIND MARGE WAY UP on a ladder. Her round figure was precariously perched on the highest rung as she hung up a framed poster with kittens wearing funny hats. A slightly lopsided poster hung beside it: fuzzy cats fast asleep in pots of brightly colored daisies.

Not exactly the kind of art that said *Techno Wizards Hard at Work* or *Tough Investigators. We'll Nab the Bad Guys Quick.*

Marge's round body dipped and swayed as she stood up on her tiptoe to hammer in a nail. Hmm. The dangers of the job came in all kinds of forms.

"Whoa, there," I said. I spoke in a soft voice so as not to frighten the unlikely acrobat in her tight pink dress. "Marge, get down from there." I held up my hand to help her down. "Ease down very carefully. How can we make a living if you break your leg?"

"Thanks, sweets. I love you too." She jumped down from the last rung with an indelicate small hop, then stood back to admire her somewhat crooked kittens.

Celeste was on the phone, furiously scribbling something on a pad. "We gave you the pinky finger. Now you give us the name." Uh oh. Someone was getting an ultimatum. Celeste wasn't happy. Was she talking to her ex?

"She's on a mission," Marge whispered. "They'll cave any minute. I'll bet you anything."

After a few more minutes of talk, Celeste slammed down the phone. "A Mr. Baxter Duvant. Age twenty-five. Of 8 Clove Street in Springston."

Marge gave me a high five.

"Great work, Celeste," I said. "You go get 'em, girl."

"Must have put a rush in to get the name that fast," Celeste said. "Remember what Agnes told us when she took the fingerprints?"

Marge nodded. "She said it might be a while."

Celeste paused. "Something's going on that they're not telling us. Why were they in such a hurry to find out the victim's name?"

"That's what we need to figure out," I said, excited – and a little scared – of the possibilities. "Plus, Alex was acting really odd." He'd intrigued me with his hints that something big and dangerous was going on in Springston. Oh, yes, our little pinky was part of something bigger. I was almost sure.

Celeste stood up from her desk. "Something's brewing, girls. But CMC is on the case. We'll figure out what's up."

"What else did they tell you about the pinky guy?" Marge hurried over to her. "Is this Baxter guy okay?"

"Well now, that's the thing." Celeste stuck her pencil in her tall mass of hair, which was now free from its scarf (since she was not on a case). "The police have no idea. No hospitals have seen him. There are no records anywhere. The police can't find the guy. Or at least that's what Bert tells me. Who knows if they're holding back with some information."

"That can't be good," Marge said. "The pinky person might be hurt! Let's go and find this Baxter." She clasped her hands and giggled. There was Minnie Mouse again. "Isn't this exciting?" She looked around. "Do you think I'll need my tape recorder?"

Celeste rolled her eyes. "Hold you horses, Marge. We're not heading out to look until we have a plan."

But where to even start? Surely the police had already checked out Clove Street. I sighed, tired already. "Well, at least this time it's a person, not a panda," I said. "We can go out in the daylight...without a bowl of pickles."

"And this subject's not as likely to fart right in your face," Marge said.

Thank goodness for small favors.

"But he could be dangerous," Celeste said. "This Baxter is not exactly some cool, upstanding dude." She glanced down at her notebook. "This guy has a record. Burglaries, theft of motor vehicles, possession of stolen property."

Marge looked disappointed. "Oh, but that's no fun. I really, really wanted to go out and save a good guy, not a thug."

Celeste put up her hand. "A crime is a crime is a crime," she said. "And an assault is an assault, even if the victim's not a person you'd care to grab a cup of coffee with. We don't discriminate." She took a green scarf from her desk drawer and tied it around her hair. "I have an idea, girls. Get your keys, detectives. Let's take a little ride."

I pulled my sweater off the hook. "I suppose we're off to Clove Street?"

Celeste nodded. "I'm sure the cops have been there already. But some of them are doofuses. And maybe this nine-fingered thief was out when they were there. The three of us might have better luck.

I'm sure the police are keeping a real close eye on the property. So we need to be extra careful. It's best they think we're off chasing pandas while the big boys handle this. What they don't know won't hurt them."

"They must know we're up to something," I said. "Since you demanded information."

"But I've promised we be cool," she said. "I said we'd concentrate on other things if they kept us in the loop."

We got into Marge's car and sped away. I had to grab the wheel a couple of times so as not to derail because Marge kept clasping her hands. That was not the way I wanted to die.

It turned out that 8 Clove Street was an apartment, not a house.

"Well, that's just great," Marge said. "Which apartment is it? I suppose the police conveniently forgot that little detail when they gave you the address. They're afraid we'll solve the case first before they even know what's up."

Celeste gave her a thumbs up. "And we will do just that. But, luckily, I have everything we need." She glanced down at a paper that she'd tucked into her scarf. "We'll find our Mr. Duvant living in apartment number sixteen."

With their peeling paint and rotting wood, the Clove Street Apartments seemed like the kind of sad place that would fit my budget. Super! I was in the income bracket of a low-life thug. I couldn't wait to meet my neighbors once I found a place.

A few older model cars were parked out in the lot, but nobody much seemed to be around. The place seemed sad and empty.

Marge studied the four-story building carefully. "Hmm. A fire escape." "Let's go up the fire escape. Very, very quietly."

"What?" I looked at Marge. "Would it not be simpler just to knock?"

"Oh hon, I don't think that's best," she said. "Because if there's something fishy with this Duvant guy, he's not likely to invite us in and point out all the clues."

She did have a point.

"Right," Celeste said decisively. "Best to take a quiet peek and then ask questions later."

But the fire escape looked more like an abandoned ruin than a safe way to get up to the higher floors.

"I don't know, you guys," I said, pushing my glasses further up my nose. "That thing looks really old. What if it just collapses?" The steel looked so corroded that I was afraid a single footstep might just do it in. "Plus, what if we get caught peering in the window? Caught not just by anyone but by a burglar-thief?" Not the best enemy to make.

As usual, my cohorts felt braver than I did. As usual, they won. So up the fire escape we'd go. Which made me nervous.

"First things first, however." Celeste spoke in her take-charge voice. "We need to go inside, look at the numbers, see which window is Duvant's. Just act like you belong here, like we're here to see a friend."

We were back in undercover mode. Marge had put on a gray coat to cover up her bright pink dress. Celeste had on her usual disguise. And me? Well, I needed no adjustments. I kind of blended in anywhere I went. I guess I'd found a job where plainness was a virtue.

The Clove Street Apartments were even more dismal when you got inside. The linoleum hallways were cracked, and the building smelled like garbage and old fish. We had to climb the dirty wooden steps to the fourth floor before we found two peeling plastic numbers, a one and a six, hanging from loose nails.

"Remember that," I told the others. "Should be second window from the left."

Marge repeated it over and over as we made our way outside. "Second window from the left, second window from the left. Hopefully that's one that we can get a good view of from the fire escape."

"Quiet, Marge!" I whispered. If somebody was listening from behind their door, that would not sound good at all. The doors were pretty thin and cheap. I'll bet sound carried in those hallways.

Outside, the street was empty. "Coast is clear," I said.

But first there was a problem. We had to somehow figure out how to get the drop ladder down. We stared up at it in silence.

Celeste was the first to speak. "Okay, this is what we'll do. Marge, clasp your hands together just like this." Celeste formed a tight web with her hands. "Then Charlie, you climb up. Our hands will be your steps."

"Do what?" I asked. "No way!"

"You can do it," Celeste said. "But you should hurry, before somebody comes."

Okay. I took a deep breath. Could I do it? I could do it!

I gave it my best go – and quickly tumbled backwards, landing on top of Marge.

"Ouch," she said, as we got up gingerly, checking to see which limbs might ache in protest or refuse to even work. "You should be okay," Marge said. "Because I was right there as a cushion. Always glad to help." She winced as she rubbed her side.

The second time went better, although my perch was quite uneven. With Celeste being extra tall and Marge being extra short, they formed a crazy kind of ladder.

Stretching my arms as high as they would go, I could just reach the bottom of the drop ladder. Then it took some effort to pull the darned thing down. I was out of breath. I added *work out more* to my ever-growing mental list of ways to improve my life. Maybe I should join in my mother's yoga group. No one was under eighty. I should have no trouble keeping up with them.

Celeste glanced up the ladder and pointed to the window of our pinky person's unit. "Okay, Charlie, you climb up there."

"Why me?"

"Who else?" Celeste said. "You're in the best shape of the three of us."

I glanced over at my friend. She seemed pretty strong to me. But I guessed all those cigarettes might have had their way with her. Still, if I was the fittest one in our little group of ladies, we were one sad lot. The bad guys could have a field day!

"Hey," I said. "Did I ever tell you I have a fear of heights?"

"We need you, Charlie. Please," Marge begged. "You're the fittest and the lightest."

"Nuh-uh," I said. "This wasn't my idea." I felt like it was someone else's turn to play Superwoman. But, still, I let her words sink in. No one had ever called me that: the fittest and the lightest.

I decided I would do it. Trying to live up to my reputation (The fittest! And the lightest!), I began my climb. The fire escape felt sturdy; this might not be so bad. That meant I got the first peek into Duvant's window. For the first time that afternoon, excitement trumped my fear. Hopefully, something would be in there to give us just a hint about what was going on and where we might go from there.

But what I saw inside the window was not what I expected. Was this really the apartment of a young guy with a long string of crimes? Why was there a grandma and a grandpa spinning around to some music from their tiny radio? They were bobbing their heads and doing jerky dance moves. This was crazy. Colored lights flashed in the background in time with the music's steady beat. I was so mesmerized I forgot that I was on a job. And that I was perched up on a fire escape I did not completely trust.

Then Celeste coughed from down below, reminding me that they were waiting for a report on what I saw. How could I very quietly describe what I was seeing? I shook my hips a little bit and did a small one-handed wave that I hoped looked like a dance move.

I could tell the others didn't get it. They looked up at me, confused, but that was the best that I could do. It wasn't easy being up there and keeping my careful balance, let alone performing some jazz dance in midair. Now was the time to peek inside, see if there was anything around the room that might be a clue. I could explain when I got down.

They looked at me, expectantly. Why were they so impatient? If they couldn't wait to find out, they could climb up and look themselves.

But should I try just one more time? What other dance moves did I know?

I'd only been to one prom, because some guy owed Brad a favor. I'd spent most of it in the corner, but I'd been impressed with this Egyptian kind of dance that some other kids were doing. They'd all stood in a line, making jerky arm movements with bent elbows, and thrusting their heads forward. Now, several flights above the ground, I gave it a try.

Marge stood below with her mouth open in amazement. Celeste shrugged and gave me her frequent frowny look that I knew meant *What the hell?*

Then I bent over and pretended to move slowly with a cane. I meant to send two messages: Old People. Weird Dance Moves.

Their mouths were still open in confusion. Then something vibrated in the pocket of my jeans. Duh. Texting would be much easier than fire-escape charades. But couldn't it wait till I got down?

I pulled out my cell.

MARGE: What the heck are you trying to tell us? Did Duvant steal King Tut?

ME: Old People dancing in the kitchen. Are you sure we have the right apartment?

Marge showed the question to Celeste, who looked thoughtful, then concerned. Was it my imagination or did that look mean *whoops*? Celeste ran inside the building and came back looking sheepish. She and Marge conferred. Then I got another text.

MARGE: Wrong place. You're at 19. The 6 came loose and was hanging down.

I shot them a look.

ME: Are you kidding me?

MARGE: Nope. Go one floor down and one more apartment to the left. Sorry, sorry, sorry!!!

Well. At least I'd had a free show. Sorry, dancing old folks. Have fun and party on. They should try my mother's classes. They'd fit in just fine.

I quietly made my way down to peek into the window that I'd really come to see (or at least I hoped it was.) Nobody seemed to be home. Although the lights were off, I could see into the bedroom as well as into the kitchen. Everything seemed to be in sight with a single glance: bedroom, bathroom, kitchen, den. So, I was pretty sure that nobody was inside to sit on the single torn upholstery chair or on the unmade bed. This guy didn't own a lot of furniture – but, sheesh, he had a lot of trash. Get it together, man. Have you ever heard of a little thing they call a garbage bin?

I texted the girls.

ME: Nobody home. Nothing much to see.

MARGE: Can you climb into the window?

Do what? Was she crazy? I would climb the fire escape and I would peek. That's where my bravery ended. This was one bad dude. I wasn't climbing in his window. I texted again.

ME: Coming down.

What were they thinking, anyway? No way could we just climb into people's windows if we didn't have a warrant. We could get in so much trouble. I knew that much from my work with the police in Boston. Plus, we were official agents of the police here in Springston. We had to follow rules.

Which was a fine excuse. Cause I didn't want to do it.

My phone dinged again as I started to climb down. Sheesh. What now?

MARGE: Just see if it will open.

I turned around and gave it a half-hearted try, hoping it wouldn't budge. Then they'd leave me in peace.

Of course, it opened easily, making a creaking noise to announce to anyone who might be passing by that something sneaky was afoot. Just great. I looked down in time to see Marge leap in the air with glee, just to make us stand out more.

I typed a message to let her know not to get excited.

ME: I'm not going in. Absolutely no.

MARGE: We will keep a lookout. This is our big chance.

ME: If you want to come up and go in, be my guest.

MARGE: But you're already there.

ME: And you could be here soon.

MARGE: I will make you cookies.

ME: No.

MARGE: Oatmeal Raisin.

I started down the steps.

MARGE: Peanut butter?

I took another few steps down.

MARGE: With chocolate chips.

I stopped.

My phone dinged again.

MARGE: You'd find out stuff that Alex doesn't know. Alex would be so jealous.

That sealed it. I couldn't believe what I was doing. I was going in.

I made my way back up, and the window easily opened – all the way this time – so that I could crawl right through. And the place was awful. Plates were everywhere with dried food crusted on them. The carpet looked like a piece of modern art with stains in every shape and color. The worst part was the smell: old food mixed with sweat. Still, I couldn't help but notice that the main room was much bigger than the rooms I'd seen that morning in my apartment hunt. And...was that a second bedroom?

I wondered what this Duvant had to pay for rent. Were there any vacancies? Could I live in this building if they had a unit open? It was roomy, not far from the office. The dancing oldsters would make for some fun neighbors. But I'd have to make sure I got a unit that was downwind from Duvant.

Heck. What was I thinking? This was not the time to ruminate on my living situation. I had to look around and leave. I glanced in corners and underneath the old couch. I tried not to touch anything if I could help it. Eww! Nothing seemed unusual besides this guy's inability to walk over to the sink and wash a dish, for goodness sake.

But the second bedroom was another story. The room was filled with empty boxes. There must have been fifty of them in there, maybe even more. But no labels or clues of any kind about what the boxes used to hold. They were piled on top of one another, almost to the ceiling, so that a person could barely walk into the room. There was a small bed in the corner with boxes stacked on top.

But wait. The boxes in the corner seemed to be taped up, still unopened. I had to squeeze through narrow cardboard pathways to make my slow way toward them. A wave of excitement hit me again and I'd be lying if I said I wasn't curious about what was inside them.

Just as I was making my way to the boxes, I heard something. I stopped and stood still. It was the front door slowly creaking open. Damn.

I was not alone.

Chapter Seven

I FRANTICALLY LOOKED LEFT AND RIGHT, hoping to find somewhere to hide. Could I hide behind the boxes? Why had I ever listened to Celeste and Marge? If it was this Duvant dude, then he might well have a gun.

I could barely hear the footsteps. My heart was way too loud, thumping like a frightened bat set loose inside my chest.

Were the footsteps heading to the spare room? Please, Mr. Thug, go somewhere else. Take a nap or make a sandwich. There's nothing to see here! Just a bunch of boxes. And a dopey girl who doesn't have the good sense not to crawl in felons' windows. Never again! Listen to yourself, not to Celeste or Marge.

With boxes jammed into every foot of space, there was nowhere to hide. Which was tragic news since – save me, please! – the footsteps seemed to be heading straight towards me. Seconds before he walked in, I ducked beneath the bed.

Thank goodness I was out of sight, although...well, just yuck! Within inches of my face were two cockroaches (who were dead, at least), a crusty piece of bread, and dust bunnies that were so huge they might just win a prize at the county fair.

Then Baxter (or someone, at least) walked into the room. I could see the cuffs of a pair of jeans and two scuffed brown boots move back and forth next to the bed. I tried hard not to breathe, afraid that the smell of old food might make me gag. Was that a dried-up piece of pizza in the corner? Plus, the dust bunny right beneath my nose made me want to cough.

Don't cough, don't cough, don't cough.

A rusty, squeaky sound came from somewhere close, then I saw four wheels move next to the bed. Well, at least I had a clue: something that had wheels. Although, who knew what the clue might mean?

Please, Mr. Thug. Hurry up. Do what you have to do and leave so I can get out of here.

But what if he didn't leave? What if he settled in for the afternoon and then just went to bed? I couldn't even think about it. Some things were just to awful to even contemplate.

The rolling and the squeaking and the moving back and forth seemed to last forever while I held my breath against the stench. To distract myself, I listed all the jobs that I might try to get when I told the girls that I was through.

I tried to think of jobs that would never, ever have you wondering if you were about to die. The girl who rings my groceries up. The man who brings the mail. The guy who cuts my hair. Did they ever have to hide from some grungy dude who might up and shoot them dead? Oh, no, they did not.

Did they lay down with their faces just an inch away from an old, dead roach? And did that roach just kind of wiggle? Could this day get even worse? I willed myself to stay still, no matter what the roach did.

Don't scream, don't scream, don't scream.

Then I felt an ominous itching in my nose. Perfect. The worst timing in the world. Now, that's the perfect skill for an undercover detective: knowing how to squelch an inconvenient sneeze. Not that we'd bothered to learn a single thing about how to keep our poor selves safe in these situations; we'd just dived right in.

A series of loud thuds sounded from the corner. He must be doing something with the boxes that were taped up and full, the ones I'd almost had a peek at before he walked into the door. I wished I'd had the time to see what was inside. At least I'd have some info for my trouble. But I'd been too slow.

Speed! Being speedy was the ticket. Next time I'd be faster.

But would there be a next time? Or would I try something else? Teacher, teller, waitress. I could sell cookies at the mall!

In my mind, I listed different kinds of cookies. Anything to distract me from the fear that was a hard knot in my stomach. Then I tried to order them by which ones I liked the best.

What was Baxter doing now? Or I supposed that it was Baxter. After all, this was his place.

I saw two hands lift a box, and a flash of white just above the wrist confirmed that I was in the presence of one Baxter Duvant. There was a bandage in the spot where once there had been a pinky. Who loses a finger, for goodness sake, and doesn't call a doctor? I pondered the question for a moment, still trying to distract myself from the possibly disastrous sneeze that was itching to get out.

Baxter stumbled over an empty box and yelled out a string of expletives. He kicked at the cardboard – which only begged the question: how much worse would he treat a stranger he caught watching from underneath the bed? Best not to think about it.

Then he left, pushing his wheely thing. I heard the front door slam shut. Yes! The knot of fear inside me loosened. I willed myself to lay still, holding my breath against the sneeze in case the dude came back. I counted to one hundred. And then I did it one more time. You couldn't ever be too sure. This guy could hurt me bad.

At the triumphant count of one hundred! (for the second time), I sneezed, then coughed, then crawled out from my filthy hiding place to go and find my friends. You know – the ones with the brave ideas. The ones who were waiting safely on the outside of the building. Those friends and I were gonna have a little talk.

Warily, I crawled out. By now, my legs were stiff. The room looked a little bit less full, but it still was a big mess. Empty boxes were scattered about the floor in a haphazard pattern, but the full ones were no longer in the corner. Where was he taking the boxes? And why? What kind of crime was this? It had to be a crime. He didn't seem the kind of guy to collect donations for the needy.

I looked around for a label that might have fallen off, a tag, anything he might have dropped. But I didn't look too carefully. I was out of there. Hopefully Marge and Celeste had tucked themselves away somewhere safely out of sight.

Before setting out the way I came, I gave the front door a try. I was counting on the fact that sometimes crooks were stupid. Yes! The door was unlocked. I slipped out quietly and tried to walk ever so nonchalantly down the silent hall. The coast looked clear to me, but someone could be watching. Even with the dimness of the hall lights, half of them burned out, I could see that my jeans were white with a thick coat of dust.

Outside in the hot sun, nothing looked amiss. No sign of a man with a squeaky cart piled up high with boxes, no sign of my two friends, which I guessed should make me glad; it meant that they were good spies. But I needed some hot water and a bar of soap, and I needed them right now. I needed Marge to show up in her little car and whisk me safely home.

Just as I was pulling out my phone to text, I caught sight of my friends' car behind the street corner. I hurried over and jumped into the backseat. I'd barely shut the door when Marge sped away.

"Never ever will I do that." I leaned back against the seat. "Can you imagine how that freaked me out? Not to mention that the guy's place is just absolutely gross. I had to hide under the bed when he came in."

"Well, we didn't send you in to clean." Celeste turned toward me from the front seat. "This is not the local garden club's Spring Fling Tour of Homes."

"If it was, I'd want a refund. How disgusting can you get? Why did I ever let the two of you talk me into that? I thought I was going to die." I let out a huge sneeze.

"Bless you, Charlie. Bless you. Oh, hon, you did so good," Marge said. "We were very, very worried."

"Next time it's someone else's turn to do death-defying stunts," I said. "What if he had caught me?"

"Oh, I can't think about it! So. Tell us what you saw," Marge cried, almost running a stop sign in her eagerness to find out what had been going on inside Baxter Duvant's place.

"Well, it was kind of strange. I was in the spare room with a million empty boxes. You would not believe the boxes. Boxes everywhere."

Marge hit the brakes hard as she came to a stoplight. "All of them were empty?"

"Most of them, I think. There was a pile over in one corner, and those were the ones that seemed to be taped shut. I guess those were packed with something." I let out another sneeze. "But packed with what, you think?"

"Bless you." Celeste patted down her scarf. "What was in the boxes? That right there, I think, is the million-dollar question. So. There was no writing on the outside of the boxes? No clues whatsoever?"

"Nada, I'm afraid. Or at least not that I could see. That was about the time I was otherwise engaged. It seemed more important at the moment that I dive for cover."

"That was good thinking there." Marge began to cough. "I think that our friend Baxter must have lost his cleaning rags. Charlie brought a pound of dust when she got in the car."

"Well, I spent most of my time beneath a bed. It was filthy. I hope we're heading to the office so I can get my car. I could use a shower quick."

Marge wrinkled up her nose. "Yeah. I didn't want to hurt your feelings, hon, but you do kind of need a bath." She picked up her speed, which was never good. I wished she'd drive more slowly. I'd had enough scares for one day.

"Thanks. So, what did you guys see?" I asked them.

Celeste lit up a cigarette. "Well, our timing kinds of stinks. He pulled up in a van. I bet it hadn't been five minutes since you'd gone through the window."

"Kind of stinks for Charlie, but, as far as getting information goes, it was a lucky break," Marge squeaked.

"Right," I said. "I feel extremely lucky."

"We knew that it was him when he pulled up and entered the building," Celeste said, "because we saw the bandage where there should have been a pinky. We started to send a text, but we didn't want your phone to ding. We hoped you'd heard him come in. And that you'd found a place to hide. We quickly moved the car around the corner, so he wouldn't see us when he came out again. That would look suspicious to him. Marge was so scared that you'd get caught, she almost hyperventilated."

I understand the feeling.

"I'll bet your boyfriend Alex has absolutely no idea that our subject, Baxter Duvant. drives a minivan," Marge said.

"With a dented fender in the back," Celeste said. "Chevrolet, I think. It's most likely a 2008." She paused. "Or perhaps a 2009."

How did she know these things?

"He's not my boyfriend!" I said emphatically. "He's...sometimes a jerk"

"Steer clear of the jerks, hon." Celeste held her cigarette out the open window. "Even the ones who look fine in their designer jeans. The jerks are never worth it."

"Back to the crime at hand," I said. "Were you watching when this Baxter came out with the boxes?"

"Oh, yeah. We saw him pull right up to the building," Marge said. "And he took this thing out. It was kind of like a big box, except it was on wheels."

"And then later, when he came back out, his little cart was filled up with all these cardboard boxes." Celeste continued with the story. "And then off he drove."

"We started to follow him," Marge said. Then she turned and made a sad face. "But we didn't want to leave you at that place all alone."

"You amaze me with your kindness."

"Always glad to help," Marge squeaked.

We tried to come up with ideas of what it all could mean: boxes being shuffled from one place to another, one little finger torn away, a possible encounter with a panda who was missing from the zoo.

"It's a puzzle. That's for sure," Marge said.

Celeste agreed. "Maybe when we're rested, an idea will come to us. Sometimes the very best ideas kind of sneak up on you like that."

"But at least we've got the license tag," Marge said.

"You do?" I asked. "That's great."

"Woo-hoo!" Marge shouted. She reached out to give Celeste a high five, swerving into the next lane. I was very thankful that rush hour hadn't started.

I idly wondered what came next. The next move might be to find the van or perhaps stake out the house. But I'd be watching from the outside, and I wouldn't get too close.

"Shoot!" Marge swerved into the parking lot of a convenience store.

"What are we doing, Marge? I don't want a snack. I just want to get back to my car." I could feel the dust bunnies crawling all over me.

"Well, you won't get there very quickly if I don't stop and get some gas." She pulled up to a pump. "Who's up for a milkshake? Anyone want soda while we're waiting to fill up? Cheese crackers? Bubble gum?"

Celeste shook her head. "Thank you, Marge. I'm good."

Cookies? Did they sell cookies? I'd earned myself some cookies. But I'd have to touch them with my hands and...there was just no way I was going to do that.

I was dreaming of lemon sandwich cookies when a Jeep pulled up beside us. Its brakes made a screeching sound as the driver pulled to a sudden stop.

Marge hopped out, seemingly unaware of the rude driver who had stopped beside us. "I'll be back in a jiffy," she said. "Oh, and, Charlie, look. It's your boyfriend!"

Please. No. Had I not been through enough?

Why did Alex always turn up when I was at my worst? I glanced down at my grimy, crawled-out-the-dumpster look. And, of course, he was looking great in a crisp blue button-down and those expressive, gorgeous eyes that made me want to melt.

"He's not my boyfriend, Marge," I said in a defeated voice.

Celeste sighed. "Your not-boyfriend's looking quite upset."

He leapt out of his Jeep and leaned into the car before Marge could shut the door and go on her merry way in search of snacks.

"What did I tell you girls about messing with my case?" he asked. "This is not a place for amateurs. This could get scary. I don't want you to get hurt."

"We can't ride through town and stop for gas without you on our tail?" I asked, indignant, as if this was something that I did daily, ride through the worst part of the city in a cloud of filthy dust. I was too tired and angry to even try to be polite.

Celeste gave him a hard look. "And where are these amateurs you speak of? I see no amateurs among the fine detectives here that you see fit to insult."

He gave her a hard stare. "So. You hang up a sign. And you're suddenly an expert?"

She glared back at him. "We're still waiting on that sign. Could you check on that for us? You people have been very slow. Bert promised us a sign."

He leaned in even closer. "You heard what I just said. Stay away from Baxter Duvant's place."

"Oh, does that guy live near here?" Marge asked breezily. "We were just on our way to do...to do a little shopping."

He smiled at me in the backseat. "I'll be watching, ladies. And the pretty one in glasses? I'll be watching her real close." He gave me a wink.

A warm feeling rushed right through me as I watched him brush his soft hair from his eyes, then strengthen his back. I felt so much all at once:

exhaustion, anger...and intrigue. What exactly had he meant by that last remark?

"No need to keep an eye on us," I said to him, flustered. "You'd be bored to death." Never mind the fact that just that afternoon he might have seen me climb into a felon's window. After performing a jazz dance on a fire escape.

Marge giggled, then she winked at me before she turned to Alex. "So, Detective Spencer, what brings you to this not-so-lovely section of our fine town of Springston?"

"You know I can't discuss investigative matters."

"Not even with other people who are investigators on the case?" Celeste asked in a hard voice. "That's so inefficient. When we're all on the same team."

He met her stare for stare. "My work is confidential. And highly sensitive."

Well, Mr. Know it All, that's too bad for you. Because we had information too. Did he know about the boxes?

"If I get some panda updates, I'll get right back to you." He gave me another slow wink. He had the bluest eyes. Was it possible to blush and fume both at the same time?

He turned and walked toward his car, leaving us staring at his well-formed...uh...posterior.

After we fueled the car and Marge got her snacks, we drove away. Ten minutes later, we pulled into the office. Thankfully, there were no more detours for milkshakes and no further rendezvous with stuck-on-themselves detectives.

"Good work, girls," Celeste said as we climbed out of the car. "Charlie, you were amazing. You were our MVP. Tomorrow I'll call Gil, see if he can trace the license tag of Baxter's van. Charlie, you remember Gil. He fixed your tires when they got slashed."

"Oh, yeah." My mind flashed back to our past case. Someone hadn't liked me looking into a set of clues that we'd discovered. So, they'd sent an ugly message that required a brand-new set of tires. Seems I was good at having close calls with angry criminals.

"Gil has some connections with the DMV," Celeste explained to us. "If the van belongs to Duvant, that won't help us much. We're already on to him. But if it comes back to someone else, then we'll have ourselves not one but two persons of interest in the case, as we say in the business."

DEANY RAY

Marge smiled. "Great idea. Oh, Charlie, I forgot to ask. How did the apartment hunting go?"

"Well, let's just say that the apartment I snuck into is just the kind of place that fits into my budget."

"Oh no!" Marge looked like she might cry. "That's so sad. And do you know what else is so sad? That our little panda is still lost out there and all alone! We need to find that witty bitty panda before he gets hurt."

"Let's meet tomorrow here at nine, and we'll focus on the panda," Celeste said. "It's the panda, not the felon, who will earn us our first check."

"But if we can figure out what Baxter's doing, that would help us too. Then every police chief in the area would want to send us jobs," I said. "Because you know he's up to no good. He's not collecting boxes to help his grandma move. He's not that kind of guy."

I'd forgotten that hours before I'd contemplated quitting as I hid beneath the bed and hoped I wouldn't die.

Celeste thought about it. "Yes, you're absolutely right. Something big is going on. And the more Alex tries to hide it, the more I'd like to know exactly what it is. And the more I'd like to solve that thing before he can do it."

132

"Well, tomorrow we're Team Panda." I fished my car keys from my purse. "And we'll be Team Felon too. But for now I'm out of here. I'm Team Charlie-Needs-a-Shower."

I got into my Corolla and, by some miracle, it started with the first turn of the key. I held my hand up in a goodbye as I backed out of the spot.

Chapter Eight

I WOKE UP TO THE ROLLING STONES wailing in my ear. I squinted at the clock. Was my mother leading class at six-thirty in the morning? I'd wanted to sleep just a little longer since the day before had been so dreadful.

The sound seemed to be coming from outside on the lawn. Sunrise exercises? I grabbed my glasses from the nightstand and eased over to the window, almost afraid to look.

Blooming butter cookies! Yep, there were my mother's students, doing strange moves on the lawn right outside my room. Who needed an alarm? And what exactly were these ancient students doing in their brightly colored clothing? I had no idea. They were jumping and waving their limbs as if the yard had been invaded by mosquitos they were trying to shake off. I had a flashback to the oldsters I'd watched dancing in Baxter's complex just the day before. Why was this a theme for me? Could I pick another theme?

Well, the sight out on my lawn had me wide awake, which I didn't want to be. Hiding on a filthy floor with dust bunnies and old roaches should earn a girl a pass to sleep as long as she would like. Plus, I'd spent much of the day before scared that I might die. That should be worth some extra points toward a morning sleeping in.

No chance of sleeping now, I thought as I peered out at the oldsters and hoped they wouldn't fall. Wasn't it supposed to be the mom who yelled at others in the house to turn the music down? Instead, mine was shaking her tushy as she pranced across the lawn in purple tights and an oversized green shirt. Where had she even bought that shirt? It was so green it seemed to glow.

An apartment with arrows flying through the window was looking better right about now.

I pulled on a t-shirt and some shorts and pulled my hair into a ponytail just as a bolt of lightning flashed outside my window. Absolutely super. Now, the ancient rock and rollers would be pouring into the den just as I made my way downstairs. And I hated to talk to anyone before that first sweet sip of coffee. Unfortunately, there was no back door to the kitchen. If I wanted to get some caffeine in my system, I'd have to go through the den.

Or maybe not if I was quick. I tried to dash through the downstairs as quickly as I could to the safety of the kitchen, but I wasn't fast enough. As if on cue, they all came filing in just as I got down the steps.

My mother looked surprised to see me. "Oh, sweetheart, I know that you worked late. I thought you might sleep in."

Was she even kidding? How could anybody sleep in when a rock concert was going on full blast beneath their window?

I gave her a sleepy smile. The students were listening eagerly, so I had to be polite in case their hearing aids were turned up.

"I was hoping to sleep late," I said, "but, well, here I am!"

A tiny woman grabbed my arm. A huge smile spread across her face. "Well, if it isn't Charlie Cooper! Why don't you come dance with us? We have the most delightful class."

Get me out of here.

"Oh. Well. Thank you very much for the invitation. But I need to get my breakfast and head on in to work." Or sneak back up to bed, if by some miracle, the class with its loud music came to an early stop.

"Well, it's so nice to see you. It's been a long, long time," she said.

Did I know this woman?

She continued to hold tightly to my arm as I tried to say my polite goodbyes.

"You would enjoy the dancing," she insisted. "Although, I have to say, you were not the most coordinated of my students way back in the day. You were very slow at dodge ball. And you always came in last when your group was running laps." She smiled. "But you were just the cutest little thing that I ever saw."

I looked more closely at her wrinkled face.

"Mrs. Beckham?" I asked. Was this my PE teacher from Waller Elementary? As if my grownup life didn't embarrass me enough, I had to be reminded of how bad I'd been at sports in the second grade. The joys of coming back to live in your old hometown.

"You're looking very well," I said. "But I know I need to let you all get back to your class. If you'll just excuse me..."

But she still wouldn't let me go. "Do you and your little friends still like to play that game?" She peered up at me. "Do you still pretend that you're rainbow-colored fishies swimming through the sea?"

Had she lost her mind? Did she not see how old I'd gotten? Did I really look like someone who spent my spare time acting like I was a fish? I pasted a smile upon my face and gently tried to pull my arm away. "No. I haven't done that in a while. But we surely had some fun at Waller Elementary."

I noticed then that everyone was staring and listening to our odd exchange. I smiled at them and waved as I at last made my way toward the kitchen.

Mrs. Beckham followed close behind me. Please. I needed coffee. She grabbed my arm again. "You were a smart one, I remember. Such an imagination." This woman liked to talk. "You all used to move across the playground, swimming just like this and making fishy faces." Of course, she had to demonstrate, fishy face and all. The look was not becoming.

Someone help me, please. Where had my mother gotten to? Wasn't she supposed to be leading these people in some kind of exercise?

Just then, she swooped in to the rescue, a savior in a flowing lime green shirt.

"This gives me an idea!" she cried happily.

My chest seized up a little. It was usually not a good thing when my mother was struck with an idea.

"When I put on the next song, let's all move like fish!" she cried out to the room.

The oldsters whooped and hollered. I guessed that it didn't take a lot to excite this little group of dancers. They likely spent their days playing cards or watching game shows. If you were retired and old in Springston, "swimming" across a den floor might be the highlight of your week.

Brad was up and making sandwiches when I made my way at last into the kitchen. I still wasn't quite used to seeing him as a normal human being who got up and went to work. He must want that paycheck badly. And the prize money.

A paycheck. Hmm. I hoped I'd get one soon. I poured myself some coffee from the pot that my mom or Brad had made. I closed my eyes and took a sip, savoring the first warm taste. Then I turned to Brad. "What time does your shift start?"

He slapped the top piece of bread onto his sandwich, then got out a baggie as if I hadn't spoken. Rude. Then he seemed to see me for the first time, and pulled an earplug out. "Did you say something?"

Earplugs! That was genius! Could it be that, after all, my brother wasn't the most moronic of the Cooper siblings? Here he was, making his sandwiches in peace while I had the beginnings of a headache brought on by the music, which was starting up again. If I had thought of earplugs, I'd still be sound asleep. Was the music even louder now? Why had my mother turned it up?

I glanced out the window while I sipped and studied my mother's garden and our big backyard. The elderly fishes were back outside by then, swimming around an oak tree. Apparently, the threat of rain had passed.

"I asked what time you had to be at work," I said to my brother.

He sat down with a cup of coffee. "My shift begins at nine, but I'd like to get there early to get a jump on things."

I stared. "Who are you exactly? You kind of look like my brother, but you can't be him."

He wasn't smart enough to get the joke. "Charlie, you're so goofy. Who else would it be but me?"

I sat down across from him. "You're not acting like my brother. He would never get up early to go do extra work. Can I see your ID?"

He still didn't get my humor. "You're not making any sense."

"Never mind." No use joking with this guy.

Thankfully, the music got a bit more mellow, and someone turned the volume down. I slowly sipped my coffee and willed the shooting pains in my head to please just go away.

Just as things were calming down, I heard someone rushing into the kitchen.

"Well, look at you two youngsters," called out a gravelly voice. "Barbara has raised some mighty fine young people. That's what I always say."

I turned to find Jean Kolcek, one of my mother's longtime students. She had retired about fifteen years before from the library downtown. Perhaps she could also share a story to humiliate me. Like the time I spilled chocolate pudding on the library's only copy of Amy's Yellow Dog.

"Good morning, Mrs. Kolcek." I smiled. "Would you like some coffee?"

"I just need a glass of water. Honey, you just keep your seat. I know where Barbara keeps the glasses. She likes us to stay hydrated. Your mother thinks of everything."

She bustled over to the cabinets with a big smile on her face. Must be that famous rush of energy you're supposed to get from exercise. Because of something called endorphins? Was that what I'd heard? Which led me to the question: what was an endorphin? I wasn't sure. I hadn't been any better with the science books than on the dodge ball field. Still, maybe I should try this exercising thing. But with people my own age, and after nine a.m.

Mrs. Kolcek moved over to the sink to fill her glass, then let out a yelp. The glass went crashing to the floor. It looked like she was choking. Then she fell – or maybe fainted. I just knew that it looked bad.

I leapt up and ran to check on her.

Brad had his earplugs back in, oblivious to anything besides the motorcycle magazine in front of him on the table. He didn't seem to be aware that this was anything but a normal day in the Cooper kitchen.

"Mrs. Kolcek!" I shouted. "Can you hear me, Mrs. Kolcek?"

Still shaken, she opened her eyes and glanced up at the window. I turned around, following her gaze. It didn't take me long to see what had startled her. In the kitchen window were two paws, a wet nose, and a pair of eyes staring out from a familiar furry face. Lou! It was really Lou, outside my kitchen window.

Very gently, I helped the retired librarian to her feet. She still looked very pale. Not that a little panda is a terrifying site. But it's not what you expect to find when you look out upon a lawn in a suburban neighborhood.

"Jean! Are you okay?" My mother rushed into the room, alerted by the noise. She put an arm around Mrs. Kolcek, who was still too startled to explain. My mother looked at me, concerned. "Do you know what happened, Charlie?"

I nodded toward the window, where Lou was watching us with interest. To him, we were a show, full of crashing glass and yelping and all manner of hysterics.

My mom let out a scream when she saw the panda. Brad continued to sip his coffee. He hadn't heard a thing. Those must be some darn good earplugs. I wanted some of those.

"What in the world?" My mother stepped back from the window. "I have been telling you and telling you – the energy in this house is seriously out of whack. To the point of being cataclysmic."

I had to think – and fast. I still hadn't had a chance to do any research on how to catch a panda. And here it was, a second chance. This was lucky, oh so lucky. I didn't have to hunt Lou down. Lou had come to me! I had to grab myself a panda. But...the scene in the park flashed through my mind. I could almost smell the funk again. I didn't want a repeat of that smelly confrontation. I glanced toward my brother. I had an idea.

143

I pulled the earplugs from his ears, causing him to jump. "Hey, Brad." I tried to keep my voice bright and calm, as if I were suggesting something fun. "You won't believe what's happened. It's the coolest thing. You know the pandas from the zoo? The ones that we used to love to watch?"

He nodded, somewhat interested. He waited for me to go on.

"Well, one of them is outside, looking in the window. Would you please go out and get him?" How crazy must that have sound?

He pondered the question a bit, as if it were the kind of simple favor that sisters always asked. Can you give me a ride? Can you hand me that book on the top shelf over in the corner? Can you go out and catch that panda?

He seemed to consider the idea, then he came to a decision. "I'd love to help you out, but I need to get to work."

Damn. I'd been foiled by his newfound interest in productivity. Who'd have ever thought? Not that he'd come to see the value of hard work. I didn't think that for a minute. He just loved the money it would put into his pocket. I knew my brother well.

Hey! That gave me an idea. "If you'll do it for me, I'll give you ten dollars."

His eyes lit up at the thought. "If you'll give me twenty, then you've got a deal."

Of course, it would be nice to have a brother who would leap up, happy to be of help. "Sure," said the perfect brother in my imagination. "You just wait right here. I don't want you to get hurt. Pour yourself more coffee. Can I bring you the cream?"

But twenty bucks to avoid another burst of foul air in my face? Best bargain of my life. That little panda had farted like a massive grizzly bear. Lou was a master farter. But that was my brother's problem now. Perhaps I was the smart one.

I went to the window to watch Brad walk out toward the panda. I was joined by my mother and Mrs. Kolcek. Now somewhat recovered, the older woman looked more intrigued than scared.

By the time Brad had made his way into the yard, Lou was halfway up the big tree that I used to love to climb. The oldsters had moved far across the yard and were huddled together, startled.

I held my breath and watched as my brother grabbed Lou from behind. Please, Brad. Don't let go. Let this be the one time that you succeed at something. Not surprisingly, the panda put up quite a fight.

Then I remembered pickles! Shoot. I should have put out pickles. That would have calmed Lou down, made him easier to hold. But my brain hadn't exactly been working at full power. So much to deal with in one morning. I hadn't even finished a single cup of coffee. Heck, I was still supposed to be asleep. The day before had been the ordeal. This was supposed to be my time to recover.

But hopefully this all would end with the panda captured: one case solved and in the books for our brand-new business. Paycheck, here I come! Hmm...turns out, I was also into getting paid, just like my brother.

It was all up to Brad now – which was really kind of scary. Still, it looked like he was winning. Surely, he would win. My brother was a hefty guy, and Lou was just a little panda. I watched and held my breath. Brad was holding on. Brad had a tight grip on the panda! Victory was in sight. He just needed to hang on until we could move the panda to...darn it! I hadn't thought this out. Move the panda where? To the backseat of my car? No way was I driving to the zoo with an angry panda. But we could keep him in the car, and the zoo could come and get him. Yes! That was the ticket.

I rushed outside and toward my car.

"Put him in my car!" I called. "Come on! I'll get the door."

Then I saw trouble brewing. I saw Lou lift his bushy tail. Uh oh, that was not good. The battle might be lost.

"Don't breathe!" I called to Brad. "It will be okay if you just don't breathe until you get him in the car."

But I was too late with the warning. I could hear Lou let loose with a big one. Eww!

Brad dropped him like the panda was a hot potato. He backed away, disgusted, trying to wave away the smell. He looked at me angrily as he stomped off to his car. "That was the worst job ever! You should pay me fifty dollars. You should pay me one hundred!"

"Pay you? Pay you for what? Do I see a panda in your arms? The last time I saw the panda, he was making his escape." I looked around, but Lou was nowhere to be seen. My brother had some nerve.

"To get a paycheck, Brad, you have to do the work," I yelled. Which I guess kind of applied to me as well. I didn't have the panda yet, so no check for me. I really needed to get paid.

Brad looked furious. "You didn't warn me that the stupid animal was gonna blow like that. And it went all in my face! That panda is disgusting."

"He's not stupid. He's just scared." But I guess I should have warned him. I had not been fair to Brad. But I'd been so sure that he could catch him. He was stronger than I was. Then our first case would have been completed, a big success for CMC.

"Sorry," I told him. "I'll get you your twenty bucks."

He brushed past me angrily on his way back into the house. "Now I need another shower. And I'll be late to work."

What a morning. What a week.

My next order of business with the girls should be to figure out a plan so we'd be prepared the next time we saw Lou. The zoo knew we were on the case; they could tell us what to do in case of another sighting. Now it seemed a little silly that we hadn't asked before.

So far, I'd had two encounters, and the score was bad. Lou: two. Charlie: zero.

But he could not have gotten that far. I had to go find Lou. I needed to grab my car keys and drive around and look. I could try to get his farting self into the backseat of my old car until the zoo could come and get him. Of course, my car might never recover from the stink. Unless my mother got in there and did the best cleanse of her life.

Could I really do that? Wrestle a panda into my car? It wasn't exactly the kind of thing they taught you to do in school. And it's not like I had backup. I looked over at the oldsters who were gathered in the yard, still wide-eyed from the Brad-and-Panda Show. These students of my mother would be no help at all. Endorphins or not, they would be no match for a trouble-making panda.

My eyes moved to my mother. She was staring, horrified, at the scene of the smelly crime, although Brad and Lou were both long gone. She did not look like she was up for some mother-daughter bonding time on a wildlife adventure. To top it off, my dad was at the diner. I was on my own.

Suddenly, my mother sprung into high alert. She ran into the kitchen, emerging with one of the spray bottles she kept around the house. I knew this one held purified water mixed with "cleansing herbs." She always had it handy since metaphysical emergencies, in my mother's mind, popped up quite a lot.

As they tried to dodge my mother's sprays, the oldsters were moving faster than they ever did in class. My mother looked frantic, like she'd almost been brought to tears. "And to think we spent so much money on panda coffee cups and panda figurines. Panda salt and pepper shakers. A panda oven mitt! The energy in our lovely home may never be the same. There's an awful, and very nauseating, aura all around that animal."

I really had to go. Lou was escaping as we spoke, getting further and further away and harder and harder to find. And my mother was wailing on and on about her foolish need to cleanse.

I massaged my aching head. "It's not an aura, Mother. It's anatomy. It's gas! Lou is not some awful creature. He's probably scared to death. And maybe pandas just have a weird...defense mechanism." Hmm. Was that what that was?

"Well, it seems to work well," an old man said, coming up behind my mom. "Maybe I'll try that particular line of defense when those salesmen get so pushy. You know the ones I mean. They follow you around the store when all you want to do is browse and pass the time of day. You just want a little peace."

Then three things happened all at once. My mother nearly sprayed me in the eye. Mrs. Kolcek almost fainted dead against me when she began to hyperventilate, the events of the afternoon sinking in at last. Then someone turned the music back on so the students could continue to move back through the yard like very wrinkled fish in brightly colored leotards. The music, for some reason, was even louder than before.

"Music!" My mother smiled. "That's just what we need." She put down her bottle and then she grabbed my hand. "Swim with us, Charlie. Swim! Like the most elegant of fishes!"

I have no time for this. I have a panda to follow.

She moved slowly across the yard, holding me tightly with one hand. With the other hand, she made swimming motions.

"Mom, I have to go. Now!"

"Breathe deeply, Charlie. Concentrate," my mother said in a deep voice. "I can see your aura's dark. You need to relax through deep breaths and through dance. Now, imagine that the sea is deep and blue and that the waves are oh, so gently rocking you along." She had to yell to be heard over the thumping music.

As she spouted nonsense, Lou was getting further and further from my reach. I had finally had it.

I pulled away. "No, Mother. I don't want to imagine a deep blue sea and go swimming through my front yard. But there are some things I do want. I want to be able to sleep in when I'm tired. And I

151

want to have a brother who might help now and then, and not just because I pay him. And I want to catch that panda who should be at the zoo."

She stopped "swimming" and looked at me, bewildered. "Oh, Charlie, don't be silly. From what I heard this morning, you were the worst at sports. How could you catch a panda if you can't even catch a ball? Plus, it's not our problem. The zoo should keep up with their pandas."

My heart rate had gone sky high. "Oh, and by the way, I'm moving out real soon."

A look of sadness crossed her face. "Oh, but you're my baby. Please don't go so soon. The house will be so quiet."

"Really, Mother? Quiet?" I looked around at all the oldsters, who were leaping and hobbling and twirling, making fishy faces, while the music played at an ear-splitting volume. I think I recognized the song from my high school days. Something about good loving and stomping my heart flat.

Too quiet. Was that really what she'd said? Too quiet at the moment sounded like my fondest dream. But it wasn't happening at this house anytime soon.

My mother frowned. "I knew this day would come, but I don't want you to move out."

"That day came already. Remember? When I moved to Boston?"

"But Charlotte, where will you go?"

"I found a nice one-bedroom. Not too far away."

She looked a little hurt. I didn't like to see that, although I was still pretty mad.

"What would you have at an apartment that you'd can't get at home?"

Had she not been listening? But I'd calmed down a little. I didn't want her to be hurt.

"It's closer to my office," I said, and I guessed that much was true. "And if I ever decide to learn the sport of archery, there's a practice range real close."

"Sounds delightful," my mother said, her face lighting up.

I didn't mention that by close, I meant in striking distance. But perhaps the landlord had just been making a little joke, which really wasn't funny. I needed to make a call that morning before the apartment got away.

Speaking of getting away, I needed to get out on the road. If I couldn't catch the panda, perhaps I could keep him in my sight and call someone with expertise in that sort of thing. Then I still would have done my job, right? Found the missing Springston treasure and seen him safely reunited

153

with his twin. Charlie Cooper saves the day. Charlie Cooper gets a check.

But first I needed coffee. Coffee for the road. I headed to the kitchen, thankful for the small orange light that indicated that the pot was still on, keeping the coffee warm. And by the stove I noticed something nice: a foil-covered pan that meant my mother had done a little early-morning baking before her class arrived. When did the woman sleep?

I peeked. Oatmeal raisin cookies and also chocolate chip. I'd earned two of each, at least. I took a bite of a soft, sweet oatmeal cookie. I would miss this in the mornings.

Just then, I heard a ping from my cellphone on the table. Please. Don't let it be a bad-news text. Don't let this day get even worse.

I grabbed my phone and checked.

MARGE: Meet us at Gil's in forty minutes. His shop is on Fourth Street North.

Hmm. I wondered what was up. And what about the panda? I had to find the panda.

ME: Might be a little late. Something has come up.

I'd explain it to them later. For now, I'd get dressed quick and brush my teeth, then take a drive around the neighborhood on a personal panda hunt before heading off to Gil's. The phone pinged again.

MARGE: What's up?

Things had been too crazy to type out in a text.

ME: Had some company this morning. Surprise guest came to breakfast.

Ha.

Where did my mother keep her pickles? That might help me lure my furry friend out of his latest hiding place. And just as if the morning had not already been insane, I could drive past my neighbors' houses, tossing pickles out the window. I'd have to make sure no one was looking. People in this town liked to talk.

Another text came in.

MARGE: Did this breakfast guest have dreamy eyes? Did his name start with an A? Did he have a crush on someone that I know with the initial C?

It sounded like a grade-school conversation from back in the day when I was a dodge-ball failure.

ME: Pretty eyes. Initial L. I didn't ask about his love life.

Then I ate another cookie.

Chapter Nine

As I drove slow circles around the neighborhood, I saw people dragging their recycling out and packing briefcases into cars. I watched kids playfully shove each other as they waited for the bus. But I saw no sign of a small red panda.

When I thought no one was looking, I threw pickles out the window, then circled back around to see if my furry friend might have come out from his hiding to scarf down his favorite snack. No luck. That elusive panda had been so close, but Brad had blown my chances of wrapping the case up right then and there. That would have been amazing.

What a nightmare of a day it had already been. Living in my childhood home was just about to kill me. I had to get out, and I had to do it now. When I pulled up to a red light, I punched in the number for the lesser evils of the places I could afford.

"Chrysanthemum Garden Manors," a woman said with a cheery voice.

Where did they get that name? I hadn't seen a single flower, and the small one and two-bedroom units weren't even close to being manors. But what were they going to call it? Flying Arrow Place? Truth might be a virtue, but it never sounded quite as lovely as a lie.

"Hi. I was calling about the one-bedroom that I looked at yesterday. Do you still have a vacancy?" Please, please, please, say yes.

"Yes, ma'am. You're in luck."

Score. "Great. I'd like to take it."

"When would you like to move in?"

Now.

"As soon as you can get it ready. It's...an emergency," I said.

There was a pause at the other end. "Excuse me? I didn't understand."

She didn't hear that every day, I bet. Emergencies weren't a thing, I guess, in the apartment rental world.

"I'd like to move in as soon as the apartment's ready."

"I see. Would you like to come by today and put down a deposit?"

I gave her my name and told her that I'd try to stop by that afternoon and leave a check. She said the apartment would be cleaned and ready sometime later in the week. A sense of relief washed over me. The day had gotten so much better.

As I pulled onto the street that Marge had listed on the text, I made a to-do list in my head to get ready for the move. It was really kind of sad how few things there were to pack. When I'd moved from Boston, I'd cleared a lot of junk. Looking around at my messy place, I had made a vow not to put anything in a moving box unless it had a place in my new, exciting life as an ace detective returning triumphantly back to her old hometown. (Ha. I was still hoping that exciting life would start at any moment. Oh, I guess I had excitement. But I wanted the kind that was glamorous and fun – not the kind that comes from thinking you might die at any second.)

Following advice, I'd heard on some early-morning show, I'd asked myself some questions about everything I owned. Does this make me happy? Would I miss this if it was gone? If not, I was supposed to toss it. Turned out that nothing much in the old apartment brought me any joy. So much of my meager possessions had gone off to Goodwill.

Along with the necessities, I'd lovingly packed a few things that I cared about: my oldest, softest t-shirts from concerts that I loved, and my collection of coffee mugs that my parents or co-workers would bring me back from trips. With no money of my own to go anywhere exciting, I had to rely on souvenirs from other people's travels. But each morning when I grabbed a mug, the picture on the front was a promise to myself. The Grand Canyon, the Golden Gate Bridge…they were all places I'd see one day when I made real money.

How sad to be almost thirty and not to even own a couch. But I guessed it was just as well. The apartment came already furnished. The stuff I'd seen inside were not exactly what you'd call luxury items: a couch, an armchair, and some tables. They would do for now.

Marge's car was already there when I pulled into the auto shop. I walked in the door to find my friends and Gil deep in conversation. A slim older man in overalls and a cap, Gil held a match between his teeth. He was looking somewhat confused as Marge yammered on and on about something or another. I couldn't hear because of all the noise. Several mechanics worked under cars or peered beneath the hoods of vehicles scattered about the shop.

I could tell Marge was excited by the way her hands were flailing through the air. As I got closer, I could hear her say "And what I'd really love to have is a turbo button. Like they have on race cars? Can you put in one of those? Like they had on The Fast and the Furious. I'm sure that you saw that one! I saw that one twice. Oh, a turbo button would be cool." She clasped her hands beneath her chin and did an excited little shuffle while she waited for his answer.

Gil looked too stunned to speak.

Celeste looked embarrassed and alarmed. "Marge. We're here on important business. Gil has work to do. And you know that we do too. We're businesswomen here."

Marge barely paused to catch her breath.

"So, how fast would that make me go?" she asked Gil. She pulled her notebook from her purse. "What would my top speed be? Could you put one in next week?"

Behind her, Celeste gave Gil a wide-eyed look, waving her hands in front of her face and mouthing the word no.

Sheesh. Marge behind the wheel of a souped-up car that went extra fast? That might kill us all before we could solve a single crime.

Gil took the match from between his teeth and stared down at the floor. "Um. I'll see what I can do."

"Yay." Marge did a little shuffle step.

Celeste gave her the all-too-familiar look that meant to settle down.

"Now. Down to official business," she said. She handed Gil a slip of paper. "Here's the license number of the van that I called you about. Can you find out who the owner is?"

He nodded. "Shouldn't be a problem. I just need to step into my office. Just hang out a minute. I'll go make a call."

Once he'd disappeared, I grabbed Celeste by the arm. "You won't believe what happened." I began the story. "My mother starts her class today before it's even light. And one of the students – they're really old – comes in to get a drink." I told it somewhat slowly, creating a kind of build-up to the big conclusion. "She's standing by the sink, and I hear her scream. And – this is just so wild – I look past her at the window. And guess who is outside?"

"Oh, I love a guessing game," Marge squeaked. "Was it the mayor? Or the mailman? Or maybe it was Elvis?" She gasped in delight. "Was it? Was it Elvis?"

Celeste rolled her eyes. "Marge, that's just ridiculous. Don't you know he died? Like a million years ago?"

Marge turned serious. "It could have been a hoax. Don't believe everything you read. That might

161

have been a way to start a brand-new life, away from all the cameras." She put her hand up to her mouth. "That would make us famous if it was really him. We'd be the detectives who found Elvis in our first month of business!"

"It was Lou!" I interrupted. "Lou was outside the kitchen with his face pressed against the window."

They stared at me in silence.

I described the way my brother had wrestled with him in the yard, only to be met with a stream of foul air aimed right into his face. Celeste gasped, and then we laughed so hard that one of the mechanics slid out from underneath a car to make sure we were okay.

"It was quite a morning," I said when I could catch my breath. "And I have some other news. I'm moving out this week. I'm putting a deposit down on an apartment. The Garden Manors one."

"That's great," Marge said, excited. "We can help you pack." She thought for just a moment. "Because we need to hang out near your parents' place ASAP. Lou might still be somewhere close."

"I did leave some pickles all around the neighborhood," I said. "So, he probably thinks it's as good a place as any to hang out." That got us to giggling once again.

"We should definitely have a look around your neighborhood," Celeste looked thoughtful. "And I'd love to see your family. I've missed your father's jokes since we quit working at the diner. And I never met your mom, although she came in just a few times when I was working there. Plus, I agree with Marge. We should help you pack."

"Oh, that's nice of you to offer," I said, "but I don't have that much stuff."

I didn't relish the idea of exposing my friends to the craziness that was the Cooper home. I did suspect, however, that Marge would love my mom. In no time flat, Marge would be dancing with the oldsters in the front yard. She'd be begging for my mother to read the color of her aura.

"My dad misses you," I said to them both. He sometimes teased me at family dinners about stealing his best help. "He says that nobody could keep the coffee refills coming like Marge and Celeste could do. Plus, he loved to tease the two of you. Some of the employees don't quite know how to deal with his weird sense of humor."

"And we never met your youngest brother," Marge squeaked. "Is he cute? I have my eye on someone, but maybe for Celeste..."

Crazy caramel brownie bites! Celeste and Brad would be the most mismatched couple in the world.

"Believe me. Brad is absolutely not the man for either one of you. I love my brother, I do. But he'd drive any woman nuts. And I should warn you. My mother – she's just...different." Was there any way out of this?

"Well, that settles that," Celeste said. "We'll set up a reconnaissance operation at the Cooper home."

Great.

"My father will be thrilled," I said.

"I have your information," Gil said, emerging from his office. He gave Celeste the paper back. "I wrote the name down here. And also an address. It's registered to some company."

We all peered down at the paper. PiJD Ltd – 34 Mill Road.

"You ever heard of that place, Gil?" Celeste asked.

He shook his head. "The company name sounds funny. In my experience, it could be a front for some illegal business. I see it all the time."

164

How did he know that kind of stuff? Just who did the guy hang out with? He scared me just a little. On the other hand, I wished that he had been around when there was a panda in my front yard who needed to be caught. I got the idea that Gil was tough.

We thanked him and headed out. As soon as we stepped out into the parking lot, Celeste had a plan. "Let's all go in Charlie's car to check out this address."

I agreed to drive us. But on one condition. "If anyone is sneaking in, it's someone else's turn."

***

Mill Road, of course, turned out to be smack dab in the rougher part of Springston. There wasn't much there except a sprawling complex of large storage units. The place was surrounded by overgrown bushes, deep ditches, and scattered limbs and trash.

"Just as I expected," Celeste said. "This little business, with a name nobody can pronounce, doesn't exactly look like a thriving enterprise."

"Let's look for 34," I said, slowing down to check the numbers. I stopped and parked when I got to 27. I didn't want anyone to link my car with whatever dubious goings on might be associated with unit 34.

Besides, I saw something a little bit further down the road that set my heart to racing. It was Baxter's van. Hmm. So, we meet again.

As we got closer, we saw no sign of anyone around.

"Look inside the van," Marge told me in a whisper.

"Not me!" I whispered back. "Our name is CMC. The M and the other C need to take a turn at the kind of spying that might get our sweet selves killed."

"I'll do it," Celeste said.

Marge and I held our breath while she walked around the van, peeking into the darkened windows. Then she shook her head. "Nobody there. Maybe he's inside?"

We gazed over at the unit. The metal pull-down door was closed. There were no windows to peek in. Like three good detectives, we looked to the left and to the right, then we tiptoed to the door. My heart was pounding hard against my chest. This could turn out bad.

A thousand thoughts ran through my head, like what an awful idea this had been for starting a new business. I also decided then and there that we should do things differently the next time we snuck off some dangerous locale. Were there websites where you could order three bulletproof vests? We should at least have pepper spray. Was it too late to go back and get my degree in teaching?

When we got to the storage unit, we leaned in to listen. We lined up in the order of our height, Celeste, then me, then Marge, the same intent expression glued on every face.

We heard shuffling. Shoot. I'd been hoping that he wasn't there, which was kind of foolish, really, given the fact that his van was parked right out in front.

We held our breath and strained to hear, then we heard something else; I wasn't sure exactly what.

"What could he be doing?" Marge asked in the world's loudest whisper.

"Shhh!" Celeste and I hissed together.

We pressed our ears more closely against the metal. We heard what sounded like boxes being dragged. Which made sense, I guess, given the scene at the apartment. What could he be putting in those boxes? I tried to come up with ideas, but I came up short. In my time with the police in Boston, no crime had ever involved a huge supply of cardboard boxes.

Still, it was a good way to distract myself from the other question running through my head: what might happen when this Baxter guy discovered three unwanted guests outside?

I had a sense of déjà vu. It hadn't been that long ago that I was in this very situation, worried about the same bad dude and the tragedy that could follow if he found a stranger snooping around his business.

Never again, I'd thought then. And now here I was. What was wrong with me?

We heard keys jingle. We heard footsteps. The footsteps were getting closer. My heart was pounding so hard that I was afraid it might jump right through my chest.

Without saying a word to one another, we made an impressive sprint across the road, leapt over a deep ditch, and hid behind some bushes. If my old PE teacher had been watching, she would have been very proud of her former slow and clumsy student. If I had known back then to imagine a felon close behind me, I would have come in first place in every single race.

From behind the bushes, we watched as the door slid up and open. We'd made it just in time.

A slouched figure slowly ambled out. The man was Baxter's size. He was Baxter's age or close. But he wasn't Baxter.

We shot questioning looks at each other. Who was this brand-new dude?

He turned his back to us and began to slowly pull down the door. I peeped just a tiny bit above the bushes to see if I could catch a glimpse inside of the unit, but all I could see was a darkened space and the tall silhouette of boxes stacked one on top of the other.

With keys in hand, the mystery dude headed toward the van. With my heart still hammering, I made a mental note: the next time I made a valiant sprint to safety, I'd head as far away as possible from the bad guy's van instead of running toward it. I tried to breathe very quietly. I hoped Celeste and Marge would do the same.

I heard the car door shut and the sound of the ignition starting up. Please. Just hurry up and leave. But the sound coming from the car didn't leave me very hopeful. It was a sputtering kind of noise that was familiar to anyone who drove a junker. The mystery dude was having trouble getting the van to start.

He tried a second time and then a third. But that's it. I heard a boom so loud my head began to spin. It jolted me hard and sent vibrations through my body.

That's the last thing I remember before everything went dark.

Chapter Ten

WHEN I CAME TO, I FELT like a knife had been plunged into my head; the ache was that intense. I tried to look around, but just the slightest movement made tears spring to my eyes.

Where was I? What had happened? Was I lying on the ground? It felt like it. But lying down good! Because I was so tired. Maybe I could sleep. I imagined two pillows beneath my head, a soft blanket bundling me against the breeze that had suddenly turned cold.

When I opened my eyes again, everything had become a blur. There was the sky. And there were a few white clouds. And there was...Alex. Alex? What was Alex doing here? And where was here exactly? I had so many questions.

Even through the blur, I could see a sad look on Alex's face. He was trying to tell me something, but he wasn't making any sound. He looked almost frantic. He looked scared to death. Had something happened with his police work that had gotten him riled up?

Something was coming back to me. Wasn't there some case we were working on together? I couldn't quite remember. Was he trying to communicate some information about that? Some new clue we had to check out, some bad guy we had to grab? Or was it a panda? I seemed to think it was panda that we had to catch. But how ridiculous was that? I must be in a dream.

Now it looked like he was shouting, but still no sound came out, only a kind of zooming somewhere in the background. This was a very quiet place. I could tell he needed help. I wished that I could help him, but it felt so good to lie there. Crime solving would have to wait while I had just a little nap. I closed my eyes and slept.

Strangely, he was still there when I woke again, and the man was looking fine. I wanted to touch his soft, brown hair and the stubble on his chin. This had to be a dream. What else could it be? Strange dream, I must say. He looked so real that I could almost touch his face.

Those eyes. Look at those eyes, I thought. I imagined him gaze at me oh so tenderly. And then he'd say the words: I love you, Charlie Cooper. Was he saying them right now as he bent over me? He looked so intense. Who turned the sound down on this dream?

I stared into his face. Then I reached up to stroke his cheek.

"I love you too," I said.

Then the sound came on full volume. Whoa, bad sound, turn it off again!

I looked at Alex one more time. Why did he look confused? I tried to sit up, but the knife inside my head seemed to plunge in even deeper.

It was at that point that things began to get intense and loud. I heard sirens and shouting.

"Quick," one voice said. "Another victim in the ditch. There's another one right here!"

"Let's collect all that as evidence. Put that in a bag," someone said close behind me. "And don't forget to tag it. Hope we can get some prints."

"Charlie!" Alex leaned closer to my face. "Charlie, can you hear me?"

Sheesh. Don't yell. My head!

"What the hell is going on?" I grabbed hold of his hand.

"You don't remember the explosion?"

Explosion? Things started to come back: a rental unit filled with boxes, a guy who looked like Baxter but who was really someone else. That's when I remembered everything. This was not a dream.

173

I stared up at Alex, and it hit me. For the love of lemon cookies, had I stroked his face? My chest seized up in panic. Had I told him that I loved him? Because I did not – no way. Well, maybe in the dream. Talk about humiliation.

An ambulance screeched to stop a nearby, and I remembered something else; my friends had been here as well when everything went down.

"Marge!" I yelled. "Celeste!" I looked up at Alex. "You have to find them now."

He squeezed my hand. "Charlie, they're okay." He glanced over to his left. "They're working on them now. But it looks like both your friends are gonna be just fine."

Two guys appeared beside me then. One of them spoke to me very gently. "Okay, we're gonna lift you up and take you to the hospital. We'll get you all checked out."

They slid me onto a stretcher. They worked very slowly, but every little movement set my head to pounding.

I was only glad that we were okay. All three of us were fine. All three of us survived.

The ride in the ambulance was a blur at breakneck speed. The two guys hovered over me, sticking a mask over my nose and mouth, and coming at me with all kinds of whatnots made of cold, hard steel. What was it they were measuring? What were they trying to prevent? Best not to even know. I was, after all, somewhat of a wuss. A problem I would have to overcome if I pursued a career of investigating.

Everything had been so lovely when I'd been asleep. If they would just stop poking at me, I'd go to sleep again.

Which I must have done, because when I opened my eyes again, I was in a bed. I looked around. The beeping monitors and drab green walls confirmed that, yes, this was the hospital. I'd never had to stay in a hospital before. I didn't think that I would like it. But everything was still a blur.

I moved my head a little to the right. Hey, it almost didn't hurt. Perhaps hospitals and doctors weren't so bad after all. I spotted my glasses on the nightstand. Carefully, I reached out to them (Ugh!) and slid them up my nose. Next, I moved my head to the left. Alex was sprawled out in a big brown chair, his head lolled adorably to one side. His hair fell across his eyes, and he was snoring just a little. A magazine dangled from his fingers. It looked like any minute it might drop down to the floor.

Since I had nothing to do but lie back and enjoy, I took my time admiring his muscled legs which were stretched out long in front of him. Then I remembered what I had told him at the scene of the explosion. Mortified, I looked away. Wait a minute. Why was he even here? Did he not have bad guys to catch, reports to fill out...something? Although, I had to admit (Damn it!) I felt somewhat safer with him being in the room.

A nurse came in and smiled. "Good morning, Ms. Cooper. How do you feel this evening?"

Evening? How long had I been sleeping?

"My head feels better. Thank you."

She poured me some water from a yellow plastic pitcher that sat beside the bed. "I'm very glad to hear it." She took a folder from a nearby table and wrote something down. Then she looked at a little monitor with lots of jumping lines. It was attached to me with a cord.

Oh, sheesh. Did she look kind of worried, or was that my imagination? Were those little lines jumping in the wrong direction? Were they jumping too fast? Too slow? Was it my heart, my brain? Don't let it be my brain. That would be the worst.

The nurse turned a little knob just below the screen.

"Everything okay?" I asked.

She smiled. "Everything is fine. The doctor should be in to see you soon. I'll let her know that you're awake. And then we should be able to send you home today."

"Hey, look who decided to wake up." The deep familiar voice was coming from the corner.

I turned to see Alex grin and brush his hair out of his eyes.

"You had a little snooze yourself," I said. "Did you know you snore?"

"You scared us all this morning." His look turned serious. "Talk about being in the wrong place at the exact wrong time."

Yes! Let's talk about explosions. And never, ever mention the things I'd done (and said!) when I thought I was in a dream.

I sat up a little straighter in the bed. "What exactly happened?"

He leaned forward in his chair. "One of the suspects in my case started up his van and the thing exploded like all get out. Apparently, the three of you were close when everything just blew. They think the impact blew you back into a big, sharp rock, and you hit your head real good. You've got some nasty scratches on your leg because of all of the debris that flew out everywhere." He looked me in the eye. "You were lucky, Charlie. Next time might be different. These are dangerous felons we're dealing here with."

Tell me something I don't know.

"How long have I been here?"

He pulled out his cell to check the time. "Let's see, we got here yesterday at four, so...we've been here fifteen hours."

Omg, I slept through an entire day? And what does he mean by *we*? What was *he* doing here? Thank you; now, please go. Seriously, he should leave. The guy looked absolutely whipped.

"Are Marge and Celeste still here, or have the girls gone home?" I asked. "You said they were okay."

"I think you got the worst of it," he told me, "but they kept them overnight as well, just to keep an eye on things. You'll all go home today. At least, that's what they tell me."

"What's the story on their injuries? Were they unconscious too?"

"Celeste might have been out for just a little while. We think that some debris may have knocked her in the head. She's got some scratches on her forehead. But she was conscious when we got there.

178

Marge is also fine – scratched up and sore, but mostly fine." His look darkened. "I told you to let it go. I told you to be careful."

Careful. That was the thing. A detective can't just stay away from where the action is. I glanced over toward him, prepared to set him straight. But he looked sad instead of angry, so I let it go for now.

"Your mom has been here too," he said. "She went home to make some kind of soup. She said it was your favorite."

Oh, yum.

"Chicken and rice," I said.

Alex looked confused. "And there's something else she's bringing, but I didn't understand." He looked around. "She said this room needed cleaning? And that she would bring some kind of spray? But, no, that doesn't make sense. I must have heard her wrong." He rubbed his forehead like suddenly, he had a headache too. My mother can do that to a person.

He smiled. "She's interesting, your mother. Not that I'm surprised. She raised the one and only Charlie Cooper." He winked. "We had a long conversation."

Oh, no. That can't be good.

He continued with the story. "She tried to help me understand the concept of *feng shui*." He knit his brow in concentration. "Did I pronounce it right? Your mother had an idea to help me fight the stress. Because lately, this job has just been bonkers. And when I told this to your mother, she said the oddest thing."

Welcome to my world.

"She said all I had to do was to move my furniture. And I'm sorry, that just seems bizarre. Still, the way she said it made it sound so...nice and warm." He thought about it for a moment. "How was it that she put it? She said that I would find a calming sense of purpose to renew the fire within me." He smiled. "So, watch out, Springston felons. Once this boy renews his fire, I'll be a major badass like they've never seen."

I couldn't help but smile myself.

"You really think your life will change because you move a desk and chair?" I asked.

What next? She'd have him swimming like a fish across the yard to classic rock and roll?

He shrugged. "It couldn't hurt to move some furniture around. Who knows? It's worth a try. But seriously, I liked talking to your mom. She took the time to listen, and she really seemed to get it, you know? There's some wisdom in her crazy. I really think there is."

We fell into a kind of silence as the scene at the rental units flashed through my mind again. I could have died out there. The thought made me want to cry. If Alex would just leave, I could sob in peace.

Since I couldn't cry in front of him, I pondered the next step in the investigation. (But no sneaking into anywhere and I'd stay the heck away from bad guys starting up their vans.) This latest chapter had convinced me that Baxter and his cohort were up to something big – big enough that someone had tried to blow one of them away.

"So, what's going on in there, in that storage unit?" I asked. "What's the latest scoop?"

He frowned. "You know the drill by now."

"Confidential police investigation. That's what you will say next."

He laughed. "And then you'll turn to me and say, *But I'm investigating too! Tell me, tell me, tell me.* Which would be irritating if you weren't so cute."

I felt my cheeks blush and hoped he didn't notice it.

"Well, at least we both know our lines." I paused. Then it hit me. "Hey, Alex, what happened to the guy inside the van?"

There was the darkened look again.

"The van was in a million pieces. He didn't have a chance. Someone wanted him to die. And that's just what he did."

I swallowed hard.

Dead. And I had been so close when it happened. Danger, danger. Alarm bells went off in my head like they had never done before. I was terrified. I couldn't really think about how close I'd come to death, so I tried to distract myself with a lesser evil. "Alex, what exactly are you doing in my room?"

Before he could answer, my mother rushed in through the door, the huge sleeves of her purple tunic wafting around her like bright sails. She carried a large tote in one arm, a potted plant in the other.

"Sweetheart! You're awake!" She kissed me on the forehead. "I've been so worried, darling. Are you sore? A little nauseous? Tell Mother how you feel."

I didn't want to admit it, but I was so darn happy to see my mom.

"A little sore, but I'm okay. And now that I smell soup, I'm a little hungry too." Now the hospital smelled like my mother's kitchen.

She opened the tote bag and pulled out a thermos and a large bowl. Soon she was handing me one of my all-time-favorite meals. I took a bite, then closed my eyes to savor the creamy concoction of chicken and rice with little bits of onion, mushrooms and celery in the seasoned broth.

She sat on the edge of the bed and pushed her long curls out of her face. "What were you doing out there, honey, in that part of town? I don't understand. What did you need to store? We have so much room in that big basement that we never use. You don't need to spend money for a storage unit. I thought you were broke."

"I was there for work," I said. I didn't even think about the undercover bit. But who can keep their guard up lying in a hospital after they almost died?

"Well, that makes sense, I guess," she said. "I suppose that every business needs a computer guru." She waved a hand merrily in the air. "Oh, these modern times! Everybody everywhere just must be *on-line* or *in-line* or whatever. I don't know the lingo of this brand new, crazy world."

"Well. Not so brand new, really. People have been online most of my life. But...uh, never mind. This soup is really good." I took another bite.

She smiled. "Which is why you girls were so smart to go into computers. You'll be always in demand." Then she looked concerned. "But dear, I hear that someone died out there. Do you think that you could possibly fix computers for business owners who don't attract...such angry clients? I'd prefer that you not be around exploding cars and such. Oh dear!" She looked suddenly alarmed. "I have to clear the air." She shivered, then rifled through her tote bag. She pulled out her spray bottle filled with sage.

I exchanged an amused glance with Alex as I dodged her energetic round of sprays. Once she had made her rounds, she sighed.

"Okay," she said. "That should make it better." She brightened when she noticed Alex sitting quietly in the corner. Alex looked amused.

"Oh Charlie, I so enjoyed my talk with your nice young man."

"Mom! Alex is not my..."

"Don't keep secrets from your mother! I had no idea about this fine young man you're seeing. See how nicely things have worked out?" She winked. "Something tells me you won't need that sperm donor after all."

I almost choked on the spoonful of soup I'd just shoved into my mouth.

Instead of being the nice gentleman that my mother was so certain that he was, Alex let out a laugh. Then he quickly got hold of himself and tried to pretend he had a cough.

My mother turned to him. "If I'd known you had a cold, young man, I would have brought more soup. But I did bring you this."

She rushed over to a corner and presented him with the plant that I'd seen her carry in. "It's a healing fern, a calming fern, a new life force for your office! To help you get back your mojo."

Mojo?

"Thank you, ma'am. How kind." Although I could hear their voices, I was way to mortified to turn and meet his eye.

Then I heard a commotion in the hall. It was getting closer, until it finally burst into my room.

"Charlie, you're awake!" Marge hurried into the room, with Celeste not far behind. Their hospital gowns matched mine.

"We're so glad you're okay," Marge said and gave me a rib crusher hug.

"That was a close one, girl," Celeste said.

"I'm so happy to see you, guys," I said. "Yeah, it takes a lot more to bring us down."

"You got that right," Celeste said.

"Celeste and Marge," I said, "I'd like you to meet…"

Marge ran to hug my mom. "We've already met you mother, hon. Your mother's so much fun!"

Sheesh. Was everybody thinking that but me?

Celeste sat down on my bed and grabbed my hand. "How are you? I heard the explosion knocked you out good."

That set my mom to chanting and running wildly about the room with extra energetic squirts of sprays.

"I'm fine. Just a few scrapes on the leg and a pounding head," I said. "How are the two of you?"

"The only good part was the ambulance," Marge said, looking somewhat delighted. "I've never gone so fast."

"I, for one, am ready to get out of here," Celeste said. "They took away my cigarettes. If there's ever a time for a cigarette, then that time is now."

"Oh, yes," Marge said. "I'm ready to leave now, too."

"Me too!" I cried.

Suddenly, we were talking all at once. About the explosion. About the near-death experience. About performing some aura cleansing rituals with some plants I never heard about.

When we calmed down, my mom brushed the hair out of my eyes. She glanced over at my friends. "Don't you think that Charlie has such a nice young man? So well-mannered and polite. And quite a body on him. That's a sexy one right there."

"Mother!" I cried, horrified.

But when I glanced over to the corner, Alex was gone. Well, thank goodness for small favors. It really was no wonder that we hadn't heard him leave, what with the chatter of my friends and my mother leaping to and fro in a cleansing frenzy.

"Has Alex been here the whole time?" Celeste looked curious.

"He hasn't left her side," my mother said proudly. "And the whole time, he looked so worried about how my baby's doing."

He really was here the whole time? For me? It was all so very strange. Hmm...maybe he wasn't such a bad guy after all.

"Well, that sounds love to me," Celeste smiled.

"Kissy, kissy, kissy!" Marge cried.

I tried to ignore that.

"Oh, Barbara," Marge squeaked. "Will you read my aura one more time? That was so much fun." She ran up to my mother, presenting herself for inspection.

My mother studied her. "Oh, this is just delightful. You're vibrating with yellow now. Which means you're full of joy."

"Hmm," Celeste said. "I guess that stuff really works. Only Marge could be filled with joy stuck in the hospital after an explosion."

Marge did a happy shuffle step. "Again! What color am I now?"

"Well it doesn't change that often, dear." My mother took her by the hand, and looked closely at my friend. "But I do see a tinge of orange now blending in with all that yellow." She winked. "Which might just mean that a new love will come into your life."

Marge gasped. "Those are the exact colors I would have picked. Love mingled into happy!"

My mother smiled. "Isn't that lovely, dear?"

While they played their little game, I finished up my soup. My mother was a master cook. I would miss that when I left. *Oh, darn it. The apartment!* I was supposed to leave a check at the rental office. I had to make a phone call, make sure they'd hold my

188

place. Or maybe there would still be time to get by today, even if it was late. Life goes on, no matter what happens.

"Mom," I said. "Could you try to find the nurse? And ask her when we can get out of here?"

As my mother left, I asked my friends if they thought that they'd feel good enough to come over the next day and help me pack.

"Absolutely, hon," Marge said. "And your mother said we could even join in with a class."

"I think I'll take a pass on the dancing or the yoga," Celeste said. "I already got my exercise for this week diving into a ditch and dodging flying metal." Suddenly, she looked angry. "We need to find the guy who did that. That guy is gonna pay!" She scowled in a way that left no doubt that the culprit was in trouble.

"I'm not sure when I'll have the energy to go chasing after bad guys again, especially considering..." I stopped just as my mother walked back into the room. "Uhm...looks like a busy week. Packing and..." I tried to be careful what I said now. I needed to be better at staying undercover. "Packing and...that big project that's coming up at work."

"And that's not all," Marge squeaked. "There's a panda to catch too!"

"How very strange," my mother mused. "I never knew technology consultation included catching pandas. Oh, but never mind. I finally found the nurse. The doctor will be in soon to talk to all of you. Then you're all heading home. Or you can come to my house. You might just find some cookies waiting on the counter."

Cookies? Did my mother just say cookies?

Where exactly was this doctor? What could be keeping her?

Chapter Eleven

THREE HOURS LATER I WAS SETTLED into a cushioned chair in my mother's kitchen. All my favorite smells mingled in the air: garlic, tomato sauce and gingerbread along with the distinctive smell of my father's pipe.

My mother had made cookies – enough to feed the neighborhood – plus lasagna and a salad with gigantic tomatoes from my father's garden.

"They grew like monsters this year," he said with a grin that took up half his face. He grabbed one from the windowsill and tossed it to my older brother, who'd come home to check on me.

"Hey, Sam, here comes a fast one," my father said as he sent the prize tomato sailing across the room. "You still got that winning arm? Or have you lost the touch?"

Sam had lettered in baseball all four years at Springston High. When they were state champions his junior year, he'd made the winning catch to get the final out. His legendary skills made all the coaches salivate to know another Cooper was entering ninth grade. But I wasn't Sam. (Neither, in fact, was Brad.) The most athletic thing that I could do was get myself to class without tripping over air.

My brother easily caught the big tomato (that looked so red and juicy that I could taste it in my mind with mayo and lots of bacon). I loved a good BLT.

"I still got it, Dad," Sam said. "I'm still the man."

"Which is a good thing," my mother said. "I need that tomato for a recipe I want to make tomorrow. If it was splattered on the floor, your dad would be in trouble." She grabbed my father's hand and gave him a playful wink.

"Now, Charlie, don't get up," she said when I tried to head across the room to pour myself more tea. "You sit down this instant." She looked alarmed, as if my legs might break if I tried to walk five feet to the fridge.

"What do you need?" she asked. "Just tell me. Brad can get it."

Ha. Would he expect a dollar? Or maybe he'd want five.

"I was just gonna pour more tea," I said.

"I'll get your drink," my mother said as she stood up from her chair. "And Brad will fluff your pillow. Bradley! You see those pillows behind your sister's back? Give them both a big fluff. But when you take them from the chair, be very gentle."

He didn't look up from his computer game. I wished he'd turn it down, at least while we were eating. There was growling, and loud sirens. I'd had enough of sirens in real life. I didn't need to hear it over the computer also.

"No way can I stop!" he yelled. "Mom, this is not the greatest time. If I kill this purple goblin, I get to level up."

"You heard your mother, Brad. Now, go!" My father took a second helping of lasagna.

Brad loped slowly to my chair and fluffed the pillows that my mom had put behind my back.

"Is this okay?" he asked in a tone that said *this sucks*. It was more like "Can I please just go kill goblins now?"

"Move it a little to the left," I said. I paused to reconsider. "Make it a little softer."

"Sheesh," he said. But, under my mother's watchful gaze, he did just as I asked. She kept a watchful eye on him as she poured my drink.

I leaned back against the pillows. "And could you get me a cookie, brother dear? Two cookies? Make that three. Chocolate chip. No...oatmeal. Oh, bring me some of both."

193

My father dug into his salad. He let out a laugh. "How are those goblins doing, son? One of them, it sounded like, was about to be blown into smithereens if your mother hadn't made you get up from your game. That purple goblin might just owe his life to the fabulous and beautiful Mrs. Barbara Cooper."

"You shouldn't be playing anyway while you're at the table," my mother said. She sat some tea in front of me and smoothed back my hair. "This is time for family." She looked at me mournfully. "Your sister's moving out, Brad. Baby bird must fly the nest. Time just seems to fly."

I sighed. "Mom. I'm almost thirty. I already flew the nest. This was just temporary, me living in my room."

I took a bite of salad, then spooned up more lasagna. I might dream about lasagna when I went to sleep that night; it was just that good. The pasta was all cheesy and filled with spicy sausage. And oh, the garlic rolls! They were crispy on the outside, and when you bit into the middle, they were all soft and buttery – a melt-in-your-mouth kind of good. Why had I been so anxious to get out of there? I was sure there'd been a reason, but I'd forgotten what it was.

I eyed the bottle of cabernet as my mother refilled my father's glass for the second time. My parents always had good wine. We loved to share a bottle during a good meal, and the label on the bottle might just inspire a story from somewhere that they'd visited or somebody that they'd met over a glass of vino. It was, perhaps, the chardonnay they'd drank while watching the sea lions play on their visit to Cabo San Lucas. Or the merlot they'd discovered on their last-minute jaunt to Pennsylvania to hear the Grateful Dead.

How had Mother Nature mixed the genes of two such fascinating people and come up with me and Brad? Sam had been slightly interesting in high school, but that was when he'd peaked. He'd settled into normal long ago, it seemed.

Of course, I could be fascinating, if I could catch Springston's favorite panda or if I could nail the evil dude who'd blown a guy away. I could be a hero if I helped put him away.

But there was a problem. No one could ever know about my daring acts of courage – if there was ever such a thing. I'd have to be a secret hero. To the outside world, I'd still be the same old Charlie.

I shifted in my seat. Ouch. A pain shot through my leg. The doctor said the explosion had knocked me to the ground with the kind of force that would have my every inch of my body crying out with pain for the next few days.

I eyed the cabernet with envy. Wine was out for now. It did not go well with my medication, which did not seem to be doing a whole lot to alleviate the aches.

The sound of gun shots rang out from Brad's laptop, causing my heart to pound. I was still a little jumpy. Almost getting blown up will do that to a person.

"Got another one!" Brad yelled.

My father jumped up gleefully and stood behind my brother's shoulder to watch the battle on the screen.

"Move your guy over to the left!" he cried. "Yellow goblin to the left!" He joined his index fingers to form a kind of gun, which he aimed at the screen.

When my father finally calmed down, he looked at me, concerned. "You okay there, baby doll?" Then he squeezed me from behind.

I usually loved to get one of my father's famous bear hugs, but when your ribs are very tender, hugs aren't exactly what you need. No one in my family seemed to remember that.

When I'd walked into the door that day, Brad had hugged me too, which had been kind of nice. That never happened – ever. But the change hadn't lasted long at all. Now he was back to being Brad.

"Hey, Brad, how's the contest going?" I asked. "For Employee of the Month? You gonna win the prize?"

He groaned. "Everybody wants it, which makes it really hard. It's tickets to the Celtics. Who wouldn't go for that? Plus, two hundred dollars. So, all the other guys are working all the shifts they can. And just a normal kind of day is bad enough, you know? Every single morning, I get up and go to work. How is that even fair? Every single Monday, Tuesday, Wednesday...this stuff is getting old."

Yeah. Welcome to the real world. Where did he think our father went when he left the house each day? Sometimes seven days a week?

"We're rooting for you," my mom said. "Oh, I hope you get your prize!"

Sam wandered over to the game. He wanted to watch as well. "Blue goblin! To the right!" he yelled, excited.

Brad's hands tapped hard at his computer. "I'm trying really hard."

To be a good employee? Or to catch a goblin? I couldn't really tell.

My mom gave me a worried look. "You go on up to bed now and have a nice long sleep. Brad and Sam will take your plate and help me with the dishes."

"But Mom!" Brad said. "It's Charlie's turn to clear the table. I did the dishes last night, because Charlie wasn't here."

Please excuse Charlie from the dishes. She was knocked unconscious by an exploding van, I thought.

"Plus, tomorrow I have to get up early! I have to go to work," he said. "Can't I just rest tonight?"

My mother handed him her dirty plate.

***

I slept just like a baby. My own bed felt so good. Well, not my own bed for much longer. Soon, I'll have another bed, but I'll have all the peace and quiet in the world.

We'd delayed the move a few days. The doctor said for all of us to rest, so we stayed in touch by text.

The next morning, I grabbed my phone once I'd had my usual breakfast of coffee with a side of cookies (this time gingerbread).

ME: My body aches all over. Help!

CELESTE: So sorry, girl. Hang it there. Do I ever feel your pain. My head is killing me.

Two minutes later my phone dinged again.

MARGE: I'm feeling great. I think I'll take a little drive, look around for Lou.

CELESTE: Hold your horses, Marge. No driving on your meds.

ME: I'll watch out my windows. Since he likes my neighborhood.

One look at our phones would leave no doubt that we were absolutely bored. Celeste and I played a word game, at which she soundly beat me. Marge kept forwarding us photographs of kittens with the corniest ever sayings printed beneath the pictures.

In between, I tossed pickles out the window. It kind of felt like work, but I could do it lying down.

***

Three days later, Marge and Celeste came to help me pack. It was moving day at last. They got there just in time to have my father's famous pancakes. We still felt sore, but much, much better. And I don't think we could have lasted one more day doing nothing.

He gave them both big hugs while keeping a close eye on the stove. "Best waitresses I ever had!" He leaned his head toward me. "If you get tired of working with this one here, you'll always have a job at Jack's."

"We miss you, boss," Marge said.

My mother was bustling around the kitchen, squeezing juice and cutting fruit.

"I just love it when the house is full," she said. "You girls are welcome anytime." She had cancelled her morning class to give me a proper send-off.

That disappointed Marge, who'd worn some flowing purple top more suitable for dancing than for a moving day.

"I was so ready to get some exercise," she said to my mother. "I'm so out of shape. Who'd have ever thought this job could be so physical?"

"Not me," my father said. "I'd think you computer types would be hunched over in your chairs almost all day long."

"I even did some warmups just before I came," Marge said.

"You just join us anytime." My mother handed her some juice. "You girls are always welcome."

Marge grinned just like a child. "Oh, Yay! Thank you so, so much."

"Come for dinner, too," my mother said as we settled at the table. "And Charlie, please tell that nice young man to join us. Why has he never been here?"

I cut into my pancake. "Alex! No! Not him."

My mother looked confused.

"Alex is busy. Very busy," I tried to explain.

"You should all come to dinner," my father said. "I'd like to meet this fellow."

"I'll invite Alex, Mrs. Cooper," Marge squeaked. "He can ride with me! I'm sure he'd love to come. Charlie's kind of shy when it comes to guys."

I shot her a death stare.

"Lovely," my mother said.

My brother Brad stood up from the table. "Well, I need to scram. Working man and all of that." He sighed as if a million people were waiting for him to do life-changing kinds of tasks.

Marge and Celeste headed up with me to my room to put my stuff into boxes. I knew I was setting myself up for some teasing by letting them get up close with my stuff.

Celeste held up a faded ribbon and studied it with a frown. "Second place in a science poster contest..." She squinted at the ribbon, whose letters had almost faded into nothing. "From 1994? You've held on to this awhile."

Well, she had that right. How pathetic can you get? But it was the only time in my whole life that I'd won a prize. I explained the project to my friends.

"Since I liked animals, I did a poster on the toad. And its respiratory system. I did all these detailed drawings and made little cards with explanations of how the whole thing works."

Marge pretended enthusiasm.

"Well, how about that?" she said. "That kind of information could come in handy at a party if you run out of things to say."

Celeste shook her head. "Marge, you know I love you, but that's the dumbest thing I ever heard. Who wants to sip on cocktails and listen to someone telling them about the gross stuff that goes on inside of frogs?"

They also made fun of my collection of Disney movies, which I still liked to put on the old VCR, mainly for the songs.

While we folded clothes and wrapped up my few breakables, we talked about our quest to find the missing panda.

With the star attraction still missing at the Springston Zoo, rumors had begun to swirl. Lou was sick, some people whispered, or the zoo had sold the panda due to mounting debts. And, of course, my mother's students absolutely swore that the panda had escaped and was loose on local streets. They've seen him for themselves!

No way, other people said. Those exercisers were just old folks. Their eyes, and their memories too, weren't what they used to be. Then management had issued several statements to assure the public that everything was fine.

Celeste's ex had filled her in on all the conversations going on behind the scenes. Some officials were in favor of announcing that the panda had, in fact, disappeared. Surely someone somewhere would spot the missing panda if the whole town was keeping watch.

Others said to keep it quiet for just a little longer. What if people panicked? Lou, or perhaps, a bystander, could end up getting hurt.

"The police have stepped up their forces to find the panda themselves," Celeste told us in a big huff. "Animal Control is working overtime. Like they don't think that we can find him."

And, well, to be honest, I wasn't sure we could.

Marge's eyes grew wide. "Let's show them what we're made of! Let's go and find that panda!"

"We absolutely will." Celeste closed the lid on one last box. "But first, let's get Charlie moved."

Although I didn't have a lot to take, we needed both my car and Marge's to get all of my belongings to my new apartment. So much of my stuff was bulky, like the old guitar I still thought I might one day learn to play.

My parents stood beside the driveway as we prepared to leave. I wished they wouldn't turn this into a big-deal thing. I was a ten minutes' drive away.

My dad gave me a hug. "We're so proud of you, my smart girl. Don't be a stranger, now."

My mom squeezed me like she didn't want to let go of my shoulders. Ouch. I was still sore. When she pulled away, there was a wetness in her eyes. Mother, what the heck?

And here's the funny thing: I was feeling strange myself. Somehow, I didn't want to do it, to drive down the gravel drive, away from my beaming parents. It felt like something big was coming to an end. Why would that even be? I'd lived out on my own before.

I turned away and pretended to adjust some boxes in the backseat so they couldn't see the tears.

This was it. It was beginning. Adulthood, here I come. For the first time in my life, I had a real career. Kind of. I was doing something on my own. And this step into the grownup world was starting none too soon. The little crinkles beneath my eyes would start to show up at any moment, along with all the other signs of disappearing youth. There's no way that was fair: getting old-age wrinkles when you still hadn't figured out how to be a real adult.

Celeste leaned into my window as I cranked up the car.

"Drive slow," she said. "And keep an eye out for that panda."

Yes! I would do just that. And be glad for the distraction.

My mother wiped away her tears. "Oh, I'd steer clear of that red panda. He has some...disgusting habits."

And then we were off.

As we pulled into the apartment complex, I studied my new home. Not the swankiest of digs, but the grounds were neat with flowering bushes sprinkled here and there. Each unit had a tiny porch for watching birds and sunsets, if you felt like dodging arrows.

The manager handed me the keys, and we carried my things up to the second floor where I unlocked the door. We were greeted by an armchair and matching loveseat in a dark green fabric, along with the welcome smell of heavy-duty cleaning products. The maids must have done their job. The kitchen held a little table and two metal chairs.

Marge hurried in to look. "Oh, this is so exciting, hon! I think the place is darling."

I looked around. "I think the place will do."

"I'll help you decorate," Marge said. "I love to decorate."

It didn't take very long to put all my things in place.

"Oh! There's one last thing." Celeste looked at Marge and grinned. Then from behind her back she pulled out a candle. "Just a little something from your business partners to make it seem like home." It was a candle that smelled like sugar cookies. "It seemed more like a Charlie gift than a baking pan."

Marge reached into her bag and pulled out a container that I recognized as coming from my mother's kitchen. "Surprise! Your mother sent you these. She said for me to pull them out once you got settled in." She reached back into her purse and the cookies kept on coming. There was a second batch. "One batch for us to eat right now to celebrate your brand-new place. And one to save for later in your brand-new kitchen cabinets. Your mother said that when you came home from a real long day, you needed to have cookies."

I wiped my eyes. Good grief. What was it with the tears?

I gave both my friends a hug. "I say we dig in now."

As we munched on peanut butter-chocolate swirls, we gazed out the back window.

"Oh, look. Here come the archers." Celeste rolled her eyes. "Better move back from the window. Wouldn't the hospital be surprised to see us back again?"

"Time to get back on the case," Marge said. "I say we go to lunch, talk a little business. Who wants to go to Jack's?"

"Are you craving a cheeseburger?" Celeste asked. "Or dreaming of a fry cook?"

Marge dissolved into a fit of giggles. Since there was nothing funny about the burgers, I guessed romance was on her mind.

***

She spotted him right away when we walked into the diner. Then she blushed and giggled her way through our business meeting.

"We don't have much that adds up." Celeste took a first sip of her milkshake. "We have a guy who lost his little finger..."

"And didn't even see a doctor, which I find absolutely strange." I twirled my fork in my spaghetti.

"That must mean he's up to something serious." Celeste thought about it. "He was more scared of getting caught than of getting an infection."

"And you'd think he'd want a doctor to give him something for the pain," I said. "You know that had to hurt."

Celeste thought some more. "He could have gone to a private doctor. But surely they would have sent him on to a hospital. With an injury like that."

"And how did he lose his finger?" I asked. "And what exactly is the deal with the ten million boxes?"

"So many questions," Celeste said. She picked up her burger. "Hey, Marge, are you writing all this down?"

Marge had unofficially become the investigative secretary, always scribbling something down in the little notebook she took everywhere.

"Writing...what? What did you say?" She was staring at the corner where the kitchen window was, tossing her hair and smiling. I still wasn't used to this new side of Marge.

Celeste pointed at her. "Get out your notebook, Juliet. Romeo has things he needs to fry up for all these hungry people."

Marge blushed. "Is he not the most adorable thing that you've ever seen?"

"Well, I wouldn't go that far," Celeste said, "but if you two became an item, I'd give my approval."

Marge brushed at her blue top. "I would have dressed more if I had only known that we'd be dining out."

Celeste picked up a fry. "Nobody dresses up to go out to a diner. No matter what they might have going on with the fry cook in the back."

Marge took out her notebook. She was giggling again. "What were we discussing?"

I twirled more spaghetti. "We were saying we have no idea what was going on with this crazy case. All of it is a mystery: this Baxter dude, the boxes, and the missing finger. We need to have a plan. Where should we look next?"

Marge stared down at her notebook, then scribbled for a while. "We have lots of clues. But they don't add up to anything; they don't make any sense. There's the rental unit where they keep more boxes. And there's the guy who..." She paused and held her hand over her heart. She leaned forward and whispered to us. "The guy who got blown away."

"And who exactly was he? That's another mystery." I stole a fry off Celeste's plate.

"And who wanted him dead? And why?" Celeste batted my hand away. "This is your daddy's place. He'll bring you fries for free. No reason to eat mine."

"The police!" Marge squeaked. "I'll bet they know. Right from the beginning, Alex seemed to know that something big was up."

"You're right," I said. "That night we found the finger, he told us to stay away. Even then, he said that things might get really scary."

"Your boyfriend wasn't lying." Marge took a sip of tea.

"He's not...oh, never mind," I said. "But he knew that this was big. And I'll bet the cops already know some things about the guy who died."

All eyes turned to Celeste. Because, as with almost any question, Celeste knew a guy. In this case, it was, of course, the chief.

She grabbed her cell, and when there was no answer from the ex, a string of colorful words came flying from her mouth. Hmm. Some of those were words that I'd never heard before.

"Shhh!" Marge put a hand on Celeste's arm.

"He knows it's me. And that's the very reason why he won't pick up. He knows exactly what I'll ask."

"Leave a message for him, hon," Marge said. "Tell him we need information. We need information now. And if not, you'll spill."

Celeste straightened up her scarf. "I don't know what you mean."

Marge had broken the unwritten rule. Celeste didn't like it mentioned that she knew something on her ex. She didn't like to talk about her past at all. Which was kind of irritating, because Celeste must know some stories.

"You can't be married to a guy and not know something that he'd rather the whole town didn't know." Marge prodded her a little.

I knew that Marge was right. Information was a weapon if you knew how to use it. Marge had her trusty pistol, and Celeste knew things about the chief...and maybe other people. You should use everything you've got. That's what my mother used to tell me when she pushed down the low-cut blouses when I was dressing for a date. Like most things my mother told me, that saying made me cringe. But I guessed she was right, when it came to guns and exes.

211

"And those boxes in the rental place?" Celeste leaned back against her seat. "The police have those, I'm sure. Took them in as evidence. So, girls, they're way ahead of us. I hate it that they know things and we don't have a clue. They know exactly what's inside all those mystery boxes."

Then I had an idea. I hated my idea. I almost didn't say it. I almost didn't say it because I was starting to (almost, just a little) kind of like my life. I had a new apartment. I wanted to enjoy it – my quiet, brand new place – before leaping once again into the path of evil. Here I am again, death. Can you catch me now?

But if I wanted to be a detective for real, I couldn't play it safe. That's what Alex wanted, for the three of us to stand back and let them solve the case. I looked around the table at the faces of my friends. We were three smart ladies; we could solve this thing if we jumped right into the action. We wouldn't solve it by eating fries.

So I said it out loud. "We should go back to Baxter's place."

Please don't let me die! My mother can barely stand it that I moved down the road.

Marge looked at me, askance. "Baxter's place? Oh, hon. I don't know if that is wise."

"Do you have a better plan?" I asked.

I was met with silence.

"Maybe he's got more boxes there," I said. "I know he emptied out the room the day that we were there. But maybe all the time he's bringing in more stuff. As part of whatever the scheme is they've got going on."

"Or I wonder if he's stopped that business altogether," Marge said. "I'll bet the whole thing with the van really spooked our buddy Baxter."

"It could have been him who died that day," Celeste folded her napkin in two.

"It could have been us." I added. "If we'd been a little closer."

"And if there aren't any boxes at his place, there may be other clues." Celeste thought about it. "As much as I hate to go there, I think that Charlie's right." She punched some numbers into her phone again. Again, there was no answer. Again, there was a string of words that weren't in any dictionary.

I took one last bite of garlic roll. "But we need to figure out a safer way to get inside his place. The fire escape? No way." I shivered at the memory of my filthy hiding place. I didn't dare to hope he'd called a maid or had a pest control appointment. He didn't seem the type. "Let's make double sure that the place is empty."

Marge nodded. "One of us will go in. And the others will be stationed at both doors. We need to come up with a signal. To say get your sweet butt out of there and you need to do it now."

The question hadn't come up of which one of us was going in.

A signal that would serve as a clear warning, but not tip off this Baxter dude that someone was inside? I wondered if there was an option to send a sound by text that sounded like a cockroach. Does a cockroach make a sound? Baxter would never notice that one. He probably heard it all the time.

Celeste picked up the bill. "Well, let's pay this thing and scram. We've got work to do."

"I hope this wasn't our last meal," I said. "I would have ordered some dessert."

"Don't worry. We'll be fine, hon." Marge gazed down at her purse. I knew exactly what that meant. The mighty persuader was coming with us, nestled among fruity gum and mints and several pairs of reading glasses. Baxter best not challenge it. Marge's inner ninja came out when the gun was in her hand.

"Let's just take one car," Celeste decided as she dipped one last fry into her ketchup.

I'd driven myself to lunch, thinking we'd all go our separate ways once we'd finished eating. My plan had been to wait another day before I started work full time. My mom had made me promise I'd get some rest that afternoon.

But then I'd had my bright idea, and we were off to catch a crook.

"I'll drive!" Marge said excitedly.

Of course. That made perfect sense. If Baxter didn't kill us, maybe Marge's driving would.

She glanced over toward the kitchen window, where Ralph was setting down some plates. I turned in time to see him wink, causing Marge to blush. I loved this romance!

"Oh, just ask him out." Celeste reached behind her for her coat. "He likes you; you like him. Why not just go out on a date? You two are killing me."

"Not just yet. Be patient." Marge fluffed her hair and giggled. "He's gonna have to wait. Cause I'm worth waiting for."

She paused to study me and smile.

"Hey, Charlie," she cooed, "I'll bet you've never asked a guy out on a date. You really ought to try it. I promise it's a kick."

"Oh, I don't think I could," I said. But then, hey, why not? At the rate that I was going, that might be the only way I'd ever get a date before I was the age of my mother's students.

"It really is the best way," Marge said. "It puts the power in your hands."

"I guess you're right," I said. That made a lot of sense. I think. "It's just a little scary."

Celeste let loose her honking laugh. "You're braver than you think, girl. If you can crawl into a felon's window, it shouldn't be so hard to ask a guy out on a date."

I guessed she had a point. But first I had to find a guy. So far, the ones in Springston were hardly to my taste. There was Alex, Mr. Know-It-All. And then there was the dude who tried to blow me up. Pickings so far were slim. If I'd had to go solely on physical attraction, then it would have to be Alex. Damn it. I pushed that thought away and concentrated on what was truly important right then. Solving the pinky-mystery.

Marge and I headed for the door while Celeste settled the bill.

"Hey!" Marge said. "I wonder if we'll see your friends from the fire escape. You remember them? The dancing granny and her man. The ones with all the dance moves." She demonstrated as we left, looking like the leader of an Egyptian conga line, causing the table beside us to burst into applause.

To be part of a profession that was centered on blending into a crowd, Marge certainly stood out. Celeste could go incognito by toning down her hair and nails, but the spirit that was Marge couldn't be contained.

She grabbed my hand once we got outside. "Come on, hon, let's dance. Do you remember how it went?"

But I didn't feel like dancing. I was too terrified.

Chapter Twelve

"Who's gonna do it this time?" I asked as Marge pulled out onto the main road. "Whose turn for the fire escape? And I hope the window's unlocked so someone can get in." I was glad I'd done my time and lived to tell the tale.

"I'm afraid it can't be me." Celeste lit a cigarette. "I have a migraine and a bad back."

"Oh, not me," Marge squeaked. "I don't have a sense of balance."

I remembered the last time I'd seen her on a ladder hanging pictures on our walls. The girl did have a point. We'd be back at the hospital for sure, and that wouldn't help our progress.

Well. This wasn't looking good.

"Sorry, girls, not me this time," I said. "This might be a little too much for my first day at work. I'm supposed to be on bed rest, not dangling in a window." Or running for my life.

Okay, that was good. It sounded more mature than No fair! No fair! No fair! Plus, it was the truth. I'd been the one who'd fared the worst when the van exploded. When the docs said I was okay to go back to work, I don't believe this was exactly what they had it mind. They thought I'd be behind a desk fixing some computer.

And so, it was decided. We'd do things the simple way. No fire escapes. No hiding. No daring leaps through windows or close encounters with roaches and dust bunnies that might win blue ribbons at some super grotesque fair. This time we'd try something different. We'd knock on the door.

"What will we say?" I asked.

"Well, we can't sell cookies, that's for sure." Celeste thought about it. "Neither of us look like girl scouts."

"We could say we work for the building," Marge said. "That we were sent to check the heater or the washer or something." She thought about it for a second. "What do building-people fix?"

"We don't look like fix-it people." I braced myself as Marge braked hard for...what? Why was she braking, anyway? There was nothing in her path.

Sheesh. I turned my mind back to our debate. "If we were showing up to fix things, then wouldn't we bring tools? We don't have any tools."

"Oh, yeah, you're right." Marge said. "We don't even have a hammer or a screwdriver."

"My father has a hammer," I said. "I'm sure we could borrow it."

"But what would we do with the hammer once we get inside the house?" Marge asked.

I shifted in the backseat. "I don't have a clue."

Had I ever used a hammer? I wasn't sure I had.

"Hey," I said. "Should we maybe take some classes? In quick repairs or something? You know, so we'd know what to do if we got into someone's house and said we were technicians or maintenance workers or whatever."

"Yes!" Marge cried. "Whoever uses hammer thingies."

"Perhaps we couldn't fix their dryers if they let us in, but we could know which parts to unscrew without making the machines refuse to ever work again," I said.

"No need," Celeste said. "I'm good with a hammer and a screwdriver and a handsaw too. I just didn't think to bring my little toolbox with me."

"Understandable," Marge said. "Who brings a hammer to a diner? We should keep stuff in the trunk: a tool box, some cleaning products, some fake census forms. Then we can pretend to have lots of different jobs at a moment's notice."

"Great idea," I said.

"I need to write that down," Marge said. She swerved way over to the opposite car lane as she dug inside her purse.

"Right now, you need to steer." Celeste put a quick hand on the wheel.

"Right now, we'll be the new neighbors," Marge said, pulling the car back in the right lane. "We won't need any props."

"That sounds good," I said. "No special skills required, and I guess we look the part."

"Oh, goodness, I hope not," Celeste said as we came in sight of Baxter's building. "I've toned down my sparkle, but do I look like I live here?"

"Okay," I said, still feeling quite uneasy. "What if he believes we're neighbors and he lets us in his place? What should we do then? We can't just say *Glad to meet you, neighbor*, then start looking in boxes. If there *are* any there." I was getting nervous. I hoped he wasn't home.

"Okay, I think I have a plan," Marge said. "One of us should try to distract the guy somehow, then the other two can snoop around very, very fast."

Hmm. I thought about how that might work. Something else they never taught in the self-help section of the bookstore: How to Distract a Thug.

I gazed outside the window as I thought some more. The streets were deserted in this part of town, except for someone's dog who seemed to be running loose. I looked closer. Such an odd dog with a striped and bushy tail. The tail was humongous. Wait...was that a dog or...?

We got closer and I pressed my nose up to the window. Shaking sugar cookies! It was! It really was. Lou was trotting down the sidewalk, happy as you please.

"Marge! Stop! You've got to stop." I yelled.

She slammed the brakes down hard, sending us forward in a wild tilt reminiscent of the kinds of rides I'd hated at the fair. Thank you, thank you, thank you to whoever thought of seatbelts.

I tried to catch my breath. "I didn't mean that quick." Next time I was driving.

"What's going on?" Marge asked. She put a hand over her heart. "Did I run over something? I didn't see a thing." She looked freaked out as well.

Only Celeste was unfazed. She looked down at her fingers. "Did I break a nail?"

"It's him! It's him!" I cried.

"It's Baxter? Where? Where is he?" Marge yelled.

Celeste sat up straight to look. "Which way is he going? Is he walking toward his place or is he heading out? If he's leaving, we're in luck. We need to get inside there now. It's safer with him gone. We only have to figure out how to get in."

"We're back at square one, I guess," Marge said.

"No!" I cried. "That's not what..."

"Oh, hush," Marge said, who had finally caught her breath. "Charlie, don't be scared. We need to be brave. One of us has to go in."

"Lou!" I yelled. "I was talking about Lou. We need to get the panda."

Celeste turned around and put one hand on my knee. "Girl, you need to calm down. One case at a time."

"No! Lou is standing right outside. He's right there on the sidewalk."

A hushed surprise took the place of all our chatter. Then we turned in unison to see what the panda was doing now. Lou stuck a curious nose into a pile of trash, then sauntered toward a giant oak that was close by.

"Well, will you look at that?" Marge said.

"What should we do?" I asked.

A horn behind us blared, as if in answer, as a pickup truck rolled to a stop behind us. Oh yeah, I'd forgotten. We were blocking traffic, I supposed.

"I guess the first thing we do is park somewhere." Celeste gave a little wave to the angry driver. "And Marge, get going quick before that guy behind you scares the panda away." The guy was laying on his horn.

Marge pulled into a convenience store with prominent advertisements for beer and cigarettes.

"Where's a good net when you need one?" I asked. "And where's a jar pickles? Hey, they might sell them in that store."

I straightened my glasses on my nose while I considered what to do. "There are some boxes that we used for my move in the back. Could we use those somehow?" Marge had lent me packing boxes, and we'd loaded them in her trunk after we moved me in.

"Why not? Go for it." Marge hit a button that opened the trunk door.

I took a nice, deep breath, and walked back to the trunk. It was now or never. I took a box and slowly made my way toward Lou, careful not to startle him. I set the box down gently in his path.

The top flap was open and facing towards him, should he care to step inside.

If this were some other person's story (someone more fortunate than I), Lou would have walked right in and made himself at home. Then I would have quickly closed the flaps and called my friends for backup.

But no, that didn't happen.

Lou stared at me, curious. *What is this crazy woman doing?* the panda was probably thinking. *Is this some kind of game?*

I moved forward with the box. Lou watched, then backed away. He trotted slowly to the right. I gently walked in front of him and put the box down in his path. Lou moved left and I did too. He moved to the right again, and I was right there with the box.

Celeste and Marge, in the meantime, had gotten out to watch.

"It's like some kind of weird dance," Marge said. "It's kind of fascinating."

I set the box down and sighed. "Do you have an idea that's any better?"

Marge got down on her knees. "Here, widdle cutie panda. Come here, come here to Marge. Come here, you cutie wootie."

Startled, Lou backed away, but, thank goodness, he didn't run. He watched Marge from a distance.

"It's not a cat, for goodness sake." Celeste crossed her arms. "You can't just call a panda."

Marge pouted. "I thought he might be lonely and glad that we were here."

That's when Celeste took charge. Very, very slowly, she approached the panda.

"He's really not that big," she said, keeping her voice low so as not to startle Lou. "I'll just try to grab him. Then we can put him in the trunk and drive straight to the zoo."

That would solve the missing panda case. Finally. How long was it safe to keep a panda in the trunk? The zoo was not that far.

Celeste had him...well, almost had him. We all held our breath. Celeste was good at almost everything.

Unfortunately, Marge had to start back up with her cooing. "It's okay, panda wanda. We'll take good care of you!" Her voice went up three octaves whenever she talked to animals or children. It was like the sound her brakes made when she screeched to a stop.

I was afraid that Lou was out of there. But, instead, he farted. Was that what he did when he was scared? So far, I'd heard him fart three times, and this one was the loudest.

We all got hit with this one. It seemed that Lou had quite a talent: he could aim his foul air in three directions all at once. The zoo officials had skipped that fun fact when they were describing to Celeste the behaviors of red pandas.

I, tragically, got a nose full (for the second time!) as did Celeste and Marge. No one was left out. Farts for everyone! The panda scrambled up a tree, looking down at us as if we were the crazy ones. Perhaps we did look unhinged. We jumped around and fanned our faces, hoping to find a way to escape that raunchy smell. If we could somehow get that stuff in a bottle and aim it straight at someone's nose, we could catch any crook in Springston with a single spray of yuck.

"This is just atrocious. What has he been eating?" Celeste asked as she gasped for air.

Marge came over to put one hand on my shoulder. "Oh, hon, I'm so sorry. I'm sorry that I laughed the first time you got a load. I had no idea." She bent down, almost gagging.

I stepped back from the crime scene, but the smell was everywhere. I thought I might throw up.

What I wanted was my mommy. If ever a cleanse was needed, it was right here on this corner.

"I think it's settled into our clothes now," Celeste touched the fabric of her blouse. "We'll have to throw these clothes away. I'm glad I didn't wear my good stuff."

And if we had to go through all of this, we could at least have caught the panda. How did you catch a panda? That should be on the list of things to do the next day: brainstorming great ideas on how to get Lou back where he belonged. So the next time that we saw him, we would be prepared. It shouldn't be that hard. He was such a little guy. There had to be some websites for zookeepers, for people who worked with wildlife...

And we also should consider buying some protection. I'm thinking hazmat suits and gas masks.

Suddenly, the wind picked up and blew the smell right back in our faces.

Marge leapt up in the air. "Whoa Nellie! Oh, my gosh. That's some wicked stuff."

I waved my hands around my face, but the funky smell refused to go away. It seemed to get worse, in fact.

"Why are we still standing here?" Celeste asked. "I think the stink is messing with our brains. Let's get in the car right now and drive far away from here."

I looked toward our car, and my day got even worse. Alex was sitting in his parked Jeep, and there were tears of laughter rolling down his cheeks.

Did he have a radar that went on, alerting him to every one of my humiliating moments? Did he not have crooks to catch? And if he was so high and mighty, why did he not get out and catch the panda himself? At least the three of us had tried.

We ran back to the car. Marge locked all the doors.

Celeste thought *that* was funny. "No need to press down on the locks like it's some emergency. That smell's not gonna waft itself on over here and try to pick the locks so it can jump right in the car."

I wished she hadn't planted that idea in my head. I might well have nightmares about that very thing. I took a long, deep breath. It felt great to breathe again. Normal smelled so good.

Marge had started the ignition up when Alex tapped hard on the window.

Marge rolled her window down. "What are you doing here?"

He leaned into the car and directed his gaze at me. He had a stern look on his face. No more gales of laughter. "I could ask you all the same thing. I'm following up on leads for a case that I'm working on. What's up with you three? This is not the safest neighborhood for three ladies to hang out."

"Thank you for caring," I said, "but don't you have better things to do than follow us around?"

"I am following leads, not ladies," he said. "I just don't want you to get hurt...again. Seriously, Charlie, there's some bad stuff going on. You need to stay away from here."

Well, if the stuff is bad, that's all the more reason to have four detectives on the case rather than just one. But when had Alex Spencer ever tried to be logical? A flashback of him sitting in the hospital chair by my bed, while I was out, came to mind. He *did* look worried about us then. Or about me. He hadn't left my room, I was told. And he did look worried right now. It didn't occur to me up until now that he was telling us to stay away because he was, indeed, worried about us. Mental forehead smack.

"Alex, we really appreciate you looking out for us. And you're right. We'll try to be more careful," I said and I really meant it.

Marge, Celeste and Alex stared at me with wide eyes.

Finally, Alex cleared his throat. "Well then...okay...then...I guess...yes, be more careful. Thank you...for...listening...I guess."

He turned and walked back over to his car like he wouldn't know what else to say.

Celeste turned to me. "What the hell was that?"

"I think someone's got a crush on someone," Marge giggled.

I rolled my eyes.

It's not like I promised Alex to completely stay away from whatever dangerous things might be going on. We were too deep now to just quit.

"Ok then. Should we call animal control?" Marge asked. "Or maybe call the zoo?"

I grinned. "Why? To pick up Alex?"

Celeste's honking laugh rang out.

"Because Lou is still here somewhere," Marge said. "Who knows how long it might be before we spot the little guy again? And I'm not going near him!"

"Put down your phone," Celeste said. "I won't give Bert the pleasure of thinking that we failed. Somehow, some way, we'll catch that panda. And we'll do it someday soon. For now, let's head to Baxter's, just like we planned."

"Let's do this," I said.

"Here's our plan for now." Celeste said. "We'll knock on the guy's door, introduce ourselves as neighbors, like we talked about before. Marge, can you find a way of distracting Baxter while me and Charlie look around?"

Marge smiled and tossed her hair. "I might have a way."

"That is just disgusting," I said.

"Not that," she replied. "I'll just flirt a little. I'd never let him touch!"

"Think of another plan," Celeste said, popping a stick of gum into her mouth. "You're not at your most alluring when you smell like Lou."

Marge backed out of the parking space. "Oh yeah, I forgot. I'll just ask him lots of questions then. Questions about himself. Most men love to talk if the subject is themselves."

"You got that right," Celeste said. "And the subject's usually so much duller than they seem to think."

Once we got to Baxter's, Marge parked across the street. We didn't want him to recognize our car. My first glimpse of the fire escape gave me the heebie jeebies.

"Does everyone understand the plan?" Marge asked.

We all started talking at once, which was the precise moment that we heard a tapping on the driver's side window. Sheesh. What did Alex want now? I'd told him we'd be more careful. But we won't back down.

Still intent on our conversation, Marge waved her hand in the air as if telling him to shoo. As for me, I wouldn't give him the satisfaction of even looking up. Whether he liked it or not, I had a job to do.

But the tapping just got louder.

Marge and I looked up at once to see a gun pointed straight at us.

I recognized the owner; I didn't have to see his face. I'd seen that hand before, and I'd seen the dirty bandage in the spot where once there was a finger.

Chapter Thirteen

"FOR THE LOVE OF COOKIE DOUGH!" I yelped while Marge let out a squeal that made me jump.

"Will you two cut it out?" Celeste spoke very calmly, as one can only do if one has failed to see the gun that's pointed at one's face. "Just settle down."

"That's a little optimistic," Marge whispered in a trembling voice.

I needed a barf bag and my mother. I could barely breath.

Then Celeste caught sight of Baxter at the window. She was struck silent for a moment. Then she rolled her eyes. "Oh, for the love of God!" I heard her breath in deep. "Okay, let's just stay calm. We've got this, girls."

Marge rolled down the window and squeaked in a tiny Minnie Mouse voice. "Can we help you?"

"Get out of the car right now," Baxter barked, moving the gun with a shaky hand so it pointed to each of us in turn.

We got out very slowly.

"You see my van around the corner?" he asked. "I want you troublemakers to head over to my van.

I'll be right behind, so no funny business, hear? I've got lots of bullets, and I don't mind shooting you."

His van? How did we not notice a van that was parked right there, pulled in all haphazardly into a no-parking zone? Like the driver had parked it in a hurry. That should have been a clue. And we called ourselves detectives. But it was way too late to make brilliant deductions now.

I looked around me wildly, but didn't see anyone that I could signal to for help. Save us! Please! Someone? Anyone? Anyone at all? A cold chill swept right through me. I had just moved into my new apartment. I hadn't slept in my new bed. I had never known real love or learned to play a classic rock song on guitar. This was not the best moment to die.

Baxter took his time ambling behind us. You'd think he'd try to hurry us along. After all, it did look a bit suspicious: a young grungy-looking dude following three ladies and holding up a gun. There were few cars in the parking lot, no residents in sight, but several cars sped by us. Hello! Pay attention, people. Kidnapping going on here! Passengers, look up from your phones. Were shootings so common in this part of town that people were unfazed by the three of us held at gunpoint?

Once we reached the van, Baxter got all up in my face. His breath smelled like very old and sour beer. "Open up the door there and climb in the back."

This was getting worse. Nobody could find us in the back of a window-less van. I was so freaking out.

It was kind of strange (and creepy) that the van looked just like the one that had blown up. How many vans did these guys have? Or was there only one now, after the explosion? A new wave of fear shot through me. What if this van was rigged too?

I couldn't think about that now. I opened the door and climbed in, squeezed myself in tightly among a sea of boxes. I closed my eyes and tried to think of cookies. Oatmeal, chocolate chip...but all I could think about was dying.

Soon Marge and Celeste were huddled in beside me. As Baxter glared from the opened door, we traded wide-eyed looks, and Celeste reached across to squeeze my hand, which didn't help to stop my trembling. Things had turned tragic just like that.

Then Marge patted her purse and gave us a knowing look. Well, that at least was something. The Persuader was on board. Probably thinking that Marge was gonna be too hasty with the gun, Celeste shook her head just slightly so Baxter couldn't see.

Part of me was wishing that Marge would pull that baby out and blow the dude away. But something kind of told me that Celeste was right. If Baxter saw that she was armed, he'd probably shoot us all before she could even aim at his ugly face. Better to wait until his back was turned.

He shot us one more evil look. "Keep your pretty traps shut or you're gonna be really sorry."

Up close, he looked younger than I'd thought he was – with bad teeth and oily hair and a small scar on his forehead.

Then he shut the door.

I held my breath when he started the ignition up. We were off and moving at a jerky pace with a lot of speeding and sudden stops. Whew. Well, at least the whole thing hadn't blown.

"What now?" Marge whispered. "How do we get out of this one?"

Celeste pulled out her cell. "Darn. I don't have a signal."

I pulled my phone out and tried as well.

"Nothing," I reported.

"Nada here," Marge said as she, too, looked up from phone.

Baxter, in the meantime, was making lots of turns that sent the three of us tumbling into each other.

"I wish he would just drive straight," Marge said. "Then if we ever get a signal, we'd have some blooming idea about where this dude is heading. Are we going north or south? Or east of town?"

"I don't have a clue," I said. I might throw up anytime. The terror and the jerky ride were making my stomach feel sickly.

"This is a mess all right," Celeste flipped her phone shut and put it back into her pocket.

What exactly would we say now if our stupid phones came on? *Come and get us. Hurry!* But hurry to where? It's anybody's guess.

She looked around the van. "Well, I guess we've got our chance to peek inside the boxes. Careful what you wish for."

She got out her lighter. Then she used her fingernail to very, very quietly slice through the flimsy tape on the box that was closest to her knee. She pulled out a large green sneaker.

"A shoe?" I asked.

"Let me see, let me see." Marge huddled closer to me.

"Whoa. This brand is majorly expensive. Bert bought a pair one time. Those things cost a fortune. Dirtball did not deserve those shoes." Celeste looked closer at the sneaker.

"Is the whole box filled with shoes?" I asked, being very sure to talk in an almost whisper.

Celeste felt around inside. "Looks like it it's all shoes. Very pricey shoes. Hmm." She paused. "What's up with the shoes?"

I pushed another box toward her, and she used her nail to slice through the tape on it. I'd thought her fingernails were just part of her charm. Apparently, those things could be mega useful. It was like a toolbox on her hands.

She reached into the box and pulled out a purse. Then another and another and another.

"This is good stuff here," she said. "Very high-end bags."

She took out a small black box and peeked inside. She held her lighter closer. "One of the most expensive brands of watches that they make."

"I want to see!" Marge said.

"Hmph. Who wants to see a stupid watch? I just want to go back home." I shuffled a little on the hard floor to try to get a bit more comfortable. At this point, I didn't care what was in the boxes anymore. I just wanted to come out of this one alive and in one piece.

Marge stared at the box with interest. "I bet all of this is stolen. That's what they are. They're thieves!"

"I don't think that's it." Celeste carefully repacked the box. "I think I know exactly what these guys are up to. They're selling counterfeits."

I had become the most disinterested detective that there ever was.

"So, nice to have a clue that breaks the case wide open right before we die," I said, blinking away my tears.

"Hon, I'll keep you safe," Marge said. "Before that creep can even open the door, The Persuader will be ready. And this Baxter person won't know what kind of annihilating super force just hit him."

"But what if he calls for backup?" I asked. "What if we're outnumbered?"

Marge winked. "Don't worry, hon. I'm good."

I took one deep breath, then two, trying to calm myself. It seemed crazy. Just the day before, I'd hated my life with a passion. But at that moment in the van, I'd have given anything to be back in my parents' kitchen, the very place I'd wanted so badly to escape. I wanted to hear a knock-knock joke, the sound of my brother's stupid game...I wanted to be safe. And to think that this was all my idea, driving to Baxter's place to sneak a peek. I should be more responsible when it comes to the decisions I make. I can't be wishing to go back home when things don't turn out the way I expect them to.

Suddenly, the van screeched to a stop. Okay, here we go.

Marge rifled quickly through her purse. "Why do I carry so much junk? Why do the things you need always sink down to the bottom? They make little pockets for phones and lipsticks and keys. Why not a pocket for your gun?"

Why not, really? No one ever needed to grab their lipstick super-fast in an attempt to save their life.

The door flew open, bringing a flood of sunlight into our eyes. Baxter and some tall guy glared inside the van, pointing guns at us. This was just great. Now there were two of them.

I stole a glance at Marge and saw that her hands were empty. Damn and double damn. Tall Dude grabbed me by my shoulders and pushed me out so hard that I stumbled. This was one rough dude. He'd left a bruise, I bet.

I looked around me warily. We seemed to have ended up in somebody's backyard. The house was large and made of brick. Kind of a classy place, not the type of neighborhood I thought Baxter's friends might live. It looked like a quiet, well-kept street with swing sets and newer model cars, grills out on big back decks: a place to barbecue steaks or throw a football, not to blow somebody's face off in the middle of the day.

I didn't dare to scream for help, what with two bad guys beside me who had their guns all cocked and ready. I bet these were the kinds of guys who shot things just for fun. Why give them an excuse?

But if someone was watching (please, please, please be watching), these were the kinds of neighbors who'd call 911. I hoped the person in this nice brick house had nosy neighbors.

"Get in the basement. Now!" our captor barked. "And if I hear a peep from you, you'll get an even closer view of my trusty little pistol." He shoved a gun into my back as he pushed me toward a back door that looked like it might lead into a basement. Was he about to rob these people? Or was this the tall guy's place? It looked too normal for either one of them. It looked a lot, in fact, like the street that I'd grown up on.

Marge stumbled, almost falling, as they herded us inside. We took the stairs down to the dimly lit basement.

"Trouble-making broads." Baxter shoved me roughly onto a leather couch.

"See what you made us do." Tall Dude pointed his gun at Celeste, directing her to sit beside me. His face turned red with anger, making his acne marks stand out. "You just had to go and stick your noses in." His face turned even redder.

Soon my friends were shoved in on either side of me. Marge kept a tight grip on her purse while she hummed a Disney song. Quietly, but still audible.

"Shhh!" I grabbed her hand. Why risk making these guys even madder? They didn't seem like Disney fans. I bet they'd never in a million years guess she had a gun in that purse. At least we had that going for us: the element of surprise.

I glanced around the room, but couldn't tell a lot about it. Only one overhead light was on, and there were no windows. I could just make out a TV and a tall lamp and I think a bookshelf.

Baxter glared at me. "Quit your crying right now. I hate when women blubber."

Well, then don't point guns right at their faces. Duh.

243

I wiped away a tear. What were the chances he would do it, that he would really kill us? *Pretty good,* I guessed. I felt a telltale tickle in my throat that meant my little bit of weepiness was about to explode at any minute into great big sobs.

I'd been due for a good cry even before two thugs kidnapped me at gunpoint. And – whoops – here came the flood of tears that might just get us killed.

Marge held tightly to my hand until my tears subsided into hiccups. Celeste picked up my glasses, which had slid down to the floor. She placed them on my nose, then she glared at Baxter. "Can you at least get us a hankie?"

"Be a gentleman," Marge said, thought that was kind of a lost cause.

"Get a wad of tissue," Baxter told the tall guy while he held the gun on us. He looked poised to run, as if he expected we might bolt at any second.

His friend came back and handed me a roll of scented toilet paper in a tasteful shade of powdered blue. This was getting weirder by the second. These looked not like the kind of guys to buy girlie toilet paper.

"Thank you very much," I said, then I blew my nose.

While Tall Dude stood guard with the gun, Baxter clomped upstairs.

Not much time had passed when he ran down with a rope. Great. It wasn't hard to guess what was coming next. He grabbed me by the arms, squeezing so hard it hurt, and tied my hands behind my back. He squeezed the knot so tightly that it cut into my skin. I glanced over to the side to see that Tall Dude had Marge tied up. He was working on Celeste next.

"Do you really have to do this?" Celeste asked him gently, as if she were making a friendly suggestion from one pal to another. "After all, you have the gun. I'm sure this kind of thing is bad for the circulation. And I'm not as young as I was once. Why don't we all just sit and talk? Let's work something out."

"Hey, I have a great idea." Baxter leaned down into her face. "Why don't you shut your ugly trap?"

"I've got something that will help." Tall Dude held out a massive roll of duct tape. "This will shut these broads up quick."

I cringed. Absolutely lovely.

While Baxter taped Celeste's mouth, Tall Dude worked on me, pulling the tape tightly around my face and hair. Then he moved on to Marge.

"Dang, man. What a day." Baxter turned on a second overhead light and flopped down into a chair, stretching his long legs out in front of him and kicking off a shoe, as if it were him, not us, who'd had the worst day ever.

I glanced around the room some more which was – again, weird – really kind of gorgeous. Signed oil paintings in nice frames were hung up on the walls, which were painted a light beige with a brand-new coat of white trim. The bookshelves were filled with hardback books as well as family photos. Someone had neatly lined up a group of porcelain figurines like my grandma once collected. Yarn and knitting needles were nestled in several boxes that lined the bottom shelf.

I looked from the two thugs to the dainty, dancing figurines with umbrellas lined in gold. Something didn't add up. Some things (besides, of course, Baxter and his friend) looked out of place. Empty plates with dried-up food were scattered about the room, along with smashed-up beer cans and greasy pizza boxes. Magazines were messily strewn across the oriental carpet. *Modern Gunman. Shooter's World.* It just didn't fit. I glanced down at the stories splashed across the cover. People who knitted things in light blue fuzzy yarn were not the type to eagerly dive into *A Guide to Ammunition. Fire Away with Confidence!*

Despite the tape across her mouth, Marge began to hum again, something from Peter Pan. Celeste leaned over to give her a shoulder nudge. Marge got the hint and stopped.

I hoped I wouldn't hyperventilate. I was feeling claustrophobic, and not being able to move my arms seemed to play into that fear. What if there was a fire? At least I could use my legs, but this rope thing, I suspected, would mess hard with my balance. And now with our mouths taped shut, there was no chance of talking sense into these guys. And, with our arms tied behind our backs, no chance of The Persuader joining our little party and saving the day at last.

Tall Dude went outside. I heard the van door close, then he came back with a laptop. He trotted over to the couch, then stopped short, staring at us with distaste. "Damn it. You're sitting in my place."

Well, if you would just untie us, we'd be glad to leave.

Very roughly, he grabbed Celeste and pushed her to the floor, then shoved me on top of her, and Marge on top of me. Carefully, so as not to rile the animals, because that's what these guys were, we rolled apart from one another. Then, with a little effort, I rolled onto my side. Lying on your back is not the most comfortable position when your hands are tied behind you. I was sorry to be a member of the exclusive club that had that information.

Tall Dude had opened his laptop and was sprawled across the couch while his fingers flew across the keyboard. I heard some familiar music. Could it be? No. That was just too weird. The awful thug was playing the alien game that my brother was obsessed with.

"Almost, almost," he whispered to himself. "I almost beat the boss's score."

Baxter got up from his chair and opened the door to another room which I could see was filled with boxes and more boxes. This operation must be huge. How much were they raking in?

I decided that one of them at least must have a few more brain cells than they seemed to. But had it occurred to them that counterfeiting held a lighter sentence than kidnapping? Or assault? Did they know what the sentence was for murder? I thought I might cry again.

I cut my eyes to Marge. It looked like she was thinking hard. How could she keep her wits about her while death stared us in the face? In this line of work, I guessed, that's what separated out the winners. Marge, with all her quirks, sometimes had a bravery that took my breath away.

So I tried to be like Marge. I tried to come up with a plan. Only, any chance at escape seemed to involve my hands or mouth, which now were kind of useless. Even if the guys were to somehow both leave at the same time (Would they be that stupid?), I couldn't dial my cell or even turn the door knob. Could I break a window with my foot? Shoot, there were no windows.

Neither guy was watching us; both were distracted. Tall Dude was staring into his laptop screen while Baxter shuffled boxes in the adjacent room.

While I tried to think of something that would get us out of there, I heard footsteps running down the steps from the main part of the house. Please. Be the normal suburban lady with exquisite tastes who must live in this home. Surely Baxter didn't live here. And surely not Tall Dude. I looked at the stack of stuff beside me. Someone else lived here, someone who could help us. Because there was no way these things belonged to Baxter, and it was not the kind of expensive stuff he'd try to counterfeit. He had no use for stickers and colored papers to Scrapbook Your

Cherished Photos, as one cellophane package advertised. Did he collect boxes of tiny wide-eyed dolls, each with the name of a month written across their pastel-colored skirts? I highly doubted that.

Perhaps the scrapbooking owner of tiny dolls was coming down at this very moment to rescue me from hell. But these weren't delicate footsteps that I heard; this was a loud clomping. Soon a guy appeared who was a little older than the others. He was dressed a lot like them, with baggy pants and massive sneakers and a ball cap that needed a good washing. He wore it backwards on his head.

By the way the other two perked up in his presence, something told me this guy was in charge. Tall Dude put down his notebook and sat up straight. Baxter put down a stack of boxes and walked into the room.

The new guy settled into the couch and looked at us lying on the floor. "Well, what do we have here?" His mouth was set into a frown, but there was laughter in his eyes. "Let's take the tape off these ladies and see what they have to say." Then he moved toward me and pulled the tape off my mouth. Whoa. Talk about a sting. But it felt good to have it gone. I'd been getting tired of having to breathe in through my nose.

Celeste winced as well as he pulled the tape off her mouth.

Tall Dude got up from his seat and went to Marge. "This one likes to hum dumb stuff. Can we keep the tape on this one?"

"Mmmmph!" Marge mumbled.

The new guy thought about it. "Nah. Just rip it off. I have some questions for these ladies."

"You're gonna make them pay, right? For messing with our business?" Baxter asked him eagerly. "Broads screwed with us real bad." He got up in my face, and that, I have to say, did not exactly leave me with the pleasantest of smells. This had been a bad day for my nose. For all of me, in fact.

Tall Dude set down his computer and let loose with a sniveling laugh. "Hey, Spike, you're the boss. But this is disappointing. Cause that's how I like my ladies. I like them with their mouths taped up so I don't have to hear their nonsense."

That's exactly the kind of talk that would on any other day earn a stream of insults from Celeste. But the girl was cool. She didn't even flinch. Because our one goal was to live. We could wait until another day to take care of assorted assholes with their bigoted opinions.

The new guy studied us with interest. I guessed his name was Spike. "Baxter called me from the road to say he was coming over with some lovely guests who'd been causing trouble for our little business." He leaned back against the back of the couch. "Hey, you guys should separate the girls. I don't want to have to listen to them chatter back and forth. You know how ladies like to talk."

Baxter picked Celeste up and carried her over to the left side of the room, where I could hear him drop her hard onto the floor. What jerks these dumbasses were. Tall Dude grabbed Marge and dropped her hard in a back corner. Absolute assholes.

Spike sat back and stared at me. "So. You're the broads from the garage."

"What?" Marge called out from her corner. "How did you know that?"

"Oh, we've been watching you," he said. "We keep a little camera at our storage place. You need to have security when your operation goes big time. And, man, we're killing it. This thing is getting huge." The goofiest-ever-looking smile spread across his face at the thought of his success. "So, we saw you snooping around our place. And then we were watching when you nosy broads hightailed it out of there." He laughed. "Garret opens up the door, and off you ladies go. You three know how to move."

"Garrett?" I asked. "Is Garrett the one who…"

Spike grinned. "The one who bit the dust. In a spectacular explosion! Wasn't it spectacular?" He made a whooshing sound. "You were there. You remember the little show that we put on. Garrett was not the best of my boys, kind of a screw-up, really." He looked me in the eye. "I had to get rid of Garrett. Nothing personal, you understand. Purely a business move."

Oh, this guy was evil. A cold chill shot right through me.

"But, I have to tell you, it came off without a hitch. He started up the van, and whoa, did that thing blow. Was it not amazing?" He looked at me expectantly. Did he expect me to say *good job*?

Well, if he was talking, he wasn't shooting, right? I had to stall for time. I had to keep this doofus talking.

He was smiling, dazed, remembering the scene. "That was some power, man." He shook his head. "That was intense. Superb."

From my place bound on the floor, I held his eye and nodded. I tried to think of some more adjectives.

"It was very, very loud," I said. "I won't forget that. Ever." Which was absolutely true. "It knocked me unconscious." Maybe that would make him happy, the idea that his big, bad explosion had knocked me senseless to the ground.

I tried to think of a question that would keep him talking. If I could just do that, I imagined (I really hoped!) that Celeste or Marge would come up with an action plan.

Then my ears perked up. What was that clicking sound I heard in the background? It was coming from the part of the room where they had dropped Celeste. I knew I couldn't turn my head. If Celeste was up to something, I didn't want this guy to turn around and look. What exactly was that noise? I'd heard that noise before.

The lighter! That was it. Was she trying to burn the rope so that she could free her arms? That was kind of brilliant, really. But also, impossible. Unless the lighter just happened to be in easy reach. I could barely move my hands from the spot behind my back where they were tightly bound. Our arms and hands were useless.

Where were the other guys? They seemed to have disappeared, trusting their boss to keep us all in line. For someone who seemed to take such pride in his skills as a felon, he was doing a lousy job in keeping a close eye on Celeste. You go, girl. And hurry!

So. How to keep him talking while Celeste did her thing, whatever that thing was?

"How did you get so good at...uh...making things explode?" I asked. I was kind of scared to hear the answer. But a girl does what she has to do.

He pointed to his head and grinned. "Because I'm brilliant, baby. This guy has all kinds of moves. Someone would be stupid to mess around with me."

Speaking of stupid, this guy never even once glanced over at Celeste. Just keep talking, buddy!

"So, what's up with these boxes?" I asked. "What exactly are you doing?" Men loved to talk about themselves, and that was working in my favor.

He gave me a proud smile. "It's quite an operation. Way more money than I ever thought. This idea was genius, if I do say so myself." He leaned forward and laughed. "I guess I can tell you. It's not exactly like you can run out and tell the cops. What we've got going on here is a counterfeiting sales ring, and you're looking at the captain." He nodded to himself, all caught up with his brilliance, while twenty feet away Celeste (I hoped! I hoped!) worked to free herself.

"You must be doing well," I said. "That's a lot of boxes."

"Oh yeah. I think of everything," he said, oblivious to the clicks, which were getting louder and steadier. "You see, the way it works is this." He leaned back on the couch. "We've got a massive warehouse, and I mean really huge, where we store all kinds of things. Purses, jewelry, watches...and then, you see, we came up with a company that sells the junk to idiots. The kind of sucker morons who pay thousands for a purse. A purse that is a fake!" He laughed. "The world is full of suckers, right? So, we're raking in the money without spending much at all. Cause, really, it's just junk. It was perfect, absolutely perfect." He narrowed his eyes at me. Uh, oh. "Till you three broads decided to waltz into the picture. Who are you, anyway? You cops or what?" He studied me with curiosity.

Nothing to lose now. "We're private investigators. We're in business for ourselves." It felt good to say it. And I was feeling hopeful – the tiniest little bit – that I'd live to say it to other people too. If anyone could get us out of here, it would surely be Celeste, who was definitely up to something.

"Investigators, huh?" he said.

It sounded so important. And, in fact, it was. If we made it out alive, just look what we'd uncovered. They'd sent us out to chase a panda from the zoo, and what would we deliver once we busted out of here? Three major crooks that the cops had yet to catch.

He let out another laugh. "You're kidding, right?" He flapped his hands up in the air. "Private investigators! Oooh, I'm really scared!"

Well, perhaps you should be. The clicking sounds had stopped, but now I heard something else. It was coming from the spot where Tall Dude had thrown Marge. I had no clue what was happening, but I knew what my job was. I had to keep diverting the fool in front of me while my friends did their thing.

Soon, Baxter appeared beside him. Great, two of them to distract. He handed a plate to Spike. "This was on the stove still hot. Pot roast. It's my favorite. She said for us to all eat up. I already had two bowls."

She? Who was she exactly? And did she have a clue what these thugs were up to in her basement while she fed them pot roast? This was some crazy stuff.

But I couldn't think about that now. I had to make them look at me and not Celeste or Marge. "How long have you been in business?" I shifted on the floor. Thank goodness for the carpet, but it was far from comfortable. When one side began to hurt, I'd roll onto the other. Well, the doc had said to lie down frequently. Although I'd much prefer a bed.

"Almost ten months without a screw-up," Spike said as he shoveled meat into his mouth. He tilted his head toward Baxter. "Then this fool messed up with a big delivery. He almost got us caught."

"It wasn't my fault," Baxter yelped. "You know that I couldn't help it that the..."

"Shut it, man." Spike turned to glare at him. "I don't pay you to make excuses. You're lucky it was just a finger I decided to chop off."

Yikes. I felt the threat of tears again, and something was rising in my stomach. Was I about to sob or hurl? Or both at the same time? Get it together, Charlie. And to make it even worse, I could barely see a thing. My glasses had slipped off my nose and rolled off toward the couch precariously close to Baxter's oversized black sneaker.

"Excuse me, Baxter," I said in a timid voice. "Could I trouble you for my glasses?"

He sighed as if I'd asked him the hugest favor in the world, but he bent down and got them and put them on my nose.

"Thank you very much," I said.

Spike continued with his story. "And then this stupid fool goes running out the door and through the park and loses his own pinky. Can you believe that shit? He trips and falls and off it flies, out of his hand. He couldn't find it, and then here come some joggers." He laughed at the memory.

Baxter winced and gazed down at his bandaged hand. "What could I do but leave? If the joggers had noticed my bloody hand, they would have asked some questions, maybe even called the cops. There was a lot of blood."

"We were there as well," Marge said, apparently, all finished with her secret business.

Baxter glanced at her, amazed. "No way, man."

"Way," Celeste replied. "We had official business in the park." She must have been finished with her noisy plan. Had she given up or was she waiting for the perfect moment to set it all in motion?

"But our business in the park had nothing to do with you," Marge said, as if this might somehow reassure them.

"*We* found your finger!" Celeste said. "The police have it for safekeeping."

"A panda we were looking for had your finger. We found the panda just as he was nibbling on it," I said.

Spike and Baxter glared at us in disbelief. They were looking from Marge to Celeste to me and then to each other like they couldn't believe what they were hearing.

"Are you high or something?" Baxter said.

"No, we are not high!" Marge cried.

"I could use a little something right about now. Does anyone have a cigarette?" Celeste asked.

"All of you shut up!" Spike said.

He was looking intently at us and thought about it. "Huh. That's some crazy shit. That's too weird for you to make up, so I suspect it might be true. Why were your there, again?"

Marge put on her official investigator's voice. "We were on assignment. We had brought some pickles. So we could catch the panda."

The two men exchanged confused looks again.

"These broads," Baxter said slowly. "These broads just ain't right."

Spike looked at me and grinned. "Too bad we have to kill them. Or should I just chop off a body part? This one right here is really kind of cute."

I got the creeps and shuddered. Okay, I needed to distract this guy a little more. The stupid happy music was still playing from the laptop that Tall Dude had left open with the alien game in progress. Spike must play it too, since the Tall Dude had been so intent on beating his boss's score.

I tried to remember something, anything, Brad had said about the game. He was always catching aliens when he should be making dinner conversation, helping with the dishes or doing anything at all.

Spike sadly shook his head. "I don't think I have a choice, boys. Pretty as they are, I think we have to kill them."

The sick feeling in my stomach rose.

"Did you know that a polka-dotted goblin from the planet Koopataka is hiding behind a mushroom in the lower left-hand corner?" I asked.

Was that what Brad has said? At least I think I had that right.

Spike looked at me, amazed. Then he picked up his friend's computer and punched hard at the keys. He let out a whoop of victory. "That's the rarest alien ever." He peered down hard at me. "How the hell did you know that?"

"Tap him on the nose," I said, "and you get Super Power X." How did I remember this stupid kind of stuff?

He tapped harder on the keys. "Super Power X! I have Super Power X! Do you know all the things a guy can do with Super Power X?"

I swear that he stared down at the laptop, with his fingers flying, for at least five minutes without ever looking up. I never thought I'd say it, but thank you, thank you, Brad.

"You three are some weird investigators," Spike said.

While Spike was busy with his game, a door creaked open from upstairs, and a woman's voice called down. "Albert Stephen Jones the Third! You promised me three hours ago that you'd take out the trash!"

A look of mortification swept across Spike's face. "I'm busy right now, Ma! I told you, it's real important business stuff."

What the...? His *Ma*? Where the heck were we? Did Spike live with his...mother? I turned to look at Marge and Celeste, who had the same I-can't-believe-what-I'm-hearing-looks plastered on their faces.

"Did you eat all the little carrots that I put on your plate? Eat your carrots, Spikey!" she sang out. "Don't just eat the meat and the potatoes. I made the carrots real soft like you like them. With butter and with honey."

"Ma!" He threw down the laptop while Baxter tried to control his laughter.

Spike buried his face in his hands. He'd lost some serious street cred at the moment. Would a boy who lived with his mother be less likely to shoot you in the face? I hoped that might be true.

"So," I asked, still shocked. "Is she in the business too?"

Spike looked up at me, furious. "No way, man! What kind of person would do that? Go into this kind of business with his mother?"

Baxter grabbed his pistol and aimed it at my face. "Don't you talk about his mother. That woman up there in the kitchen? That's woman's one good lady. That woman feeds us real good. She ain't into crime."

"She thinks we're watching TV and playing games on the computer," Tall Dude chimed in, who had reappeared during the commotion. He handed

263

Spike a bowl of carrots. "You mother said eat some more of these."

"And don't think she's gonna come down and save your stupid asses," Baxter said to me. "Cause she's got real bad knees. She hardly ever comes down here."

Tall Dude sunk down into the couch. "Which means that we can store stuff and not get barraged with questions."

I couldn't believe what I was hearing. If I screamed, I bet she'd come down. Not that I planned on trying that soon. That might be Plan B if Marge and Celeste weren't up to something. A scream might anger these short-fused guys with pistols at the ready.

Still, it made me feel better to know that she was up there washing dishes or whatever, living a normal life. It made it seem less likely that I would die down in her basement.

I glanced over at Celeste, wondering what was up with her. She still had her hands behind her back as if they were tied up. Of course, that might just be a ruse.

"Spike!" His mother called again, causing him to bristle. "I can't squeeze another thing into this smelly trash. When are you going to take the trash out? And I can't reach the top shelf to get my pills for vertigo."

Spike shot a look at Tall Dude.

"Okay, I'm on it, boss." Tall Dude trotted up the stairs.

But Spike's mother wasn't finished. "And ten more minutes of video games, then you need to practice your piano."

Spike sunk back into the couch, one hand covering his face.

His mother continued. "That was our agreement if you came back to live at home."

Tall Dude stopped short on the stairs and shrugged. "I can't help you out with that one. I don't have an ear for music."

"I can help!" Marge said. "I know lots of lovely songs."

Once again, the upstairs door flew open. "Is something squeaking down there, Spikey? I thought you fixed the doorknob. That squeaking hurts my ears."

"I fixed it, Ma," he said, glaring across the room at Marge.

"What? I didn't hear a thing," Marge said.

"Spike!" his mother called. "There it is again, that squeaking."

He stared angrily at Marge. "That was another problem that I'm just about to fix."

Baxter went back into the room with all the boxes, leaving us alone with Spike.

"Okay," Spike said, standing up. "The time has come for us to go for a little ride. It's time to say bye-bye world. Your little adventure as spies is coming to an end. You three are going down."

He pointed the gun at me, then he wildly looked around the room, pointing in at Marge and then Celeste in turn. "Stand up, ladies. Head on out. This was supposed to be my day off." He glanced at the TV. "Football starts in thirty minutes. First you screw with my little business with your snooping around and then you make me miss my game."

"Why don't you let us sneak on out?" Marge asked. "Then you won't miss the kickoff. And everything you told us will be our little secret."

I watched her wiggle on the floor while she tried to stand up with her hands behind her back. I hadn't managed to get myself up either. It wasn't the easiest thing to do.

"We won't say a word," Celeste chimed in. "If you'll please just let us go. Think about it. You don't want to do what you're about to do. Right now, your only worry is a counterfeiting charge. And kidnapping, if they find out. Although we'd never tell. But if you got charged with murder?"

"Three murders!" Marge squeaked. "You'd be locked away forever." She kept bobbing forward, then falling back as she tried to get up off the floor. I hoped that, secretly, her hands behind her back were free from any ropes.

"You'd miss a lot of football," I tried. This guy seemed to like his games.

Spike stopped and scratched his head. "Shit. You're messing with my head." He kicked the couch. "Head out now, but quietly. If you'd kept your noses out of my business, I wouldn't have this hassle. Bunch of nosy broads. Here, let me pull you to your feet."

He was heading my way when I heard footsteps thundering down the stairs.

"Hey, Spike, hold up!" Tall Dude yelled.

Spike kicked the couch again.

"What the hell?" he yelled. "I got business to attend to. And the game's about to start. Plus, we're all out of beer. Which idiot forgot the beer? This day really sucks."

"Tell me about it," Marge said, who sounded close to tears.

"Your mom says you have lawn to mow," Tall Dude breathlessly reported. He spoke in a soft voice, afraid to be the bearer of bad tidings to an already angry Spike. "She says you've been promising for days. She says she's mortified about what the neighbors think."

Spike got up in his face. "I'm a man of business. I don't have time to mow no lawn."

Still fearful, Tall Dude shrugged. "I think the lawn looks fine."

"Spikey! Do it now," his mother yelled.

"I just have to run an errand," he called up the stairs. "I'll get it done today."

"No TV till you mow the lawn!"

He kicked at the couch again.

"The garden club is coming over in the morning," she called. "It has to be done this instant. I can't have them thinking I live in a field of weeds. I'd be so ashamed."

And she'd really be embarrassed by the fine young son holding three victims hostage in her basement and threatening to shoot them dead. You can't live a thing like that down, no matter how fine and delicate your petunias might be in the spring.

"Baxter's coming up to do it," Spike called. In the adjoining room, Baxter turned around, surprised, three boxes in his arms.

"No! You're coming up yourself, and you're coming up right now. We had an agreement when you moved back home. And today's the flower show. You said that you'd take me and help me pick some flowers for tomorrow's little party."

He paused. His face turned even redder. "Yes, ma'am. I'll be right up. I just have to drive some lady friends back home. It won't take long at all." My chest seized up with dread.

"Oh, send them up!" his mother called. "They can give me their opinion on the new colors for the kitchen."

"They're kind of busy, Ma!"

"No, we're not!" Marge squeaked.

I don't know who glared at her harder: Celeste or the seething Spike.

"I'm really good at colors," Marge whispered, somewhat cowed.

"Would your friends like some ice cream while you mow the lawn? Are you coming now?" came the voice from the top of the long staircase.

"Can't you give me thirty minutes?" Spike walked up two steps and called. His voice took on a pleading tone.

"I made your favorite mac and cheese last night," she said angrily. "And you give me attitude."

"Today! I promise, Ma."

"Promises are golden; hard work is even better! Hard work gets results! Remember Helpful Harry from your favorite little book?"

"Please. Just let me run the girls home." He turned to look at us and pointed the gun straight at my face as if to remind me of my fate. More of an Evil Ernie than a Helpful Harry. Then he climbed up two more stairs. "Just fifteen minutes, Ma. They don't live very far."

Okay, we might have a shot. His back was turned and the gun was hanging loosely at this side. I glanced around the room. Baxter was still distracted in the next room with his boxes; Tall Dude was on the computer playing around with Super Power X. I wondered how exactly to grab this tiny chance to escape our date with death.

But my friends were faster. Marge leapt in front of Spike who turned around to find a gun pointed in his face. Celeste sprinted across the room and locked

Baxter into the room with the load of boxes. One less thug to deal with.

Then it got even better. Because – how exactly had this happened? – Celeste had Tall Dude's gun and held him at gunpoint! She must have grabbed it from the couch while he was killing goblins. How stupid could a guy get? How did these guys dress themselves, let alone make a ton of money from a counterfeiting scheme?

"Who's the stupid broad now?" Marge asked, her voice composed, her eyes full of concentration.

There it was! We had our ninja back.

Spike dropped his jaw and stared at Marge. "Don't kill me, lady! Please. I don't want to die."

Marge moved a little closer. "Don't you move a muscle, or I'll blow your dimwit brains out – what little brains you have." She looked down at his feet. "I'll blow them to pieces all over your fancy shoes. Hmm. Are those real or fake? Drop the gun. Right now!"

He did exactly as she asked, and held his hands up in the air.

Seconds later, some sort of ruckus seemed to break out in the upstairs of the house. Slamming doors and running footsteps and a sea of angry voices startled our little group. And just when things were getting good.

What was up with that? Were more thugs on the way? We had to leave – and fast.

Spike's mother let out a frightened scream.

"Who are you?" she yelled. "No! Don't shoot! You must have the wrong house. Not my little Spikey and his little friends!"

Then the door from the outside burst open, spilling a tangle of uniformed police, who rushed at us with guns drawn. Thank you, thank you, thank you. I'd live. I'd really get to live!

Silently and quickly, Marge slipped her gun into her bag.

At the same time, more officers rushed down from the upstairs, followed by Spike's startled mother. She watched the action with one hand over her heart and one hand caught up in her blonde-gray hair. "Oh Spikey, what is this?"

An officer grabbed me roughly by the shoulders and then reached for his handcuffs.

"Hold up," a deep voice said that I knew very well. It was a voice I should have known that I'd hear at that very instant, a voice that was present for all the most troubling moments of my life. Alex shot me a weary look.

"The girls are on our side," he said to the officers. "Don't mess with them."

He stared at me for the longest time with a strange look in his eye. Was it relief? Or worry? For just a crazy moment, it seemed like he might reach out to grab me in a hug. But when he put his arms around my waist, it was to free me from the ropes.

"We meet once more, Charlie Cooper," he said. "Why am I not surprised?"

I looked in his eyes and man, was I glad to see him.

"We tried to be more careful," I finally said.

He looked at the ropes, which he still held in his hands. "I'm glad that you're safe now, but it doesn't exactly look like you had the upper hand. Exactly who was holding who?"

Amid the commotion, Celeste had appeared beside me. "Me and Marge had guns aimed at the criminals that you've just arrested. Charlie distracted the main guy while we did our work." As if to prove her point, she still held Tall Guy's gun tightly by her side. Not for long though, as a police officer took the gun from her.

"And we've got another suspect locked up behind that door." I pointed my eyes toward the room where Celeste had Baxter trapped. I couldn't help but let a little pride creep into my voice. "And we got confessions too."

Then Marge joined our little party. "Alex. Well, hello. So glad you guys could make it for the grand finale. If you'd come a little earlier, we could have put you to good use. But you have to admit it now: we do some fine work."

Alex rubbed his temples and let out a sigh.

"Radio the chief," Alex called out to an officer who stood beside the door. "Tell him we caught all three."

"*We?*" I raised an eyebrow. "Did you just say *we?*"

Alex looked down at the floor. "Yes. We."

I couldn't help but smile at him.

He gave me just the smallest grin and I felt my legs getting shaky. The guy was looking fine, even when he was reluctant to give credit where credit was due after three new detectives had just bagged a death-defying victory.

"I was worried about you, Cooper," he said. "You've got to stop scaring me like this."

"Sorry," I said sheepishly.

"And you owe me an aspirin. You gave the bad guys fits all right." He massaged his forehead. "But you gave this good guy a whopper of a headache."

Chapter Fourteen

I WOKE UP THE NEXT DAY TO TOTAL silence, which never, ever happened. That's when I remembered: Oh, yeah! I was at my new apartment.

I settled back into the softness of the covers, burrowing into the pillows for a luxurious, quiet snooze. No rock-and-rolling oldsters, no loud guffaws from my father as he drank his coffee in the kitchen, no noises from my brother's room. Brad sometimes (the times when he had a job) failed to turn off his alarm, which made weird monster sounds.

Something else was different too. Every single bone in my body ached and ached. I did not feel well at all. But what a dream I'd just been having. Alex was the star. I nestled into my pillow and tried to will my way back into the dream. I was still in that sleepy place where the dream world seemed so real. I felt like I could close my eyes and slip back into the story. At least I wanted to.

In the dream, I'd been with Alex on the beach. We were dancing at the spot where the waves barely touch your feet. Things had started to get steamy when something woke me up. Life, give me a break. If my love life has to suck in real life, don't jolt me wide awake just when some gorgeous hottie is about to make a move.

The dream had been so good. Alex had been stroking my back and whispering in my ear…something about detectives getting sexier in Springston. Then he'd kissed my neck and said something about boxes and fake purses and somebody's mother's basement…

Whoa. I sat up, wide awake. Everything from the day before came rushing back at once. No wonder I was sore. And I hadn't yet recovered from the previous fiasco when I'd been almost blown to bits. I felt around for a scrunchie to put up my hair, moving my arms gingerly. Every movement hurt.

I glanced over at the bright red letters on the clock, which read eight a.m. So much for sleeping in. Nothing like waking up to the memory of a gun jammed right in your face. I wasn't sleepy anymore. A memory like that will jolt you wide awake every single time.

I laid back and remembered, glad to be alive. Most people might have died if they'd been tied up like that by three thugs who were determined to kill them off. But we'd done some kick-ass work, Marge and Celeste at least. They were full of surprises, those two. Who else would have thought to use a lighter to get their arms free from ropes?

And okay, I'd have to admit it. Sometimes I'd had my doubts that we could do this thing: solve crimes for a living. But my partners always seemed to pull out hidden talents – hidden until the moment when we had to save our lives.

The police had filled us in after they'd led the guys away in handcuffs. For weeks, the authorities had been watching Spike's mother's house, driving by at frequent intervals. Of course, how close had they really been watching? They'd missed the whole shebang in the backyard when Baxter had led us in at gunpoint.

Then, later that afternoon, Celeste's ex had made the call for the officers to go in and arrest Spike. They'd been hoping to do it for a while, and the evidence was at last in place, thanks to the explosion at the rental unit and the boxes that they found there full of counterfeited items.

Of course, we already knew all of that; we were way ahead of them. Spike had told me the whole story about setting up the business to sell the stuff for massive profits. And while the officers rushed in to point their guns at him, we already had that covered. Plus, we had two bonus suspects. Who said we weren't good?

They'd been expecting to get Spike. Tall Dude and Baxter were surprises. The police had known they were involved with the operation; they just didn't think they'd be so lucky to find all three of them together in Spike's basement.

Very slowly, I got out of bed and looked around the almost empty room until I found my glasses. Then I moved into the kitchen. Please. Let me have remembered to pack coffee.

I found it, thank goodness, along with an old chipped mug. I poured some creamer in while I waited for the coffee to finish making.

Too bad that I hadn't been all up in Spike's face with a gun like Marge's when the officers rushed in. Story of my life. I was the one tied up on the floor while my friends did their thing. Why did Alex always show up when I looked like a doofus?

Only now he knew the whole truth.

"Charlie was the hero," Celeste had graciously explained. "She kept Spike distracted while I was busy getting myself free from those stinking ropes."

I thought we'd all been heroes. And when Alex found me on the floor, he hadn't given me his usual look of pity like I was some fool. He'd looked...kind of soft and tender, like he'd looked in that dream. The memory of that dream still made me kind of weak.

Something was up with real-life Alex. He could be a pompous jerk; he'd still prefer we stay the heck away from stealing his thunder in some case. (And, boy, had we done it this time.) But it had been a while since he'd raised his voice at us. He'd seemed less controlling and more...caring.

I could take care of my own self, thank you very much, but being swept up in his muscled arms? Well, I think I'd dreamed that too, sometime in the night.

He'd stuck very close to me while the house was searched and while the guys were led away. I remembered how his hand had felt, warm against my arm. "Be gentle with her; check her out good," he'd said to the paramedics. "I want to make sure she's okay."

Then we'd all gone down to the station to give the police our statements.

Now, as I sipped the first warm taste of coffee, my thoughts turned to Spike's mom. So many people got hurt at a time like this. Of course the victims did, but so did the families of the bad guys. His mom had seemed like a nice lady; she'd made Spike's favorite foods and read to him as a child. And still the poor thing ends up with a moron for a son. Maybe I could stop in for a visit, take her to a flower show or something.

She'd even let him move back home. Moms are nice like that, no matter how old their children get. Hmmm. I bet her overgrown grass was the last thing on her list of mortifying bits of potential gossip. I was sure the neighborhood was buzzing with all kinds of talk that had nothing to do with weeds.

Once we'd told the police all kinds of details that they didn't know, an officer drove me back to my new apartment. Another officer took Marge to get her car from Baxter's place.

I poured a second cup of coffee and took it back to bed. We had all agreed: no work for us today. But it was a funny thing. Despite helping bag three real life bad guys, we had yet to solve our first official case. We could foil three guys with pistols, Celeste could break out of restraints, Marge could outmaneuver a hardened criminal in a lively round of Who Has the Gun Now. But we couldn't catch that little panda.

Which meant no paycheck yet. Perhaps Celeste could get the ex to pay us for our work the night before. Celeste could be persuasive. I wouldn't put it past her.

I looked around at my bare walls. I needed pictures, posters, art..., something. The place was small, but it would do. Best of all, it was all mine. Right then, it felt a little stuffy. I needed some fresh air.

I opened the window by the bed. I breathed in the air. That felt *really good*. A little cool, just the way I liked it. And I heard voices, too. Neighbors! Maybe new friends, even. Things were looking up.

But what was that whizzing, whistling sound somewhere near my ear? Like really, really close. I heard a kind of thud; thuds are never good. I turned toward the noise to find a massive arrow plunged into my new beige wall. Absolutely lovely. I wasn't killed the day before by three felons with guns, but I might die today by an arrow coming from an archery range.

But life was good, I told myself. Never mind the arrow. I quickly shut the window. Some problems had quick fixes. Just close a little silver latch and, just like that, you're safe.

After that, I showered and dressed to meet the girls for breakfast at the diner, which was a good thing, really. There was no food in the apartment. I put on a t-shirt and capris, grabbed my keys and thundered down the stairs of the building.

***

Marge and Celeste were already at a table by a window when I pulled into Jack's. They each gave me a wink as I got out of my car, and Marge looked extra happy, even when you considered the huge feat we'd pulled off the night before. Too much caffeine? I wondered.

I smiled at them and waved, then turned to find Alex right in front of me. Where had he come from?

He grinned and watched me closely, like he was thrilled to see me.

I blushed, remembering my dream, which was silly, really. He couldn't read my thoughts.

"What are you doing here?" I asked him.

"Oh, I just picked up a sandwich to eat back at my desk. No time for a real breakfast. There's all kinds of paperwork once we wrap this case up." He sighed happily. "Yep. Last night we did good. The police reeled in some big ones."

"The police?"

He smiled. "I'll give you that one, Cooper. You girls had 'em cornered before we burst into the door." Then his face turned serious. "Charlie, you're a smart detective. But you can't keep putting yourself in that kind of danger. If you got hurt, I'd..." He frowned, looking thoughtful. "I'd ask you to be careful. But I know that's not your style."

I was too worn out to argue, but I hoped he'd go on talking. I loved that soft look in his eyes when he looked at me.

"Are you okay now?" he asked.

"A little sore but fine. What's the news this morning from the station?"

"The three of them are still locked up. I don't think they'll be making bond. We'll probably hold them all until their trials."

"That's a relief," I said.

As I was looking into his eyes, I saw a shadow moving behind his shoulder. I looked closer. It was too short and pointy eared to be a person, too bushy tailed to be a cat. Alex turned around to see what had made me gasp.

Lou sauntered about the parking lot as if a panda hanging at a diner was a normal kind of thing.

Alex stared, amazed. "Hey, look. It's your little friend." He began to laugh. "Look who decided to show up for your victory breakfast."

Ha ha. Very funny.

I had to act, but how? I had to catch that panda. He kept showing up everywhere I went, that should have made it easy. And I blew it every time. I needed to pull the kind of fast trick that Marge or Celeste might try. I needed my own ninja move.

But instead of the ninja move, there was only blabber that came out. "He runs off every time. Because of the fart. The fart! How can anyone stand that fart? Then every time we look up he's just gone. And we even tried to trick him with a bowl of pickles, which I thought was really smart. Because the panda loves pickles. And one time I got my brother to chase him in the yard..."

Alex held up a hand and laughed. "Slow down! What? That sounds like one strange panda. Pickles? Really? Pickles?"

"And I know that it's a lame case and that you probably think is funny. But I still need to solve it. Because I need a check. And because the kids, they get so sad when the panda's not at the zoo. The kids were all so sad that day the monkey jumped up on my head."

He stared. "The monkey? On your head?"

I suddenly felt tired. "I've been tied up and gagged and almost blown up too, and it's just no fair

284

if I get farted on today. I just want to go inside and order Jacks Egg Special Number Two."

Alex laughed again. The nerve. Couldn't he see this was important? That we absolutely had to grab our town's most important panda?

He just looked at me and shook his head. "That's a lot of words." He took his cell out of his pocket and punched something in. He handed me the phone with a number on the screen. "Just hit send and you'll be speaking to Animal Control. Tell them to get here stat."

Well. I guessed that did make sense. As badly as I wanted to be the hero who had nabbed not only three elusive criminals, but a celebrity panda to boot, this might be the best that I could do. Lou would be home safe. That's what was important. As long as he didn't get away before the experts could arrive.

The panda darted toward the diner door, then ran a little to the left, looking around with curiosity and sniffing the pavement. Was he looking for something to eat? I had to keep my eye on him. I couldn't let that feisty thing get too far from my sight. I pushed up my glasses, which had slipped down on my nose during the excitement. I willed my heartbeat to slow down. I'd had enough drama for one week. I just wanted my plate of scrambled eggs with bacon and mini flapjacks, maple syrup on the side.

Alex, to my amazement, took his sandwich from the bag and began to unwrap the paper. The most wanted panda in all of Massachusetts might escape anytime. And what exactly does he do, this guy, this officer of the law? He unwraps a sandwich.

I glared, but he just winked. Then he removed two pickles from the sandwich and slowly approached our furry fugitive, laying the pickles on the ground. As the panda began to eat, Alex did the most amazing thing. He very gently stroked the panda's back.

And, surprisingly, Lou let him. No running off. No farting.

Alex made it look so easy. I guessed he didn't have that desperate, got-to-catch-you vibe. He just fed him pickles. Like they were just two guys hanging out in the parking lot on a lazy afternoon.

I took in the way that Alex brushed his soft hair from his eyes and the way the top button of his shirt strained against the muscles of his chest. Then I glanced at the diner window, where I knew my friends were surely taking in the show. They stared at me, wide-eyed.

After Lou had quickly gobbled up the pickles, Alex picked him up like a baby and walked over to stand by me.

I moved a couple of steps away, and then I braced myself. I was on high alert. A fart bomb would be erupting any second now. I waited a few seconds before breathing. Hmm. Guess this is my lucky day. Lou seemed to be digesting his snack with no smelly tummy issues.

And so I wasn't (that) worried when Alex put him in my arms. Lou snuggled up against my chest and promptly fell asleep. I hugged him to me and gently rubbed the soft fur behind his ear. When he wasn't farting in my face or hightailing it away from me, the little guy was kind of cute.

Soon, the Animal Control van flew into the lot, jolting Lou awake. Two uniformed guys got out and were quickly at our side. The tallest one reached out to take the panda from me and secured him in a cage in the back of the van. I couldn't even look. The back of a van would probably always bring up bad thoughts. Now I knew Lou would be fine. I was sure he missed his twin.

"Whew." The shorter man shook his head. "Someone did good work. We've had training in this kind of thing, but that's one hard panda to catch." He scrunched up his nose. "I know the kids all love him, but I've never seen a panda pass wind like this one does."

The other guy came up beside him. "I almost resigned. I couldn't take the smell. We're not trained to deal with that stuff. Highly unusual. This little furry guy kept giving us the slip. One of you must be a genius."

Alex glanced at me and smiled. "And she's a pretty genius too."

I felt my cheeks getting hot.

I knew he should get the credit. I gave him a smile. I guessed Marge and Celeste weren't the only ones capable of surprises.

"Thank you," I said when the van was gone. "I don't know what to say."

He winked. "Congratulations, Cooper. You wrapped up your first case. I'll tell the boss the news when I get back to the office." He looked down at his sandwich. "I never was a fan of pickles anyway. Just as long as I have lots of mustard."

"Stay away from pickles." I grinned. "They're bad for your digestion."

"Take care, Charlie. I'll see you around. Most likely you'll be in trouble, and I'll show up just in time. Isn't that our pattern?"

I lightly touched his arms. "You can be a nice guy, Alex. Who would have ever thought?"

"Well, if you really want to thank me, you can buy me dinner." Was that a flirty smile, or was that just me hoping? I had never been any good at understanding guys.

"Sure," I said. "Dinner. Absolutely. Uh...just tell me when and where."

He was looking at me in a way that made me blush some more.

"It's only fair, you know," he said. "You already stroked my face and told me the kinds of things you really shouldn't say until at least date number three. Any self-respecting guy would at least want dinner first."

I was mortified. If there ever was a good time for the earth to form a giant hole that could suck me in, then this was it. He'd heard what I said to him after the explosion after all. I so wished there was a way to melt into the pavement.

He winked and reached out to straighten my glasses and smooth down my hair. "See you around, Charlie Cooper. Make sure you get some rest."

At last, I made my way into the diner and took my seat. A plate of food was waiting for me; my friends knew my favorite order.

Marge and Celeste just watched me eat, glancing at each other and giggling to themselves. Celeste was not the giggly type. Today, she looked like her old self with her hair as big and red as ever.

I looked up from my eggs. "Just come right out and say it. Let the teasing start." Was it about the panda? Or Alex? Most likely, it was both. I'd get a double whammy.

"Oh, hon, I just knew it." Marge grabbed some bacon from my plate. "Alex has a thing for you. And he has it bad."

Celeste took a sip of coffee. "Congratulations. Your man is super hot."

"He's not my man," I said. But I, Charlotte Cooper, of Springston, Massachusetts, had a real-life date. That didn't happen often.

"Well, girls," I continued. "I guess we can turn this breakfast into a double celebration. I'm sure you noticed out the window that I just wrapped up our first case. With a little help from Alex."

Celeste held up her mug. "Cheers!"

I touched my orange juice glass to their coffee mugs.

"I'm so glad that Lou is safe," Marge cooed. "Fuzzy wuzzy, cutie wootie, panda wanda."

"Marge. Please," Celeste said. "I'm getting a headache when you talk like that."

"How are you girls feeling?" I asked, changing the subject before Marge could think of even one more rhyme.

"My back is killing me," Marge said. "Boy, that floor was hard. But that was an amazing night. We should call some TV people. Wouldn't it make a great plot? With the fake bags and guns and all?" She thought about it a little more. "Which star would play me? Would she come here to meet me first?"

"You did great work, Charlie." Celeste took another sip of coffee. "We all were on our game. I can't believe you kept that guy talking like he did. He didn't glance over even once to see what I was doing. Because he'd rather talk about himself."

"We best rest up," Marge said. "I'll bet business will come rolling in. Now that they know what we can do."

Celeste nodded. "The chief and I are going to have a long talk tomorrow."

Oh, boy. I bet he was dreading that.

"Now we just need that stupid sign," Celeste said. "How hard can it really be to put up a stupid sign?"

My mind wandered back to Alex. I just had to share my news. "I have a dinner date with Alex." I poured syrup on my flapjacks.

Marge's squeal caused heads to turn. "Oh, this is so much fun! When, when?"

I thought about that. "Actually, I have no idea. He suggested I buy him dinner. But he left before we could make something out."

"Hmm," Celeste said. "You better stay on your game, girl."

"I have no idea how, but I'll try," I said.

"Don't worry. We'll help you," Marge giggled.

"What about you?" I asked. "When's your first date with the fry cook?"

"Saturday night," she said with a proud smile on her face. "I went up and asked him out while you were busy outside, scoring a date with Alex and rescuing our panda."

"Wow." I said. "So, you just asked him out?"

She shrugged. "You should go for what you want. And what I wanted was a fry cook with a cute behind." She pointed her spoon at me. "Remember that next time, Charlie. If you want something bad enough, just go out and get it."

Hmm. It sounded simple. I wished I was that brave. At least the woozy, injured Charlie had a kind of bravery. She'd reached out to touch a guy's face in a suggestive way and declared she loved him right there at a crime scene. But the real Charlie? She was a wuss.

"Good for you," I said to Marge.

"Charlie!" My dad hurried to the table and caught me in a hug.

I winced, unable to tell him I was sore from being kidnapped and tied up.

"How's your new place?" he asked.

"It needs decorating. And I could do without the archers right outside the window. But I think I'll like it there."

"Well, we all miss you at the house." He looked around the table. "And it's good to see my favorite waitresses. Once you work at Jack's, you know you're always family."

"This is our favorite place," Marge said. "Best pie in all the world."

"How are Mom and Brad? "I asked. "Did Brad ever find out if he won? You know, the Employee of the Month?"

My dad slid into the booth beside me. "Well, it's a funny thing. One of his colleagues wanted to win the thing about as much as Brad. They're both big Celtics fans. Brad thought he was about to lose. And your brother wasn't happy. They've both been pulling double shifts. But right before the grand finale, your brother pulled ahead."

"He won? That's great," Marge said.

"Yeah. The colleague came in as usual, drank his coffee like he always did, and promptly got..." My father looked around the diner, then he whispered the last word of the sentence. "He got diarrhea. And I guess we've all been so unfortunate as to know what that is like. The guy couldn't do his last shift. Too many interruptions."

"That's just so sad," Marge said.

And also, quite suspicious. I wondered if Brad had anything to do with it. He could be sneaky, when he wanted something bad.

"How's the job?" my father asked. "I have to thank you ladies for bringing my girl back home to Springston."

"It's exhausting," Marge said. "But we're doing very well. Yesterday was brutal." She touched her arm. "I don't think I've ever been so sore."

"Yeah. We sure got knocked around." I said.

Celeste kicked us both beneath the table.

My father looked confused. "Huh. Technological consulting must be a lot more physical than I ever thought. But what does this old man know? I can turn my computer on and off. And everything else confuses me almost every single time." He smiled. "But it sounds like you three girls do a real fine job."

Celeste smiled at me across the table. "I think we're the best in town."

***

Thank you so much for reading the second book in the Charlie Cooper Mysteries series.

TAKE A SNEAK PEAK of *Diced* (A Charlie Cooper Mystery, Volume 3) by Deany Ray:

Chapter One

"THIS IS THE LAST BOX." Celeste set it on the twin bed. "I think you're all moved in."

Marge studied a poster on the wall of the bedroom where I'd grown up and which I thought I'd left for good. "New Kids on the Block!" she cried. "I never could decide which one was the hottest."

"I wouldn't mind spending time with that one in the middle." Celeste walked over to take a look. "How did that song go?" She sang a few bars of one of the old tunes I used to play nonstop. Then she bumped hips with Marge as they danced across the room.

"But New Kids on the Block?" Celeste looked at me with curiosity. "Aren't you a little old? "

Marge sank down on the bed. "And just think. They're old like we are now. Isn't that the weirdest thing?"

I folded some t-shirts into a drawer. "Well, it's not like I exactly put the poster up last week. This hasn't been my room since I was in high school."

Celeste gave me a look. I saw that look a lot – whenever I tried to dance around an inconvenient truth.

I grabbed some hangers and some jeans. "Okay. Okay, you're right. We all know I moved back once not that long ago. But this time is the last time. And I won't be back for long. I see money in our future." I pushed my glasses further up my nose.

"You got that one right." Celeste took some books out of a box and headed toward a shelf.

I was humiliated to be moving back in with my parents at the age of twenty-nine. But it was all part of the plan for starting my dream business with my two best friends. I was no longer a secretary for the police in Boston. Marge, Celeste and I were undercover spies for hire. And we were pretty kick ass, if I do say so myself.

One reason that it worked was that we really looked the part. Nobody would suspect that we were working for the cops. Marge, with her softly rounded figure and constant wide-eyed smile, looked like she'd be more adept at making flowered wreaths or clipping coupons from the paper than pulling out her trusty gun just at the perfect moment.

Celeste looked like anybody's neighbor once she covered up her bright red hair, which she wore in an elaborate updo when she was Celeste Ortiz, and not the worst nightmare of any bad guy who dared to disturb the peace in Springston, Massachusetts.

And as for me, I'd always been plain, easy to forget. Who knew that could be a talent? But now I guess it was.

The only trouble was that I was pretty broke while I was waiting for my bank account to move from almost empty to borderline dirt poor. And here in affluent Springston, being poor won't buy you much in the way of housing. Apartments in my budget were...well, to say that they were dismal would be a compliment. So, I'd moved in with my parents a couple of months ago, when I'd come back from Boston to start up the new business. Then I'd decided to move out and into my own place. Because I was twenty-nine. And living with my parents. But the apartment was so bad, I was only there for three weeks.

Celeste frowned as she looked down at the stack of books she was arranging on a shelf. "Charlie, why did you buy this? *Stop Being Such a Loser, a Guide to Love and Life.*"

It would have been better, I supposed, to have unpacked my things myself.

Marge frowned. "Why buy a book that sounds so mean? You get enough of that from people."

"It was on sale?" I tried. "They had it for half price."

"Well, I guess they would," Marge said thoughtfully. "Winners wouldn't buy it, and losers have no money." Then she linked her arm through mine. "You are not a loser, hon! Do you know how smart you are? And sometimes, of the three of us, I think you are the bravest. And we have seen some bad stuff since we went undercover."

Embarrassed, I tried to change the subject. "Hey, are you guys hungry?"

Celeste looked down at another title. "*How to Find Your Va Va Voom and Make the Men Come Running.* Now, that's a book I'd like to read. I bet that one's from your mother."

I sat down on the bed. "Can you believe she gave me that? Now do you understand why I have to get my own place as soon as possible? Can we please make some money soon?"

Celeste frowned. "Well, Bert's been kind of vague about what kind of case he'll send us next."

Bert was her ex-husband – who apparently had a secret he hoped she would never tell. Conveniently for us, he was now chief of police. He sent cases to us so Celeste would keep her mouth shut about...well, I had no idea what the secret was. Marge and I had begged, of course, to get the information, but Celeste would never tell. I loved her sense of loyalty to a man she kind of loathed – but I wished she'd bend it just a little.

"I think your mom is fun. But if she drives you crazy, you can always live with me," Marge said. She brushed at the colorful top that covered her oversized figure.

"And I have lots of room." Celeste finished with the books.

She did have quite the big house. And a swimming pool! And a charming porch that wrapped all the way around the house and overlooked a stream. An overly generous settlement from her divorce from Bert? Celeste was very private. No one really knew.

"You know I love you both," I said. "But you see enough of me already."

Before I met the girls a couple of months ago, it had been a long time since I'd had close friends. And I wasn't anxious to ruin the friendship with too much time together – even more important when you go into business with your besties. That meant there was no other choice. For now, this was my home.

Distressing situations always made me think of cookies. So I had a thought – a thought covered in white chocolate with just the right amount of crunch and drizzled in white icing.

"Let's eat," I told the girls. "Anybody up for Jack's? I might just order my dessert before I order lunch."

"Oh, Jack's. Absolutely!" Marge squeaked. "I think there's a meatloaf sandwich calling out my name."

"Today is Tuesday. Pork chops," I said. "Monday's the meatloaf special." I should know. I am, after all, the only daughter of the one and only Jack. My father's diner has held for decades an honored spot among Springston's favorite places.

Marge put on her sweater. "Oh, they don't put it on the menu. But if you ask real nicely, they'll fix you up a sandwich if they have any meatloaf left. It tastes better on a Tuesday when the flavors all had time to meld." Marge and Celeste had both spent time as waitresses at Jack's.

"Oh, shoot," I said. I'd remembered something. "We unpacked everything from Marge's car, but we forgot about the TV in my backseat. Maybe Brad can help."

Most likely, that meant we'd have to talk my brother into getting off the couch, which meant he'd give me grief. How dare I interrupt a good nap or a computer game?

"Brad is here? What happened to his job?" Celeste asked, surprised.

I sighed. "It lasted just about as long as any of his others."

Brad's last attempt at working was a job sorting mail at the post office here in town. At first, things had gone well. But his spurt of productivity came to a crashing halt as soon as he was named employee of the month. Without an incentive (tickets to the Celtics! And a two-hundred-dollar bonus), there really was no point, according to my brother, who soon got fired for laziness. The story of his life.

As we made our way downstairs, none of the usual sounds were coming from the couch. No soft rumble of a snore building into a crescendo. No fake-sounding gun shots as he took aim at some bad guy on his gaming system.

Hmm. I checked in the kitchen. Perhaps Brad was hungry too. Bingo. There, indeed, was Brad – or the back of him anyway – grabbing an armload from the fridge. Massive sandwich coming up.

I glanced over at the counter to see if my mom had made some cookies. There are some advantages to living back at home. My mother loves to bake. But I saw something else instead: there was booze everywhere. Rum and gin and whiskey, along with other bottles that I didn't recognize.

"Party!" Marge said. "Can I come to the party?"

"What is up with this?" I turned to my brother. My parents liked to entertain, but usually just in small groups. This seemed extreme.

He turned and grunted in acknowledgement when he saw Celeste and Marge. "Mom's taking some kind of class," he said, "to learn to mix fancy drinks. Or some crazy thing like that."

"What?" I asked. "But why?"

He shrugged. "Since when does she need a reason to do the stuff she does?"

True enough, I thought. Why did my mother teach fitness to elderly students who looked too frail to stand up, let alone twist themselves into yoga poses I wouldn't want to try myself? Why did my mother respond to any piece of bad news by spraying herbs into the air to perform some kind of cleanse? I should know by now never to ask why.

I gazed at the supplies which would make a lot of drinks. Who was supposed to drink them all? The exercisers who were often in the backyard doing awkward-looking dance moves? My mom and dad and Brad? Even when they were sober, I had a crazy family. Please, I thought. Don't let them all turn into drunks.

"Where's Mom? Is she here?" I asked.

"She's gone to see a student who wasn't feeling well. She left you cookies. Oatmeal."

Score. I grabbed a handful for myself, then passed them to my friends.

Brad agreed to help with my TV, sighing as if I'd asked him to carry eight TVs up ten flights of steps, and to do it with one hand. All I knew is, I needed to somehow get my TV up the stairs. I needed to be able to hole up in my room all by myself and watch my favorite shows.

"You're lucky I was here," he said.

"When are you not?" I mumbled.

***

Marge got her meatloaf sandwich, and I tried one as well. Celeste had her favorite omelet with sun-dried tomatoes, cheese and spinach.

"Thanks for the help today," I said. "At least I didn't have much stuff."

Marge took a bite of her sandwich. "Too bad it didn't work out. Your place was really cute. I was working on a welcome gift." She smiled. "A paint by number! You should try it, Charlie. It's so much fun." Sometimes Marge seemed twelve years old. Unless you were a bad guy at the wrong end of her gun.

"Yep," I said. "The new place was a bust."

At first I'd been excited. It had all the trappings of the kind of upscale housing I never could afford: exposed brick in the living room, a well-manicured front lawn, a spacious bedroom with a high ceiling and lots of closet space. Too bad that right below my window was a great big field set aside for the sport of archery. Who knew that shooting arrows from a bow was a thing?

That shouldn't be a problem, I thought. I'll just keep the windows shut. But a couple of times the arrows had hit hard enough to pierce right through the glass.

One late afternoon I'd opened a window briefly to get some fresh air and sunlight. The apartment felt so stuffy, and all seemed quiet down below. Apparently, the arrow throwers must all have other plans. Then, stupidly, I forgot to close the window before I went about my day, surfing the internet for an hour, then taking a long, hot shower.

Then, as I stepped into my room to get my clothes, an arrow came hurtling through the living room and straight onto my bed. It missed my head by half a foot. What an embarrassing way to go that would be. They would have found me naked with an arrow stuck into my head, in the stupidest place on earth to have chosen an apartment.

My line of work can be really brutal. But perhaps the most dangerous thing that I have ever done was to live at Chrysanthemum Garden Manors. Without a helmet. The apartment manager said that I'd lasted longer than other tenants that faced out toward the field. She said the apartment owners were thinking about a suit against the owners of the field. They were losing money fast, and I could tell they'd invested lots of cash into making the units attractive, high-end living spaces.

So, that was a nightmare. But things were looking up for me. I loved the challenge of my new job. I was part of a good team. When a set of clues would seemingly lead nowhere, I would see a certain look come over Marge's face. Or Celeste would suddenly grow quiet. And I'd know a great idea was brewing; we soon would have a plan.

I took a sip of coffee. "I'm sure it won't be long before I can afford a decent place. Because I have faith in us to make this business work. It's really so much fun to watch the two of you in action."

Celeste took a sip of tea. "But Bert's gonna try to mess with us. He'll send us oddball cases, and he'll do it just to spite me."

I knew she was right. Most likely, he'd keep sending business in the future to buy his ex-wife's silence, but he would not be glad to do it. He would not be glad at all.

Celeste stuck her fork into the small bowl of fruit that had come with her order. "But no matter what he throws at us, just keep one thing in mind: there's a way to make it work and get to the bottom of each case. There always is a way."

"We just have to think of it in time," Marge squeaked.

Just a few weeks ago, we'd been chasing a missing panda who had slipped off from the zoo. Talk about a cross between an assignment and an insult! But we not only found our furry subject, but in the process found a clue to a much bigger case. We solved a counterfeiting case before Bert and his officers could catch the crooks themselves. That was really fun. Except for the explosion that sent us to the hospital and the bad guys kidnapping us.

"Has Bert paid us the bonus yet?" Marge asked. "For helping with the other case?"

"He paid us for both matters." Celeste gently wiped her mouth. "So that's enough for next month's rent. We just need to get more cases."

In addition to hitting up Bert for work, we'd taken flyers to other law enforcement agencies in towns that were nearby. So far, we'd had no takers. But with a huge victory on our resume, Bert could vouch for us. And I had no doubt Celeste would make sure that he did.

"The bad news," Celeste said, "is that Bert didn't bother to return my calls and now he's out of town. Of course, I have his cell just for emergencies. I have a good mind to call him anyway, disturb his nice vacation." She cut a bite of omelet.

Marge shot me a grin.

"Alex might help us this time," she said in a singsong voice. "He'd do it for Charlie."

Hmm. I doubted that was true. Alex Spencer was a (gorgeous!) lead detective that we crossed paths with quite a bit. And he never seemed exactly happy for the help. More like annoyed that we interfered with his investigation. Which (Guess what?) we did.

But something seemed to change as we closed up the investigations, delivering the crooks to jail and the panda to the zoo. When I looked into his eyes (Those blue eyes! They were so very blue!), I no longer saw exasperation and an ego that was bigger than a house; I saw something else instead. A genuine concern about my safety? That made sense in a way. I was prone to land right in the middle of the most unsafe situations. And it didn't help that I was clumsy.

Marge had other thoughts about what Alex had in mind. Now she folded her napkin in her lap. "I've been watching that boy a long time. He's got it bad for you."

I wished. I loved the way his soft brown hair was always falling in his eyes. I loved the ways he sometimes broke into a grin like the world was just so funny. And I loved it when he wore his white shirt that stretched tight across his muscles. Alex was not the kind of guy who went for Charlie Cooper.

309

Although he was fun to think about. And sometimes it almost seemed that he looked at me as if...No! That was wishful thinking.

"What happened to that date that you two were gonna have?" Celeste broke into my daydream.

I stared down at my mashed potatoes. "It wasn't supposed to be a date. I think. And who knows if he really meant it."

Alex first brought up the not-date in the parking lot of this very diner not too long ago. He had just helped me distract the panda till Animal Control could make its way to where the little guy was scarfing down some pickles – from a sandwich that was meant to be the hot detective's lunch. It was a funny thing: the panda had a thing for pickles. Alex said that I could thank him by taking him to dinner some evening in the future.

"Okay," I have said nonchalantly while my mind was screaming *Yes, please! Can we do it soon? I'm available all week.*

"It was probably just a joke," I said to Celeste. "Because it was just this crazy day. With the panda. And the pickles."

But was it? Was it just a joke? It was true that Alex liked to flirt. And wasn't that sometimes just the start of something much, much more?

Marge looked at me with determination. "It's time you take some action. You can't let that one get away. I can tell you really like him. Sometimes guys are just so slow. A girl has to make a move."

No way could I do that.

"Well, Marge, I don't know."

"Oh, I have an idea!" she squeaked. Her voice rose to such a high pitch that people turned to stare. "Have you read that book your mother gave you? About your va va voom?"

I wondered if my face was red.

Celeste gave Marge a gentle nudge. "Can't you see that she's embarrassed? She doesn't want to read about a book about her...about her...well, you know, whatever."

"I'm just saying." Marge shrugged. She did a little shoulder dance. "Charlie needs to learn to work it."

Good grief. I was always disappointing someone – either my mother or my friends – with my inability to ever get a date.

After lunch, we stopped in at the office. We had some calls to make to sheriffs and police chiefs in surrounding towns. We had some bragging rights now that we'd bagged some big-time bad guys that the police here couldn't catch. Oh, the police had had their eyes on them all right. But we were the only ones who could deliver on the evidence they had to have for a conviction.

As we pulled onto the street, I was glad to see our new sign that was finally in place. CMC Services. The police had taken their time in getting it put up. To the outside world, we were technology consultants. Whatever that means. Guess it's a fancy word for computer repair. We'd even borrowed old broken laptops to scatter around the place so we'd look legit if anyone stopped in. What if my mother came with cookies? (I hoped!) What if one of Marge's friends spied her through the window? Marge seemed to make a new best friend anywhere she went – standing in line for coffee, filling up her car with gas.

Celeste had called a friend in the industry who'd lent us some equipment that seemed to have something to do with our chosen field. No matter what the question, Celeste always knew a guy. Some of them, I have to say, seemed quite shady. How did she know these people? I didn't have a clue. It was all a part of the mystery of Celeste.

As I sat down to make my first call, the door suddenly flew open and a man walked in. We all stopped and stared. That had never happened.

Shoot. He was carrying a laptop. Could it be a customer? Not for the actual business we were desperate to grow, but for some computer problem. Sorry. No can do! When it came to that kind of stuff, we were lost. I could barely work my phone.

Of course, we'd known that this might happen, despite our very unobtrusive sign and the fact that our "repair shop" was never advertised. And so we had a plan – to be so very, very busy that any customers who showed would surely take their business to another shop. Because people need their laptops and they need them now. Computers hold your whole life. So it wouldn't be a problem. At least, we didn't think it would.

The man looked upset. "I don't know what's wrong with this thing. The keyboard stopped responding. And it kept making this loud notice. Now the thing won't turn on. What do you think that means?"

We all exchanged glances.

Finally, Marge picked up the laptop and pretended to give it a good look. She had been practicing her lines for this very kind of moment. "It could be the hard drive going bad. Or you might have a virus." She opened up the case, pounded on some keys and frowned. "I really hate to say this, but it could be your motherboard. You just never know."

He let out a breath. "But why would that have happened? It's really fairly new."

"Happens all the time," Marge said. "Could be the software or the hardware, or it could be the malware. The AC adapter even. Or perhaps the AC/DC."

Good grief. She'd been sounding really good. But AC/DC was a band. Hopefully this computer dude was not into rock and roll.

"Can you fix it?" he asked desperately. "It's got my novel in there. Eighty thousand words. And all my contact information. And, well, just everything."

Wow. That was terrifying, to have something that important trapped inside a small machine that just decides one day that it's not gonna turn back on.

"Well," Celeste chimed in, just like we rehearsed. "We're super busy right now. We're on quite a wait."

"Oh, no worries," the man said. "I leave tomorrow on a big hike in Myles Standish Forest. And then we'll do some camping. So I won't be around to use this baby anyway."

Shoot. What do we do now?

Celeste shot me a panicked look.

The man ran his finger sadly across the laptop. "If this thing's gonna flake out, I guess now's the perfect time," he said.

Yes. Absolutely perfect.

Celeste glanced down at her cellphone. "Oh! I just got a text. The parts have come in early for...that big new system they've just put in at...Springston Best Electric?" She glanced over at the man. "And I'm just so sorry. But I told them we'd get on the job as quickly as we could. Who knows when we'll be finished?"

He shrugged. "It's cool. Like I said, I'll be off the grid. How much will it cost?"

It seems we couldn't get out of that one. The girls and I exchanged looks one more time.

"Seventy an hour," I said. We'd researched prices too.

"And this could take lots and lot of hours," Marge said in her best cautionary voice.

"Well, I'll spend what I have to spend. I've spent years on that novel that's in there. This is a valuable machine."

Great.

He touched the laptop with a kind of reverence. "You ladies have to promise me you'll take good care of this."

Marge studied it again. "Sir, you might consider a firm that specializes in…" She stared down at the name on the computer label. "In this model that you have here. And in motherboard stuff and keyboard things and…A-B-C-D issues."

The man waved away her suggestions. "It's all good."

No sir! It is not. It's all, really bad.

Celeste tried to look official. "But you know that there are firms that specialize in…the type of repairs that…cause a laptop to stop responding."

"But I don't know the people at those firms. And I trust you girls," he said.

"Well…thanks," I finally managed. But why in the world would he trust us?

"My girlfriend said to come here." He smiled. "Said she's known one of you for some time. From the karaoke girls' nights out. At Ted's in the square."

"That's me!" Marge squeaked.

Oh, this is getting better and better.

"My girlfriend says your songs are always…entertaining."

Marge blushed. "Oh. Well, I'm very flattered. What is your girlfriend's name? And does she hike as well?"

316

My heart began to race. Did it really matter if his girlfriend liked to hike? We were absolutely screwed.

"She's not one for the outdoors," he said. "And her name's Katrina. She works sometimes at the music store down the street. She says she's seen you through the window with a lot of laptops all around. She thought you must do repair work. And that's why I'm here."

"Oh," Marge squeaked. "Katrina is the best. I hope she likes the little dances I add in with my songs. I do that because..."

Celeste put a hand on Marge's shoulder. "Why don't we take this nice man's contact information, and then we have to get to work. We need to go and get those parts for the electric company."

"Oh, yes," Marge said then wrote down his name and phone number and sent best wishes to Katrina.

"See you in a week!" he said cheerfully as he headed out the door.

"Sheesh," Celeste said when he was gone. "What do we do now?"

No one said a word.

"We'll have to fix it somehow." I finally broke the silence. "We have to fix that man's computer."

"Well, I really don't know all that much about that kind of thing," Marge said. "Except how to turn one on. And how to play that fun game with all the little candies. And I'm thinking that won't help."

"And it's not something you can Google and learn everything there is to know in a how-to video." Celeste sat down to think. "Why weren't we hairdressers? Or bakers. Anything but this."

"Since we don't have a clue," I said, "we should find someone who does." The only problem was, who could we ask? We were supposed to be the experts, not the ones who asked for help.

The door swung open a second time and an angry-looking woman strode into the door. What was up today? Was her laptop broken too? If only our real business would draw in the customers like our fake computer shop did.

This woman had a hard look, as if any minute a string of expletives would come flying from her mouth. She marched up to me and frowned. "I hear you girls are good detectives."

I couldn't speak for half a minute. Business! This was great. But so much for staying undercover. How had she even found us? When I finally caught my breath, I began to speak. "Well…"

But she didn't let me finish. "I need you to

snoop around for me. I need to know the truth. The truth about my husband."

Chapter Two

"THE TRUTH ABOUT...?" I stammered.

Marge stared at the stranger, wide-eyed. "But first, how did you know..."

"That we were detectives?" Celeste finished Marge's question.

The woman nodded her head toward Marge. "I heard this one talking. This one likes to talk."

Celeste and I turned to face our friend, who looked back sheepishly – like a kid caught with all the candy.

"So sorry, so sorry," she squeaked.

The woman continued to explain. "She was telling the hairdresser all about it, how the three of you took down some tough jokers. Like James Bond, but in cute shoes. I think that's what she said. Sounded like a bunch of nonsense. But then she said you wrapped up two big cases all at once. That's when my ears perked up."

Marge gazed down at the floor as Celeste fixed her with a hard look.

"Not that I'm one to eavesdrop." The stranger held up a hand as if to wave away the very thought. Other's people's troubles aren't that interesting to me. I've got problems of my own; I don't need their drama. But when a woman aims two fingers at the shampoo girl? And makes this kind of weird sound like she's firing off three rounds? Well, you put your magazine down so you can hear what's going on."

Celeste stared at Marge, appalled.

"Well." Marge spoke in the teeniest, tiniest voice that I had ever heard. "She asked me how my week had gone. And I got excited. And I just...forgot."

"We would gladly hear your story," I said to the woman. "Would you like to take a seat?" I rolled my desk chair over. I wondered then if we should think about guest seating. We weren't expecting guests. I'd thought that being undercover would cut back on the walk-ins. But then again...maybe not.

Marge pulled up her chair and I perched on top of her desk.

Celeste leaned against the wall. "Before you tell us about your husband, let's make some introductions." Having had a chance to catch her breath, she morphed into a professional, hoping to seal the deal with a prospective client. "My name is Celeste, and this is my partner Charlie." She nodded toward me and smiled. Then she turned her gaze to Marge. "I believe you've met Annie Oakley here. She also goes by Marge."

"Deborah Bickford," the woman said in a raspy voice. "And my problem's name is Stanley. The sorriest excuse for a husband that ever walked the earth. I hope that you can help me." She gave me a pleading look, and I got the feeling that her tears had long been all cried out. She just had that look: of holding lots of sorrows in the deep furrows of her brow. "I was stupid, stupid, stupid to ever say *I do* to a clown like that. But I was only nineteen. And by the time I realized that the guy was just a pompous jerk, he had knocked me up."

Celeste grabbed her hand. "The only thing worse than a bad man is a bad man that you're stuck with, a bad man that shares your name. Sometimes, a woman has to just take out the trash. If you get my drift."

Deborah looked her in the eye. "Isn't that the truth? I've been thinking the same thing. Our daughter's grown and gone now. She's off in California. And we were never really happy, can't agree on anything." She sighed. "He wants to buy a boat. A boat! How can we buy a boat? We don't have the money for that kind of stuff." She ran a hand nervously through her short dark hair. "And he complains about my flowerbeds. Now, can I just ask you this? Who in their right mind argues against flowers? Did a flower ever do a single thing to make his life any harder?"

"No!" Now, Marge was angry too. "It most certainly did not!"

Deborah leaned in toward her. "And now, I have my suspicions that he's seeing someone else. Can you believe that?" Her eyes took on a steely look. "Isn't that just crazy? Because the joke's on her! This man is not a prize."

He did sound like a dud. But then again, this Deborah was not exactly the most pleasant person on earth. Was she like that before she met him? Or did Stanley turn her into a cold and angry woman? It was hard to say. All I knew was that this wasn't the kind of case I had in mind when I quit my job and moved to Springston. I wanted to rid the town of danger, not to chase down every cheating spouse sneaking out to misbehave.

Celeste cleared her throat. "So, how exactly can we help you?"

"Well, if he's really cheating, I'll divorce him just as quick as he can holler at me when I set down his dinner plate. *Is this all the measly supper that you're gonna feed me? Who taught you how to cook?* The man is never satisfied. And when the courts divide the assets, I want to make good and sure they have all the information about…his activities. I deserve whatever they will give me, after all the utter nonsense the man has put me through."

"But…" I was confused. "It doesn't sound like there's much money for you two to fight about."

"There's a little bit of savings. In case of emergencies – and to retire one day. Not much of a nest egg, but we've managed to throw a little bit into savings now and then." She sighed. "You see, here's the thing. He's been taking chunks of money out. He doesn't think I know. He thinks I'm clueless about finances. But I look at the statements. Because it's my money too."

"Absolutely," Marge squeaked.

"And he goes somewhere in the evenings. Claims he's off on errands. Or to watch a game with friends."

"Does he have a lot of friends?" I asked.

She paused to think about it. "To be honest, I'm not sure. We don't talk much anymore. No more than we need to. But I feel sure he's lying. I can always tell because he sweats so much when he's hiding something from me. It's been that way since high school – when I should have said *no way* when he asked me to the prom. But I had to have that new black dress with the silver sequins that my mom said she would buy me if I went to the dance."

Marge leaned forward in her chair. "Did it have spaghetti straps? What shoes did you wear?"

"It had off-the-shoulder puffy sleeves. I had nice shoulders way back then. I liked to show them off. And I wore some real nice silver heels." Deborah's look turned angry. "What kind of questions are these? Who cares about the stupid shoes? It was my date who was the biggest heel. I just didn't know it yet." She paused and took a deep breath. "So. Will you take my case?"

"Well, it's not the usual thing we do," Celeste said. "But we have some free time at the moment."

"I've saved some money of my own. I have my own account. My mother always said that's a good thing for a woman. In case of emergency. Or in case of assholes." She stopped to clear her throat. "All of that to say I can pay you for your trouble."

"Well, we need some info first," Celeste said. "Marge, can you grab your pad?"

Marge rifled through her flowered purse, finally pulling out a notebook and a small silver pen. "Okay," she squeaked. "All set. Tell us more about your husband. Where does Stanley work?"

"He used to own a store in town, King's Electronics at the mall. But that went bust last year, which made things worse at home. The man was super stressed. That's when I went to work – at the uniform factory. I'm sure you know the one? Down past the new hospital, over that little hill. And with overtime and all, I don't have time to chase him down to see what the man is up to. Plus, I don't want him to catch me watching. I'm no good at undercover."

Neither were we, apparently. But I guessed she'd forgotten that.

"Where does Stanley work now?" I asked her.

"At the convenience store on Holberton. You probably know it as the place with the guy dressed like a hot dog standing out in front. I don't understand their thinking. Like someone in their right mind might drive by and say, *Hey, I'm gonna pull in here and stop – because a man dressed like a giant hot dog is waving like a fool.*" She frowned. "That would make me speed right up."

Sometimes I thought my job was bad. I'd been farted on by a panda that I was trying to rescue. And there'd been more than one occasion when I thought someone might kill me. But at least I'd never had to dress up like somebody's dinner.

"Is Stanley…" I began.

"Oh, no. He's never worn the costume. Although that would serve him right. Then there'd be no way the fool could find another woman. I'm sure it kills the romance once you've seen a man dressed up like a hot dog that's on special for a dollar. But, no. Stanley's just a clerk."

Celeste pulled up her office chair and took a seat. "What hours does he work?"

"He works till seven most nights. He's the one that closes up. And then on Fridays and on Saturdays, they're open until nine. And he stays until they close. Somehow I just know that man is up to something." She fixed each of us with a hard look.

Hey lady, don't glare at me. I don't even know this Stanley.

I looked down at my watch. It was just past two, which meant we had quite a while before Stanley would be off to…wherever Stanley went. "Do you expect him home for dinner?" I asked our newest client.

She responded with a bitter laugh. "Supposedly, he's meeting up with some guys over drinks. That's tonight's excuse. I'm hoping you can call tonight and let me know what's up."

Tonight?

"I don't want to fool around," she said, as if she could read my mind. "I need answers. Quick."

She wouldn't be an easy one to please.

"We'll work as quickly as we can," Celeste promised her. "It's all dependent on a lot of things. Like where he decides to go and when."

"And how easy it is to follow him." Marge wrote something down. "We don't want to blow our cover." As if there was no way she'd slip up and do a thing like that.

"I know this might not be your biggest case," Deborah said. "But I need to have it solved. Because if he's up to no good, then I deserve the money. It wouldn't be a lot, just enough to buy myself a little treat every now and then."

This woman didn't look like she'd ever met a treat. But I'd give her a break. How very sad her life must be. It made my endless string of dateless nights seem...well, luxurious.

While I studied her, Deborah reached into her large black purse and pulled out a photograph. She handed it to me. "That's the fool you're looking for. He'll have on that green vest. He wears it all the time."

I straightened my glasses and gazed down at the photo. A man about Deborah's age was sitting at a table with a can of beer. He was looking up as if surprised by the camera's flash.

Celeste stood up and signaled that the meeting was now over. "We'll stake out the scene today. We charge forty-five an hour. Does that work for you?"

Actually, we charged much more. Or at least we had charged more for our first case. And Celeste had ways to make sure that Bert would pay a nice fee when new cases started rolling in – which I hoped would happen any day.

I knew what Celeste was thinking now. If we named too high a figure, then we might lose this job. We had to have the job.

Marge collected a deposit from our client and took down her contact information.

"I've thought this out," the client said. "I want you to call my cell, but we have to be careful. Because sometimes I'll catch him listening when I'm on the phone. Like I'm the one with things to hide. I hate that about a person, when they're always so suspicious."

Like when they hire three private eyes to see what their husband's doing?

She continued with her plan. "So if I don't pick up, that means that he's around. If that happens, send a text, and I'll call you back once I can get to somewhere safe. Also, we have to use a code text in case he glances at my phone."

I saw Marge's eyes grow wide. There were certain kind of words I knew she absolutely loved, and Deborah had just hit her with a whole string of them: stakeout, code and somewhere safe.

"Okay, what's the code?" Marge asked, leaning forward in her seat.

"Well, I've thought of two for now," Deborah said. *"Meet Me in the Moonlight for a Millionaire Romance.* And also, *lima beans."*

Marge looked at her, confused. "The second one is cute, I guess. I do love lima beans. And the first one sounds exciting. But, I have to say, that might get Stanley all riled up. It sounds like things are bad enough without making him think you're out under some full moon..." Her voice trailed away. Whatever she was thinking made her grin, then blush. "Is there a rich dude, really? Because if there is, I'm thinking there's a better way out of your situation. Why not drop Stanley for the millionaire? If Stanley's such a loser?"

Deborah sighed. "The rich dude is in a book. That's the easiest place to find the good ones, am I right? In the shelves at the library? Stanley knows that every month I get together with the book-club girls." For the first time that afternoon, I saw the woman smile. "We like to read romance. It would seem a normal thing for one of the girls to text me with the name of next month's book. And the hostess assigns each of us a dish to bring. They like my lima beans."

Marge nodded. "Very, very clever. Is that book any good? *Meet Me in the Moonlight*?"

Deborah's scowl returned. "I didn't say it was a real book. It's just something I made up."

Marge looked disappointed. "I was gonna check it out."

"Well, that would be kind of hard." The client buttoned up her coat and headed toward the door. "Call me, then. Or text."

"Oh, and one more thing." Celeste held up a hand, signaling for her to pause. "We'd appreciate it if you kept it confidential – that we're in the business of undercover work."

"Understood," Deborah said. "I won't say a word. But you best have that conversation with your partner over there." She nodded her head toward Marge.

"We will," I said. "Very nice to meet you. And we'll be in touch."

After she had left, Celeste turned to Marge. "Marge, what in the world? You have to be more careful. If people know what it is we're up to, then we can't do our jobs."

Marge looked down on the floor. "I am so, so sorry. Lesson learned. I promise!" Her gaze fell upon the laptop that awaited our "repairs."

"I guess if I had to open up my big mouth and let the cat out of the bag, it should have been at karaoke," Marge said. "If Katrina knew the truth about my real profession, then we wouldn't have that problem." She nodded toward the computer with the novel locked inside.

"Yeah." I frowned at the machine. "We've got to figure out how to whip that thing into shape." Mystery number two: what was wrong with the computer and how the heck to fix it?

"Okay, let's deal with Stanley first," Celeste said. "At least we have a case." She glanced at her cell to check the time. "We've got a while before he gets off. But I say we head on over there, see who comes in and out, and look for anyone suspicious."

"Works for me," I said. "And we don't know for sure that he'll really stay until seven. That's just what he told his wife."

"Oooh," Marge said, impressed. "That's really, really good."

Celeste opened the top drawer of our small filing cabinet. "We need to take something with us. Just in case we get asked why we've been sitting there so long in the parking lot. Or if someone's catching us staking out the convenience store." She rifled through some files and plucked a folder from the drawer. "Okay, this is perfect. Girls, we're selling real estate." She held up some brightly colored brochures with brick houses and plush lawns. "And we're waiting on some clients calls. About some nearby houses. So we thought it would be easier if we parked close by."

Marge thought about that for a while. "First let's drive around the area. And make sure some houses are for sale. The market's hot near there, I heard. People like to live on the west side. Once a house goes on the market, it gets sold quick."

"Good point," Celeste said. She grabbed another folder. "If you girls prefer, we can sell *On the Town Cosmetics*. I think they're selling and they're in that area."

"Oooh," Marge said. "I love *On the Town*."

"That means we're rip-off artists," I said as I grabbed my coat and purse. The products, I supposed, were good, but they were overpriced. One of the secretaries sold the stuff at the police station in Boston. She was always telling me I needed to try a pinker shade of blush and that I should wear more lipstick. But if I did decide to do that, I'd buy it at the drug store where a tube of lipstick didn't sell for $18.99.

***

Five minutes later, I was being jostled in the back seat while Marge sped around the corner.

"I'm hungry. Who's hungry?" she asked. "Jack's is on the way."

"We just got back from there," I said.

"But that woman made me hungry when she said lima beans. And we might be there a while, waiting for this Stanley to make some kind of move."

"She's got a point," Celeste said. "We can get sandwiches to go. The food offerings at Stanley's store might not be to our taste."

I shrugged. "I hear the hot dogs are real cheap."

"I just want a smoke." Celeste lit a cigarette and held it out the window.

I thought I might order some of the sugar cookies that were so good at Jack's. They weren't actually on the menu, but came free with any kid's meal. Still, my dad had let them know to give me all I wanted whenever I came by.

So, for the second time that day, Marge pulled into Jack's. The parking lot was fairly full despite the fact that it was too early to eat dinner and too late for lunch. The retirees liked to stop in at this time of day to have some pie and coffee. Church committees, PTA groups – the real movers and shakers of the town – would rather meet at Jack's than in some dusty, over air-conditioned room at their church or school.

We walked in and placed our orders. We had not been waiting long when I felt a strange sensation, something tickling at my neck. Ewww. Was that a bug? I jumped, then turned to see my father, who never could remember that I had long outgrown the tickle-monster game. I yelped just loud enough for the diners closest to the counter to turn their heads and stare.

"Whoa, Dad, will you cut it out? You'll scare off the customers."

"Ah, they know ol' Jack is crazy. That's just one of the million reasons that they love the place." He turned to a group of women at the table next to us. "This is my daughter, Charlotte Cooper, with her cohorts. They're computer fix-it girls. If your machine gives you any trouble, you take that thing to Charlie and my girl will fix you right up."

Thanks, Dad. Thanks a lot.

"Do you have a card?" One of the women frowned as she put down her coffee cup. "My screen keeps going blank."

Absolutely perfect.

"We're having some new ones printed up," Marge chirped happily. "But we'll leave some cards with Jack as soon as we get them in."

Hmm. She could have left out that last part. My dad would be all over that. He loved to brag about his baby girl. He didn't seem to notice that I hadn't really done...much of anything.

"These other two, they used to work right here for me," my father told the woman. "And I had no idea I had computer gurus serving up the soup." A new thought made him grin. "Oh, hey, I got a good one." He winked at the customer. "Here we go. Knock knock."

Great. You knew the food here had to be the best. Because customers kept coming in despite my father's jokes.

As always, Marge thought that they were funny. "Let me answer! Let me answer! Okay, Jack, who's there?"

"Dwayne!" He always laughed before the punch line.

"Dwayne who?" Marge asked gleefully.

"Dwayne the tub. I'm drowning!" He flailed his arms up in the air.

Marge clasped her hands with joy.

The nearby customers turned to stare again, smiling at the scene.

"Well then," my father said, "what can we get you girls?"

Celeste smiled. "We've already placed our order. They're working on it now."

Dad stepped into the kitchen to see how our food was coming. I saw a familiar face peeking from the window where the cooks set out the plates. It was a shy, softly rounded face with large and hopeful eyes.

Hmm. Did Marge still think my father's fry cook was just 'the sweetest thing'? The status of the budding romance seemed to change from day to day.

"Someone's watching you!" I said in a teasing voice.

"Well," she said primly, "I will have to be very careful not to look that way."

"Playing hard to get?" I asked.

"Oh, hon," she whispered to me, "it's absolutely over. Big mistake right there. That man can go from *It's nice to meet you* to *Let's pick out a ring* in thirty seconds flat."

"He proposed? Already?" Celeste grabbed her arm and smiled. "Marge, you vixen, you."

Marge frowned. "Well, no. Not exactly. But he was moving way too fast." She looked around, then whispered, "He asked me if I wanted children! And if I'd like to meet his mother. No! I don't want to meet your mother. I want to dance with other guys! I want to kiss one guy on Tuesday at the movies, and on Saturday I want to beat another one at bowling. I want to play the field. Is he looking? Is he looking?" She squeezed her eyes shut as if that would keep him from seeing her and not the other way around.

"It's okay." I touched her arm. "He's nowhere to be seen."

"Good," she said. "I told him it was over. But I did so hate to hurt him. I hope he's not too sad."

Well, I thought, that one was over quickly, but the girl knows what she wants. I liked that about Celeste and Marge. If there was something that they wanted – a man, perhaps, a new career – they just went out and got it; they found a way to make it work.

Celeste patted down the pockets of her sweater. "This thing today could take a while. I need to make sure I'm all stocked up on smokes."

"Well," I said. "That shouldn't be a problem. At a convenience store."

"Guess you're right. But do we want to go in right away?" she asked. "Or just watch and wait at first? And not draw attention to ourselves?"

"Good question," Marge chimed in. "Hey, I brought my binoculars. And a tape recorder." Her voice got louder and rose to a squeak when she got excited.

"Quiet, Marge! Remember?" Celeste frowned at her.

"Oh, yeah. Right. I got it," Marge said sheepishly.

I hadn't brought a thing. I really didn't have a clue what it was that we might need. The cops I knew back in Boston said that working on stakeout jobs could be brutally boring. The main thing I remember was, they drank a lot of coffee.

So...I was bringing cookies. And I'd ordered a sandwich too in case we were still being super spies when it came time for dinner. Because, after all, who knew? We might end up following this Stanley guy to stakeout number two. Next time I'd bring a book. For now, I guessed my cell would have to do. A couple of word games were loaded on my phone. And another one with a little mouse you had to move through a maze of blocks before the clock ran out.

Marge cut into my musings with a round of giggles. "Hey, Charlie," she said happily, "a very handsome cop just walked into the place."

A warmth spread across my chest. Alex. Alex with the sexy smile and the arms that felt so strong when he pulled me out of danger. Did I mention he was always there when I was at my clumsiest? Alex who teased me with a date and then never followed up. My heart sunk at the memory. Who needed that guy anyway?

It was no big deal, I told myself, to run into Alex Spencer. But why had I worn this old white shirt? Was that a chocolate stain? And I wished I hadn't pulled my hair back quite so tightly.

Stop it, Charlie. It didn't matter. If the man could not be bothered to just pick up the phone, that was absolutely fine. Because I was busy too! Why, I barely even noticed that he'd walked into the room.

DICED

I turned to Marge and changed the subject. "When is the Sweet Pea Festival? And did you bring a sweater?" If he didn't want our "date" to happen, well, that was cool with me. I'd forgotten it already.

"Hello, you." The familiar deep and playful voice was coming from behind me.

"Alex," I said, turning around slowly. "I didn't know that you were here."

His hair caught the light from a nearby window, and he had on a crisp blue shirt that exactly matched his eyes. There was a soft look in his eyes as he grinned at me. Why were the gorgeous ones always the biggest flirts? That kind of wasn't fair.

My smile was small, polite, before I glanced over toward the kitchen. I had no time to talk. We had to get our order and head on out of there. Big case in the works. If I did have time to stop and look at Alex, I'd see how soft his cheeks were and imagine how it might feel to touch the stubble on his chin. But just never mind. Because. I. Did. Not. Care.

He caught my eye and winked. "What do we have here? This looks like big-time trouble multiplied by three."

Then he touched my arm, and I tried so hard not to melt right then and there.

Chapter Three

"NO TROUBLE," MARGE SAID, taking out her compact mirror to see how her lipstick looked.

"Just three girls at a counter waiting for a bite to eat. Nothing to see here." Celeste adjusted the navy scarf that covered most of her signature bright hair. Flaming red hair is not good at all when you're working undercover.

Marge put on a bit more lipstick, then peeked around the mirror to see if a certain fry cook might be watching from the kitchen.

Ignoring the other two, Alex kept his eyes on me, a small smile on his face. Did he like me after all? Of course not, I decided. He was probably just afraid we were messing with some case he wanted to solve all by himself. Men don't like to be shown up. And we'd proven we were good. In our own special way.

A waitress appeared to put our orders on the counter. Celeste took out her card to pay.

"Oh, I think you're up to something." Alex reached into my paper bag and plucked out a cookie. "You owe me food, remember? This can be a small down payment."

I pretended to think about it. "Oh. I'd forgotten that whole thing." I closed the bag and moved it further from his reach. The cookies at Jack's were too good to give away for free to Alex.

He turned to Celeste and Marge. "Whatever it is that you're up to, just be careful." He lightly touched my hair, which should have made me mad. Who had given him permission? But – jumping jelly doughnuts – the man was looking fine. I wished his hand would stay right there.

He gave me a wink. "Now, where are you fine ladies really heading off to this afternoon?"

Did he somehow already know we had a new case in the works? Was he that good?

Celeste picked up the bag of food and sighed. "No need for you to worry over the three of us. You just run along. Don't you have some crime to fight? We're just helping a wife and mother with some family concerns."

I could tell that she was starting to get angry. Her bad feelings about Bert seemed to extend to all the cops in Springston.

Marge frowned dramatically in a way that showed off the Temptress Red lipstick she'd just reapplied. "Such a sad state of affairs. The poor woman is just distressed."

Affairs? That might be the perfect word. Only Marge had made Deborah sound like the most delicate of flowers instead of a hurricane.

Alex pointed at me, then spoke in a whisper. "Just keep this one from getting knocked out or tripping into an open grave until I can come to save her." Both were references from true-life misadventures starring me as klutz extraordinaire and Alex as rescuer.

"Fair enough," I said, red-faced. Why did our cases, few as they had been, always bring us face to face with Alex at my exact worse moments?

"It's not dangerous police stuff," I tried to reassure him.

"She's absolutely right," Marge said, standing up to go. "And we'll look out for your girlfriend."

I gave her a look.

She responded with a giggle. "Alex, you be careful too." She looked around and whispered, taking into account, for once, the need to keep our work confidential. "If you need some backup, you know we have mad skills. If you need rescuing one day, then we're your girls right here."

We were interrupted by the waitress, who looked at Alex with a bashful smile. I guess I was not the only one who'd noticed those blue eyes.

"What can I get you, sir?" she asked.

Alex smiled back at her. "Cheeseburger to go, and hold the pickles please. I'd like some fries and a coke, too."

"Bon Appetite," Celeste said, standing up. As she turned to go, she ran straight into...my mother.

"Well, if it's not my favorite girls!" my mother cried, pulling the three of us into a hug. Then she kept her arm around my shoulder. "I missed my Charlie so much. I don't like it when she's gone."

"Mom! I lived ten minutes from your house. And I didn't live there long."

She waved my remarks away with one sweep of her arms, which that day were draped dramatically in a maroon and purple scarf. "Too far!" she cried. "Too long! Now everything is set to rights. Did the move go okay this morning?"

"Charlie's all moved in," Marge reported proudly.

My mother smiled at me and pushed some of her long curls from her shoulder. "I wish I could have been there to help you get settled in." She dropped her voice to a whisper. "But Mrs. Horton's in a bad way. They had to move her into what they call *a home for active seniors*." She made air quotes with her fingers. "I didn't see a soul who I'd describe as active. I swear! Even the caretakers looked like they were half asleep."

My mom not only taught exercise classes for the over-eighty set, but she took an interest in their lives. She continued with her story. "I just had to get her out of there for a little while. We decided to come out for lunch." She turned to wave at an older woman at a corner booth. She smiled cheerily at Mrs. Horton – who, by the way, looked to be about one hundred and seventeen – then turned the smile on us. "So! What's new with my girls?"

"Well," I said, "I'm glad not to have to cook my own dinners anymore." I smiled in anticipation of my mother's gourmet meals, which appeared on the table every night, no matter how frantic her schedule had seemed to be that day. "What are you making today, Mom?"

She kissed my cheek. "I thought we'd have spaghetti casserole. I know that's your favorite." She turned to Marge and Celeste. "And how are you two doing? Anything exciting happening in your lives?"

Marge thought about the question. "Well, of course, there's work. Then I thought I might hit up the bookstore. I've never been a reader, but there's always time to start. I love a good romance, don't you? And I think that while I'm there, I'll buy a book about computers – on how to fix one quickly when you have no idea what's wrong." She frowned. "Such a mystery, those machines."

My mother looked confused. "But aren't you girls the experts?"

"What she meant to say," Celeste said, "is that we're getting manicures! Electronics work can take a real toll on nail health."

Beside me, Alex laughed. He held up his hand to study it. "Oooh. So can chasing crooks. Just look at these fingers. Whatever will I do?"

My mother burst into a fit of girlish giggles. "Charlotte, isn't this the nice young man who was so sweet to sit beside you at the hospital that day?" I'd been injured pretty badly in the last investigation, and Alex had stepped right up to make sure I was okay. That had been the moment when I saw him in a new way, this tall, well-built detective with the disarming grin. Despite his man-sized ego, he was really kind of sweet. He made me feel…well, safe. He also set my fantasies to spinning in all kind of fun directions. Which I couldn't think about right then with my mother standing there.

Now he'd turned back into the kind of man who'd propose a date, and then just drop the idea altogether. Like it had never ever happened. I knew all about that kind of drop-dead gorgeous man. They knew how it made you feel when they looked at you with those eyes. Those eyes were a weapon. It was just a game to them, to play with your affections. From now on, as much as possible, I'd stay away from him.

My mom reached out her hand to him. "It's so nice to see you again. You took such good care of my daughter. I want to thank you for that." She thought about it. "I'll cook you dinner! Some delicious lobster tails maybe."

Noooooo!

"I'd be honored, Mrs. Cooper," Alex said.

Thanks, Mom. Thanks a lot.

My mom looked at me and smiled. "He has lovely manners, Charlotte." Then she turned to Alex. "Please, won't you call me Barbara? Are you free to come to our house on Saturday? We've got the whole family gathering. Of course, being young and handsome, you might have plans already."

Sheesh. Was my mother really blushing? She must be under the spell of those Alex Spencer eyes. Then, hey! I thought of something. I was also young. Why did my mother just assume that I was free to come to her lobster dinner? Because my mother wasn't stupid. Because my dating life was kind of non-existent.

"Oh, lobsters. Really? Lobsters?" Marge clasped her hands together. "Do you dip them in butter?"

"Oh, yes. Jack makes the most delicious garlic-butter sauce. Marge, you should come on Saturday. And Celeste, we'd love to have you, too. I do love to have a crowd. It can be a party!" She clapped her hands together as her plan took shape.

"Oh, I absolutely will," Marge said. "Tell me what to bring. I can get my hands on a recipe for some lovely lima beans. But I don't suppose that goes so well with lobster..."

Celeste interrupted. "Oh Barbara, we're so sorry, but Marge and I have plans. She must have just forgotten." She shot Marge a look.

Something seemed to dawn on Marge. She blushed and winked at me. "Oh yes, that's right. We do have plans already. We'll come another night for sure. Alex and Charlie, I just know, will have a lovely time." She gave me a not-so-subtle wink.

Great. I finally got my date, if you could call it that. And now – big surprise – it would include my mother.

"I will look forward to it, Barbara." Alex nodded his goodbyes.

"Seven o'clock," she said. The fingers of her left hand did a little dance that was her special wave.

"Well, this is absolutely lovely," she said as she watched him walk out the door. She stared at him as he left. "Did you girls notice that young man has a very nice behind?"

"Mother! Please. Just stop," I said. Sometimes moving back to your hometown could kick you in the gut.

"His behind is okay," Celeste said. "His attitude is not."

My mother stared, transfixed, at the empty place that had recently been occupied by Alex. Was she going into some trance, channeling some enchanted spirit who could turn an old-maid daughter into someone's wife? And maybe add two children dressed in fresh-pressed clothes who loved their grandma best of all? My mother believed in strange things. You never knew what she was thinking.

"Girls." She finally spoke. "Let me ask you a question."

"Shoot it to us straight." Celeste tilted her head to wait.

"If this Alex were a beverage, would he be a rum and coke? A martini, dry? Or just a frosty glass of beer?"

I stared at her. Say, what?

Marge leapt up in glee. "Me first! Me first! What drink would I be? Can I be a Mai Tai? With a little green umbrella? I collect the umbrellas from everybody's drinks. I have every single color."

Celeste looked at Marge first and then at my mother. "I don't understand. Why in the name of the Tuesday Pork Chop Special would Alex be a drink?"

"It's my brand-new hobby," my mother said with a smile. "I'm taking a cocktail class. Our teacher said that mixing drinks is more than just a matter of choosing the ingredients and measuring just right. He said the best bartenders, the most delightful hosts, know how to match the perfect drink with a personality."

For this she was paying money?

"Not to burst your bubble," I said, "but wouldn't it work better just to ask them what drink they'd prefer? What if you decided they were a pineapple margarita, and they were allergic to pineapples? What if they were really in the mood to just have a nice merlot?"

I stopped myself. Why was I even having this stupid conversation? What kind of person looked like a pineapple margarita? And if you met that kind of person, would you make them a drink, or would you run the other way?

"Oh, Charlie," my mother said. "Don't be so serious. Have a little fun."

"That sounds fascinating." Celeste leaned against the counter. "What made you decide to take the class?"

My mother lowered her voice to a whisper. "It's this thing with Mrs. Horton. It made me determined to stay as youthful as I can, to do the things that young folks do."

Celeste looked skeptical. "You don't think that old folks drink?"

"Well, yes." My mother thought about it. "But they just drink the same old things. They don't try new drinks with every meal. They don't try the new and the exciting. They stick with the old and boring."

Celeste nodded to herself. "Makes sense to me, I guess. I'll have to drop by one day. You can pour me a surprise."

"I'll look forward to it. Well, I guess I better go order up some food before Mrs. Horton needs her nap. Toodle-oo. It was so much fun to see you girls."

She returned to Mrs. Horton, who, indeed, was napping at the table.

"Let's get out of here," I said, "And hurry. Before we run into someone else."

***

Stanley's store was located in a busy part of town. The sign out front was flashing bright despite some missing lights. *Busy Bee's*, it said. *Tobacco, Food and More*. A small lighted cartoon bee danced above the words.

There were cars in every space in the tiny parking lot. Marge circled the block five times before a truck pulled out of a space along the street just across from the Busy Bee. We had a perfect view. I looked at my cell to check the time. It was just past three. We could be here a while. I stretched out in the back seat and watched people come and go. Cars idled in the parking lot, their drivers hoping for a space.

I checked my email and played the mouse game on my phone. Then I ate two cookies. Hmm. Time was passing slow. I watched people go into the store and guessed what they might be buying. Then I

Googled alien sightings in Massachusetts. Nothing interesting came up.

Marge and Celeste were talking about people they had known when they worked as waitresses at my father's diner. I halfway followed the conversation, but lost interest. Most of them were doing boring things, like moving to Vermont to work in medical transcriptions. I Googled *Do Cops Make Bad Boyfriends?*

I still had more cookies. I opened the bag and took a bite. So sweet. I kicked off my shoes and shifted my position. The button for the window pressed into my back. For my next undercover mission, I would have to bring a pillow. Or a blanket even. Hey, I'd make a list.

"Marge," I called up to the front seat. "Could I have a sheet of paper? And a pen?"

"Sure thing, hon. Will do." She took a bite of her sandwich, then set the wrapper on the seat to dig into her purse. She tore a page out of her notebook and handed it back along with her silver pen.

"Thanks." Hmm. What to bring the next time? I wrote down magazines and brownies and fuzzy socks. Then I crossed out the first entry. Magazines could be distracting. I had to stay alert. Should I look out of the window more? What should I be watching for?

"Hey, could you hand back Stanley's picture?" I asked.

Celeste handed me the photo Deborah had left with us. "Keep this face in your mind," she said. "We need to make sure this guy doesn't slip away unnoticed."

"Right." I stared at our mystery man. He was short, stocky and bald and had on the olive-green vest that Deborah hated; she said he wore it all the time. That was good at least. Most people on a stakeout have absolutely no idea what their target might be wearing. Yay for bad fashion sense.

"Okay," Marge sighed. "This is super boring. Why don't we drive around for a while and then come back before it's time for him to leave?"

"No way," I told her. "When a client's interests are at stake, we don't make decisions based on whether we are bored. What if he decides to slip off early? What if he's been lying about when he gets off work? Maybe the mistress will decide to show up. Or the mob boss or the secret second family. Or whoever or whatever this guy's big secret is."

"Charlie's right," Celeste said. "We're here on a stakeout, not a fun girls' day out."

Because that would just be pitiful – a girls' day out at the Busy Bee.

The time stretched out very slowly.

***

3:42.

"What time is it now?" Marge asked.

"Do the math," Celeste said. "Six and a half minutes later than the last time you asked."

"My whole body's getting stiff," Marge said. She wiggled her shoulders in a little dance. "Is anybody thirsty? I think I'll go inside, see what they've got to drink."

"Can't do that. Remember?" I asked her. "We said that we weren't going in. We don't want to show our faces."

"Right."

***

4:02.

Why did Marge have to mention drinks? Now I was absolutely parched.

I turned around to look behind me. "We aren't too far from the mall," I said. "It might feel good to stretch my legs. Why don't I go for drinks?"

"Soda, please," Celeste said.

"Make that two," Marge said.

I opened the car door and gratefully stretched my legs out onto the pavement. The fresh air felt good against my skin. As I began to walk, my knees felt kind of creaky from my time in the back seat.

Soon I was back with sodas for my partners and a caramel latte with whipped cream for me. Because caffeine! And cream!

***

4:22.

"I know some songs," Marge said. "Let's have a sing-along."

Celeste leaned back in her seat. "Here's my idea: let's don't."

***

4:45.

"I have to pee," Celeste said.

"Me too," Marge said.

"Me three."

Celeste turned around to face me. "You too? Couldn't you find a bathroom at the mall?"

I shrugged. "That was a while ago. I didn't need a bathroom then."

Once they'd mentioned the, um, problem, I had to go real bad; I had to go so bad it hurt. They never showed this in the movies. The cops in the movies were always on surveillance. And never – not one single time – did they need to pee. What were they, robot cops? In real life, this surveillance stuff was brutal.

"Well, you know what's down the street, right?" Celeste looked at her phone to check the time. "I hope that Pete's is open. You both have been there, right? *Pete's Uptown Sombrero*."

Oooh, I knew the place. Their tacos were superb.

"I'll go first," Celeste said. "I know the guys at Pete's." Well, of course she did. "They'll let us use the bathroom. They owe me a favor."

It was Celeste, so I knew not to ask. I was just happy for a potty.

***

5:15.

We played *I Spy*. Which was kind of funny. Because we were...well, we were spies. We played word games on our phones. Then we sat in silence for so long that I wondered if one or both of my friends might just be asleep. I wasn't sure, but it didn't matter. I could keep watch while they napped. I ate another cookie.

***

5:45.

Marge began to sing in a sleepy voice. "The little green frog went hopping by..."

"No," Celeste and I said together, my mouth full of cookie.

***

6:03.

"What time is it now?" Marge asked.

No one had said a word for twenty minutes. I was out of cookies.

"If I were a drink, what drink would I be?" Marge asked.

**

6:10.

Celeste sang in a high-pitched, quiet voice. "Hop, hop went the froggy..."

Hmm. Who knew Celeste could sing? She was pretty good.

Marge and I joined in. "The cat said 'Can I come along, come along, come along?' The cat said 'Can I come along to the big green meadow?'"

We remembered the movements too. Pointed fingers to make cat ears, waving hand motions for the snake...

**

6:22.

"I've got to get out of this car," Marge said.

She walked three times around the car. I wondered what kind of cookies they sold in the Busy Bee.

***

7:03.

My mind drifted off to Alex. I imagined we were on the beach, and Alex was...well, let's just say I'd finally found a pleasant way to make the time go by.

But what was that kind of roaring sound? Was it a motorcycle? If it was, the driver was getting way too close.

Then I saw Celeste startle in her seat. She turned and shook Marge by the shoulder. "Wake up, Marge. You're snoring."

"What?" Marge jumped up. "Did Stanley come out yet? Did I miss everything?"

"No, Sherlock. He's still there." Celeste leaned back in the seat. "First rule of surveillance: you have to stay awake."

"Sorry. So sorry," Marge squeaked, then she stifled a big yawn.

That's when I looked past them and noticed the figure by the door at the Busy Bee. "Look guys, there he is."

We all watched as he flipped the small square sign to *Closed. Please Come Again.* It was him for sure, bald head, green vest and all. He disappeared back inside the store, but we never once let our eyes wander from the door. He'd be out any minute.

Celeste, who'd taken a turn behind the wheel, started up the engine, ready to follow Stanley to his mystery destination.

***

7:40.

I leaned forward, trying to get a glimpse into the darkened store. "What on earth could he be doing?"

"Should we take a peek?" Marge asked. "Maybe the secret stuff he's doing happens right here in the store. After business hours."

I thought about it for a while. "I guess he's in there by himself, right? Nobody went inside after he closed up."

"Unless they were there already before he closed the store, and they never left." Celeste said. "Or he might come out any minute. How long does it take to count the money? What else would he do in there? It shouldn't take a long time to close the place up and leave."

"It wouldn't hurt to just stroll by," I said. There were plenty of people on the street, walking to the bars and cafés. We'd blend in, no problem.

We all got out. Ouch. My knees creaked again, like I was Mrs. Horton. We made our way toward the Busy Bee and slipped into our roles.

"I'm gonna have the Taco Plate," Marge said for the benefit of anyone who might be listening. "But we have to get the cheese dip, too."

"You can pick the appetizer." Celeste smoothed down her scarf, which was looking kind of skewed. "Just give me a margarita."

We slowed down as we walked past the window of the store. Oh, so very casually, we turned our heads to glance inside. Then we turned around and glanced again. Was that...was that a pair of legs splayed out on the floor, just beside the counter? Marge gasped and Celeste beckoned us to come a little closer and get a better look.

The shape came into clearer focus. It was a human shape for sure. With a knife stuck in the neck. In a pool of blood.

I felt a little faint. There was too much blood.

Made in the USA
Coppell, TX
22 April 2022

76888737R00215